Disrespecting Lela

By

Julie Williams

DISRESPECTING LELA

Copyright: Julie Williams
Published: August 2013
Publisher: Julie Williams/JXW Communications

ISBN-13: 9780615877051
ISBN-10: 0615877052
Library of Congress Control Number: 2013915910
Julie Williams JXW Communications, Akron, OH

Dedication

PARENTS
SALLY P. & JERRY (RUDY) WILLIAMS
UNITED IN FOSTERING A LOVE OF THE ARTS AND
RESPONSIBLE FOR IGNITING AN IMAGINATION THAT IS
WITHOUT BOUNDARIES.

SISTERS
ETHEL VINSON & CARMELA RENTAS
WE WERE BORN WITH A BLOOD BOND THAT HAS BEEN
PROVEN TO BE UNBREAKABLE.

SISTER FRIENDS
DEBORAH VINSON-MILBRY, DEBRA WALTERS-GRAVES,
NELLIE PRYOR-ROGERS
TIME, TEARS, LAUGHTER, & LOVE THROUGHOUT THE
YEARS HAVE MADE US SISTERS FOREVER.

THANK YOU
KENYA HOLLEY
MY CREATIVE AND TECHNICAL ASSISTANT

Whoso findeth a wife findeth a good thing, and obtaineth favour of the LORD.

Proverbs 18:22
(King James Version-Public Domain)

DISRESPECTING

LELA

one

Genesis

The sound of Ashley's lungs struggling to breathe had finally surpassed the sound of her heart beating faster and faster. Sweat streamed down her temple. Her legs fought hard not to fold and send her to the ground.

Ashley had only run around the corner and up the street about six blocks to create this trauma to her body. When she turned the last corner, her determination helped push her unexercised body to move a little faster.

Ashley's abnormal motion caught the attention of Mrs. Goodman. Mrs. Goodman was in her front yard trying to prevent this extreme dry heat from destroying her annuals and perennials. The spray from her water hose went in an unintended direction as she became fixated on Ashley's intense struggle to run. Mrs. Goodman's eyes locked with Ashley's eyes. There was an unspoken message conveyed.

Mrs. Goodman knew instantly that something was wrong.

Ashley could not stop to provide any comfort for the horrible possibilities that were passing through Mrs.Goodman's mind. Her destination was far more important than the need to provide Mrs. Goodman consolation.

After pounding only once, the door flew open.

Mavis stood looking at Ashley with the seriousness of the situation written on her face. Mavis was a voluptuous woman with hips that indicated her African American ancestry. She stepped back to let Ashley stagger inside still searching for more breath. Once Ashley walked into the living room, Fran was standing in front of the couch with tears filling up in her eyes. Fran, a thin, light-skinned woman, seemed visibly shaken. Lela sat calmly in Curtis' easy chair watching the cable news on the television. Her sweet honey skin seemed so smooth and clear. She looked cool and unusually beautiful in one of her summer dresses. She never even looked around as Ashley tried to speak.

"What's the matter? What happened?" Ashley managed to get out.

"You need to go look in the bedroom," Mavis firmly instructed.

Ashley looked at Fran who could only shake her head in agreement with Mavis.

"Why?" Ashley wanted to know.

"Just go look in the bedroom," Mavis commanded.

Lela continued to ignore Ashley's sudden appearance.

Her full attention was still directed toward the television. Ashley slowly walked past the women and toward Lela's bedroom. She hesitated at the door. When she looked back at Mavis and Fran, Ashley realized she had no choice but to enter.

What was in the bedroom sent Ashley rushing back into the living room. She fell to her knees and fought the urge to eject the contents of her stomach.

"Oh my God! Oh my God!" Ashley shouted in disbelief.

She jumped up and ran to the telephone. She tried to lift the receiver. Mavis quickly put her hand over Ashley's hand slamming the receiver back down.

"What are you doing?"

"What are you doing?" Mavis said as she stared in Ashley's eyes.

"I'm calling the police. You know what is in that bedroom. We have to call the police."

"What do you suggest we try for, life in prison or lethal injection?" Mavis asked.

"What do you suggest we do?"

"He's dead! Oh my God!" Fran finally shouted out. "We have to do something."

"Look at her," Mavis instructed.

Ashley looked at Lela who was continuing to ignore the presence of her friends. Ashley had not noticed before the large bath towel folded several times in Lela's lap.

"She has a gun inside that towel Ash!" Fran shouted out.

"Where are the kids?" Ashley suddenly realized.

She began looking wildly around this immaculate living room. Lela had always been able to buy the finest things to display in her home. It had become an obsession for her to maintain this house and the surroundings as the showcase of the neighborhood. Scanning this beautiful room found no evidence of children.

"They have locked themselves in Kelly's bedroom," Mavis said.

Ashley ran to Kelly's bedroom. She tried to open the door, but it was locked. She pounded on the door. There was no response. Fear almost made her faint as she pounded on the door again. She could hear the muffled sound of crying coming from inside.

"Kelly, open the door. It's me, Auntie Ash."

There was still no response and Ashley had no strength left to pound on the door again. Suddenly, the door unlocked. The door slowly cracked open. Ashley only saw one of Kelly's eyes peek through the small opening. There were no tears or sign of fear in the eyes of this twelve-year old. Kelly had suddenly been thrust into the role of sole protector and had not backed away from her unwanted, new responsibility. At this moment, she did not even trust her beloved Auntie Ash. Kelly's only objective was to insure the lives of her three smaller siblings and all things now were a possible danger to this goal. She was cautious, but willing to listen to Ashley's plea.

"Open the door Kelly. Everything is going to be all right." Ashley tried to assure her.

"There is blood everywhere. He's dead you know."

"I know."

"She's going to kill us next."

"No, Kelly. She loves all of you."

"She loved him."

Kelly slammed the door in Ashley's face. Ashley felt the presence of what had caused Kelly's sudden action and turned around. Lela stood with the gun in her hand.

"That's why I asked them to call you. I wanted you to see for yourself, so you would understand. Everything I have worked to create and love is now gone. It's all gone," Lela said.

Lela turned and walked back to the kitchen. Ashley tested the door. Kelly had locked it again. She followed Lela to the kitchen. As she passed through the living room, Fran sat on the couch now crying uncontrollably. Mavis had sat down in one of the chairs and lit up one of the cigarettes she had recently vowed to stop smoking. Mavis seemed to be savoring the taste of this small lit up stick as she cut her eyes in Ashley's direction.

When Ashley entered the kitchen, Lela had laid the gun on the counter by the sink. She had gotten a plate and was filling it with food out of pots on the stove.

"I'm fixing you a plate Ash. Curtis did some barbecuing this morning. I know how much you love his barbecue. Sit down."

Ashley slowly sat down at the kitchen table. There was silence for a moment as she tried to find the right words.

"What have you done?"

Lela stopped fixing the plate of food and looked out the kitchen window for a brief moment. She came over and placed the plate of food on the table in front of Ashley.

"What do you want to drink?"

Ashley looked in her eyes, but could not respond. Lela went to the refrigerator and got out a can of ginger ale.

She filled a glass with small blocks of ice. She put the glass on the table and slowly poured the soda until the foam fizzled to the top of the glass. Lela sat down at the table in front of Ashley.

"Eat as much as you want. We have plenty."

Ashley had known and loved Lela for many years. She had never seen her this calm. The look in her eyes was causing Ashley to shiver. Lela's soul was lacking something. There was something cold, something unfamiliar staring back.

"He came in here, spoke to that dog, and did not even say a word to me. You hear me Ash? He gave more respect to that damn dog than to me, his wife. I told him and he just looked at me and walked away. Like I was nothing. Like I was nothing at all. He was going in there to get ready to go see his woman. He just thought I was stupid. Like I didn't know. As if I didn't know about the first one, and like I don't know about the one he has right now. It would have gone on forever Ash. He would have never left and he would have never stopped. He was mean and cruel to me Ash.

What had I done to him to deserve all this disrespect?

I gave him four beautiful children. I made this house a shrine to him. I cooked his food morning, noon, and night. I loved him every day since the day I met him. He walked in here, spoke to that damn dog, and didn't say not one word to me. He was not going to disrespect me like that ever again. Not ever again."

Lela sat back in her chair as if a load had been lifted from her shoulders.

"There was another way Lela." Mavis said standing in the doorway of the kitchen. The smoke from her cigarette could not mask the look of disgust in her face. She turned and walked back into the living room.

Lela sprang from her chair, grabbed the gun from the counter, and followed Mavis back. Ashley rushed behind her afraid of what she might do. Lela walked up close to Mavis who quickly turned to face her.

"How dare you say one thing to me. You with two former husbands and one man after another. I built a family and a home," Lela ranted.

"You call this a family and a home. Your husband is in the bedroom with his throat cut from ear to ear. Your children are locked in their room afraid their crazy-ass mama will kill them too. That's a family and a home? Bullshit!" Mavis hollered.

"At least I'm not a whore," Lela retaliated.

"At least I'm not no damn murderer. Every man I ever fucked is still alive," Mavis informed.

"Stop it! Stop it!" Fran leaped from the couch. "We have a dead man in one bedroom and some traumatized children locked in another bedroom. Stop talking about shit we should have fought about years ago and start concentrating on the shit we got going on right now. Ash, what are we going to do?"

"Always calling on Ash," Mavis said insulted. "Like she is the great Buddha. Mohammad reincarnated. Jesus Christ almighty. How the hell does Ash know what to do? Has she ever slaughtered her husband before? Hell, she don't even have a husband."

"You're absolutely right. I have no idea what to do," Ashley said mentally and physically exhausted. "What did you say my choices were? Life in prison or lethal injection for a woman that I have loved like my own flesh and blood."

"If you loved her so much, you should have done something before this happened," Mavis reminded Ashley.

"We all should have done something," Fran reminded them all. "We all saw this coming. He didn't start being a bastard this evening. He was a bastard from day one. I don't know how in the world she was able to stand him this long. He wasn't just a jerk. He was the king of jerks."

"If we went around killing men for being jerks, they would all be dead," Mavis shouted. "You should have told her to just leave his ass."

"It wasn't my place to encourage her to leave her husband and break up her family," Ashley tried to explain.

Mavis walked right up to Ashley's face. The smoke from her cigarette made Ashley's eyes water.

"It wasn't your place. Then whose place was it Ash?" Mavis wanted to know.

"Her marriage was created by God. She needed to look to God for the answer."

"And God told her to cut his throat? Mavis rebutted.

Lela had sat down on the couch by Fran with the gun still in her hand.

"Whores don't have any religion do they Mavis?" Lela said.

Mavis walked over to Lela and smiled.

"And saints don't have any damn sense," Mavis told Lela. "Did it ever occur to you that maybe God expects you to have some damn sense sometimes and do something for yourself? If Curtis was making you so unhappy, so unloved, so disrespected, you should have had enough guts to pack up them brats and walk out the front door. But no, not for little Miss Perfect. That would be too hard. It wouldn't look right to the community. And God forbid you ever have to struggle. Everything has to be nice and easy, even if it meant putting up with that son-of-a bitch."

"She has children Mavis," Ashley said softly.

Mavis turned around slowly in attack mode.

"Children that will never erase the blood in that bedroom from their minds. This was better Ash? I'm just an old stupid whore, Ash, so clarify this for me. Till death do us part? Was this what God meant?"

"Why did you come over here Fran?" Ashley asked trying to alleviate some of the building tension.

"Lela said Curtis did some grilling. Mavis and I just came over to get a plate of barbecue. If I had known Lela was over here cutting up her husband, I would have never come," Fran said with regret.

There was a moment of silence and then they all started to laugh.

"Did he grill a lot Lela?" Ashley asked.

"Ribs, chicken, hot dogs and burgers. You should taste it. It is some of his best ever," Lela proudly reported.

"That man can barbecue better than anybody in town and you just killed him."

Mavis began laughing again. They all could not resist laughing with her.

"For just a few seconds, I wanted to stop the pain of him. What I did not know was that destroying him meant destroying me as well."

Lela brought them back to the dilemma they were still confronted with.

"What are we going to do?" Fran reiterated with tears coming back into her eyes.

"What happened Lela?" Mavis finally inquired.

"When he walked passed me not even speaking, I followed him into the bedroom. The kids were watching television in the family room. He went into his preparation routine for going out at night. I tried to tell him he couldn't disrespect me like that anymore. That I could not take this any longer and he had to treat those kids and me better. That we were a family and he had to treat us like one. He just started smiling. He was not even listening to me. I looked around and he was looking right at my children. They were standing in the doorway watching him do that arrogant little smile he does to indicate to them that I am, as he says to them all the time, a silly woman. I did not even know I had that knife in my hand. It slid across his neck like a knife on warm butter. I tried to stop the bleeding. The blood went everywhere. It all started because he did not speak to me. At the end, he fought so hard to say something to me. The blood choked him into permanent silence. I had hurt him and then I tried so desperately to save him. I watched him choke to death on his own blood. I have loved him so much for so long, but all I felt was relief that he was gone. The worst part of it all was the look in my children's eyes. It was horrible. I instantly went from being their mother to some type of monster. My husband is gone physically and my children are gone mentally. My life is over."

Mavis sat down in Curtis' easy chair and lit another cigarette.

"Curtis loved this chair didn't he?" Mavis said as she adjusted her behind for maximum comfort.

"The kids and I gave it to him for one of his birthdays," Lela said staring into the past. "He doesn't like anybody to sit in it, but him. It's like his personal throne. He really hates it when you sit in it."

"Good," Mavis said with joy.

"What about the gun? What are you going to do with that gun?" Fran wondered.

"Kill myself."

"And what about the kids?" Ashley questioned.

"I would never hurt my kids. I love them way too much. I didn't mean to hurt him. I loved him even more than I loved those kids. That's horrible to say, but I did. Look what I have done for him over the years. Have I ever done that much for my kids? Now look what I have done to those children. It has always been about him. What he wanted, what he needed, what would make him happy. That was all I ever thought about."

Lela seemed to be talking to herself.

"Was he good in bed?" Mavis asked with a snicker.

"Mavis!" Ashley said with scorn.

"Shut up Miss Holier Than Thou. Answer the question Lela," Mavis stated.

"I am not even sure. It got to the point that anything he did with any affection toward me I soaked up like water."

"You have always loved him, but when did he stop loving you?" Ashley requested to know.

Ashley did not know a simple request for information was really more lethal than one of the bullets resting in the gun in Lela's hand. She was not sure if Lela thought, despite it all, that

Curtis still loved her or if she had just never confronted the idea that he may have really stopped loving her.

"Ash," Fran scolded. She sensed the question had delivered a fatal blow to Lela. Even Mavis sat up in the easy chair and put out her cigarette sensing some adverse reaction.

"He never had to stop loving me because he never started loving me."

Her friends did not realize that Lela's answer would hurt them more than it would hurt her.

"Why did you both get married?" Fran was puzzled.

"I was pretty and a good Christian woman. I loved him and it didn't hurt that he could take care of me and my children and still have change left over for a few new cars and a cup of coffee too. It was the right thing to do for both of us. At least, that was what we thought at the time. Then it slowly over the years became unbearable for both of us. I needed him to love me even if he had to pretend and he just could not do it. It was all a lie. A lie that turned into anger and hatred. What did you say Ash about my marriage? A marriage created by God. Then what is God? I have killed my husband and damaged my children forever. He was my whole world and my world is gone."

Lela looked at the gun in her hand as if she just realized a precious object was in her possession. Her new obsession with the gun made her friends freeze with terror.

The doorbell suddenly rang. The sound of the doorbell startled them all. None of them could move, but Mavis. She got up and slowly opened the front door. Mrs. Goodman stood looking concerned.

"Is everything all right over here? Where is Lela?" Mrs. Goodman asked.

Mavis did not respond to her concerns.

"I'm Mrs. Goodman. I live across the street."

"I know who you are," Mavis said in a dry, nasty tone.

Ashley gently pushed Mavis away from the door.

"Hello Mrs. Goodman. How are you?"

Mrs. Goodman struggled to look inside the house as she talked. Ashley positioned herself to prevent any entry.

"Hi Ashley. I saw you running. I got a little worried. I couldn't rest so I thought I had better just come over here and ask if everything was okay."

Ashley looked directly into Mrs. Goodman's eyes before speaking.

"Everything is fine Mrs. Goodman."

"Are you sure Ashley?"

"Everything is fine."

Ashley slowly closed the door on Mrs. Goodman's investigating eyes.

Mavis went and sat back in Curtis' easy chair. She lit up a new cigarette. Fran sat back on the couch still quite nervous. Ashley walked to the middle of the living room and turned to see one of Kelly's eyes peeking around the doorway. Kelly was trying to determine the status of this bloody situation. Ashley turned from Kelly to see Lela first check the gun for bullets and then take the safety off the weapon. Lela glanced over at Kelly and then looked up at Ashley and smiled.

"What do we do now, Ash?"

two

The Other Son

In one split second, Charles Mercer had went from being the other son to being the only son. Charles had found comfort living all his life in the giant shadow of his brother, Curtis. Now that shadow was gone. A spotlight was now focused directly on the other son.

Blue lights from all the police vehicles outside the house pierced through the kitchen windows. The lights illuminated the tears running down Charles's face. There was tremendous commotion outside and inside his brother's immaculate home. Charles had found an area of peace sitting at the kitchen table. He needed just a moment to digest this entire situation. He needed just a moment to collect his nerves and, most of all, his strength. The fact that his big brother was dead was going to be terribly inconvenient, but the thought of possibly loosing Lela forever was almost unbearable.

Guilt rippled through Charles' body. Every muscle began to stiffen. He struggled to prevent anyone from noticing that he was fighting insanity.

Charles tried to block out the chaos and concentrate on his wife. His beautiful wife, Eden, was just weeks away from giving him a firstborn son. Eden was the type of woman that most men would be honored to have her call them husband. Not only was she beautiful, but also well-educated and very devoted to helping Charles make his dreams come true. It could not have been easy marrying into his family. Both his mother and sister were domineering women who rarely remembered that Eden was his legal wife. Then there was Curtis. Eden had to constantly fight his flirtations and tried to hide Curtis' inappropriate gestures from Charles. Charles should have told her there was no woman immune from Curtis. She did not need to worry about hurting his feelings. Flirtation was a natural reaction Curtis had to any living, breathing woman.

Charles continued to sit in silence. He wondered why, just like his brother, he did not appreciate his own wife.

When Charles had come home one night and told Eden he had been approached by influential members of the community to consider making a run at becoming the city's first African-

American mayor, there was no hesitation in her response. Eden had assured him that they could win an election together.

Charles was always the one with all the doubts. Trying to run the entire city seemed like an impossible task. He struggled daily to run the Mercer Health and Beauty Supplies Corporation.

His mother, Doris, had started the company without a dime and turned it into one of the highest grossing African American owned businesses in the state. Doris had taken her children from living in housing projects to living in mansions. In words, Doris said she was now ready to start relinquishing power to her youngest son. However, her actions demonstrated she had no ability to relinquish power to anyone.

Charles truly felt his mother would really have preferred to pass her crown of glory on to her oldest son, Curtis. However, Curtis was not having any part of the family business.

Curtis was not the type of man to wait in the shadows for his chance to be fabulous. Curtis was already fabulous.

The first day Curtis brought Lela to his mother's house flashed in Charles's mind. His heart almost came out of his mouth that day. He felt Lela was the most beautiful creature that he had ever seen on this earth. That day was over twenty years ago and he still had that same feeling every time he looked at Lela.

Charles fought hard to focus. He needed to focus on what was happening now. He needed to stop thinking about his lack of love for his wife and his endless love for his brother's wife. Think about what Lela has done to your brother he kept saying to himself. Think about what was needed to preserve his own family. He tried to remember Eden's smile, her perfume, and her touch. Why could he not love his wife? Why would he not let his beautiful wife stop the Lela madness that was constantly raging in his head? Everything he was working so hard to achieve was all being blocked. Lela was totally consuming him. He was being devoured whole by this love for his brother's wife.

Charles clinched his fist and pounded them on his knees. He wanted to make his six-foot body stand, but there was no strength in his legs. He wanted to rip the shirt from his dark brown body and scream Lela's name. He needed to stop these thoughts. He needed to stop his heart from racing and start breathing regular. He needed to stop a growing urge to go to Lela and take her in his arms. He wanted to let her know that he would make all this horror vanish. Curtis was gone. They could just leave and be together now. Unlike his brother, he would protect her, cherish her, and love her.

Charles was paralyzed by reality. Only his tears continued to move down his face. He was not going to be able to smother this raging fire. In fact, resolving any type of problems was not his duty in the family. These types of situations were always for Curtis to resolve. Curtis was the son who knew how to change all wrongs into rights. Curtis was the son who had charm and a larger-than-life personality to soothe all necessary souls. Curtis was the son who was taller, more handsome, and whose voice was always like a calm river that flowed through everyone's soul. Charles was known only to everyone as the other son.

If only he had been honest with Lela from the very beginning. If only he had let her, and the entire world, know how much he cared. His silence all these years had caused his brother's death and Lela's misery.

Police detectives periodically came into the kitchen and tried to ask him questions. They attributed his lack of response to grief. They did not know that Charles was terrified to speak. He did not want them to realize that his tears were not for the murder victim, but for the murderer.

three

Soul Less Sister

If Mrs. Goodman had not called the police, who knows what those bitches might have done. That thought kept racing through Tracey Mercer's mind. Thank God that nosey old woman had sniffed around the house like a hound dog. When she saw Junior crying in the window, Mrs. Goodman had the police finish her unofficial detective work. She demanded the police go into the house just to satisfy her intuition.

Tracey felt that Ashley's ability to talk Lela out of killing herself was no accomplishment to brag about.

Curtis' children had already seen their father slaughtered. They should have had the satisfaction of seeing his murderer blow her brains out. However, Tracey's wish had not been fulfilled. She knew there was no way Lela could ever kill herself. It is always easier to kill others than to kill yourself. Lela had no real guts to carry out any type of self-inflicted physical harm. Tracey realized that her lack of respect all these years for Lela was now justified.

Tracey had not been able to cry yet for her dead brother because her increasing anger was blocking her grief. She was alone now. Curtis was gone and Charles would never be any help to her. Her younger brother was in the kitchen crying like a baby. Tracey knew Charles' tears were not due to the death of a family member. Charles was crying over the death of any chance for him to have that poor excuse for a woman. Tracey had never been blind to Charles' love for Lela. In fact, the only person that did not know Charles loved Lela was Lela.

She stood with her arms folded like a statue on the front lawn. Barricades had been put up to restrain the media and other curious neighbors. Despite all the police and paramedics going in and out of the house, Tracey knew they would not be able to stop her mother when she arrived. There was no way Tracey was going to let her mother see Curtis in this condition.

She stood on the front lawn like a statue and waited.

Tracey was tall, bronze, and beautiful. She was almost a total duplication of her mother. Almost no one ever noticed how glamorous Tracey looked. Unlike her brothers, Curtis who was flamboyant and Charles whose heart was kind and gentle, Tracey had no redeeming personality traits. She was mean. She was downright mean. The intensity of her evilness was what caught and kept people's attention. Anyone stupid enough to let her looks distract them were doomed to pay the consequences.

Unlike her ambitious mother, Tracey had always equated ambition with being ruthless. It had currently served her well as a vice president for the largest banking institution in the city. Although her mother now seemed to want her to soften, Tracey had never been allowed to show weakness while growing up.

Her brothers were allowed to have all types of flaws, but not Tracey. Her mother demanded that Tracey be strong, focused, and determined at all times. No one ever thought it would reach this level of intensity, including Tracey. Tracey knew she should change for the better, but she no longer had any control over her thoughts and actions. Just like Charles was consumed by his love for Lela, Tracey was consumed by her anger about everything.

Tracey continued standing like a statue waiting for her mother to arrive. She would have to tell her mother that Lela had killed her beloved, oldest child. Curtis was dead. After that task, Tracey would have one other immediate task. She would have to make sure that Lela burned in hell.

four

Heartbreak

Doris Mercer came charging up the middle of the street like a bull that had seen a red flag. All the barricades had prevented her from getting her automobile any closer to her son's house. Police officers tried to stop her steady stride with gentle words. They did not dare touch Doris or try to physically restrain her in any way. Their tactics were useless. Doris had blocked out all sights or sounds and headed straight for the front door of her son's house.

Doris Mercer was now in her late sixties, but still gorgeous. She was the original mold for her daughter Tracey. Doris was tall, bronze, and beautiful. Hair that flowed down her back and makeup applied just right. Jewelry that only accented the style of her attire.

Long ago, Doris had realized that mixing beauty with brains was a good cocktail for success. Her initial business venture was trying to use marriage as a way out of poverty. Her first husband was only able to give her regrets and failed at being a father to her first child, Curtis. Her second husband only gave her more regrets and only gave his name to two more children, Tracey and Charles. Then Doris realized men would not be her road to riches. She re-directed her focus away from men and into what she knew best, fashion and beauty.

She started out in the kitchen of a two-bedroom apartment of a housing-project selling Mercer Health and Beauty Supplies. What was almost forty years ago seemed like just yesterday.

Mercer Health and Beauty Supplies and her children became Doris' main concern. Her business empire and her children were her only true jewels in life. Now something was wrong with one of these precious gems.

"Get out of my way," Doris commanded.

"Mother, you cannot go in there," Tracey said.

"Where is my son?"

"Mother, Lela has done something horrible."

"Where is my son?" Doris demanded.

Police officers had surrounded the two women. They looked anxious because they did not know at what point to intervene. Tracey did not respond to her mother's question. She was not sure how to delicately tell her this terrible news.

Doris tried to storm passed Tracey. Tracey grabbed her mother by the arms and pushed her backward. Doris staggered back.

"I want to see my son right now!" Doris shouted.

Doris tried to storm passed Tracey again. Once again, Tracey pushed her backward.

"Curtis is dead. Lela killed him."

Tracey spoke the words with the tone of a woman who had never given birth to a child.

"No! no! That is not true. My baby is not dead!"

Doris tried to rush Tracey again. This time the police officers felt they needed to restrain Doris. Tracey was unable to provide any comfort to her mother. She could not reach out to embrace her. She did not order her mother's immediate release. Doris, in the strong grip of strangers, looked in her daughter's eyes. There were no tears of pain or sorrow. She only saw the cold stare of anger and hate.

"Where is my son?" Doris said desperately.

"Curtis is dead. Lela cut his throat. He is dead."

The police officers did not need any order to release Doris from their grip. They felt Doris go weak and limp. When they backed away, Doris staggered onto the grass.

"Lord no! Please Lord, not my baby! Lord no!"

Doris fell to her knees. Tracey could not move. She just continued to stand like a statue watching her mother disintegrate before her.

Doris fell flat on her back on the front lawn. She let out a scream that echoed through both heaven and hell.

"No! No! No!"

Tracey and the police officers stood in silence.

Doris was lying on her backside on the ground pleading.

She pleaded with God to give her son back and pleaded to the Devil to undo this evil deed. Neither responded to her request.

Doris Mercer's firstborn child was gone forever.

Curtis James Mercer was dead.

five

Ada's Assignment

"Miss Ada.......... "Miss Ada."

Ada Stinson could hear her name, but could not seem to open her eyes.

"Miss Ada.......... "Miss Ada."

The voice was becoming more clear and familiar.

"Miss Ada, please wake up."

Ada was startled when she finally opened her sleepy eyes. She had forgotten that Keisha's new hair color was now blond. Actually, Ada liked this color better than prior colors. Ada thought she might have to fire Keisha during the pink and green hair color periods. Ada realized that young people today just have no sense of class. Ada was far from the best lawyer in town, but she did try to maintain a little sense of style and dignity.

However, this blond hair color matched Keisha's light brown skin. Ada felt she could tolerate this blond hairstyle. Now she would have to concentrate on getting Keisha to wear clothes that were more appropriate for a lawyer's office. Ada would need to get the words tight and short out of Keisha's wardrobe closet.

"Miss Ada we have a client, "Keisha whispered.

"What are you saying," Ada mumbled.

"She is trying to tell you that you have a paying customer."

This unfamiliar voice brought Ada back to total consciousness. She first looked in the eyes of a nervous Keisha. As usual, Keisha had on a blouse that barely managed to contain her abundant bosom. Her skirt was about two inches away from being considered a headband.

Ada tried to straighten up her full-figured body in her office chair. She tried to fluff up her massive black curls of hair. Ada took a tissue from the box to wipe away sleep from her eyes and touch up makeup and lipstick. Then she focused her eyes on the stranger in the doorway.

Ashley Powell stood in the doorway like a statue chiseled in stone. Her firm, slender body filled out a tan business suit with perfection. Sunglasses covered eyes that were red from continuous crying. The tone of her voice indicated she was there strictly for business.

"I am Ashley Powell. I have a legal issue I need to discuss with you."

Ada began to shuffle papers on her desk to try to pretend as if she were working. She stood up to greet her visitor.

"Yes, Miss Powell, come right in and have a seat. This is my assistant, Keisha Johnson. Keisha, please get Miss Powell a cup of coffee."

"Cream and sugar?" Keisha asked as she walked toward the door.

"No coffee for me," Ashley replied as she sat down in one of the chairs in front of Ada's desk and removed her sunglasses.

"Hold all my calls Keisha," Ada commanded.

"Yes Miss Stinson," Keisha said as she walked out of the office.

Ashley waited to hear the door close before she began her explanation for this office visit.

"Do you know who I am?"

"I think the entire town knows who you are, Miss Powell. I think they have shown that news clip on television with you dodging news reporters about a thousand times now."

"I guess that is true," Ashley admitted with a brief smile.

Ada sat back in her chair.

"Exactly what can I do for you Miss Powell?"

"I'm sure you are also aware that my best friend, Lela Mercer, has been arrested for murdering her husband?"

"I think there may be two people in China that have not heard the news yet?" Ada said smiling.

"You're a comedian and an attorney," Ashley sternly replied.

"I'm sorry Miss Powell. This is not a very big city. You can't kill Doris Mercer's son and keep that a secret."

"I need you to represent Lela Mercer."

Ada could not stop her laughter from spontaneously coming forth.

"Now I'm a comedian," Ashley responded.

"I'm sorry again Miss Powell," Ada said. "A case like that would be a little too high profile for me. In case you didn't notice when you came in, I'm a storefront lawyer. I mainly handle little punks who think they can get rich selling drugs. I represent poor, nameless bastards who shoot each other after an all night drinking binge and don't even remember what they did the next day. I represent stupid hookers who picked up undercover cops instead of real johns. I'm the lawyer who represents crackheads who really need to go to treatment centers. I try to get them minimum-security time or a halfway house. I'm a poor man's lawyer, Miss Powell. Doris

Mercer is one of the richest black women in this state and maybe this country. She is going to spare no expense to have a public crucifixion of that pitiful, young girl. You definitely don't need me, Miss Powell. I would be happy to give you some recommendations of some big time lawyers you probably should consult."

"I need you, Miss Stinson," Ashley firmly reassured Ada.

Ada's humorous attitude quickly transformed into a state of confusion. Then Ashley made it all clear.

"Portia Lee is your niece, correct?" Ashley asked.

Ada sat up straight in her chair and took a moment to determine in her mind how she wanted to answer that question.

"Portia Lee is your niece, Miss Stinson?" Ashley reiterated.

"What makes you think that?" Ada finally responded.

"Some of the members of my church told me that you are Portia Lee's aunt. Is that true?"

Ada hesitated again with her response. She was not sure how to reply without putting herself in harm's way.

"Portia Lee is one of my brother's daughters," Ada slowly replied.

"Good," Ashley said with relief. "I need Portia Lee and I need you to get her for me."

Ashley took out a checkbook and began to write.

"You have got to be crazy. There is no way Portia Lee would take this type of case. That idiot killed Doris Mercer's son."

Ashley sprang from her seat like a tiger after prey. She slammed the checkbook down in front of Ada. Ada quickly pushed back her seat from the desk not knowing what Ashley was capable of doing in her present state of mind.

"What did you say?" Ashley said in a tone of voice that had gone low and dark.

Ada was unable to hide her discomfort.

"I did not mean to offend you, Miss Powell," Ada quickly apologized. "I'm merely trying to point out that your friend has a very cut and dry case. She killed her husband. There is not a bit of reasonable doubt in this case. Her own children saw her kill him. You definitely need a lawyer, but I don't believe Portia Lee is the lawyer you need."

Ashley stood up straight. She ripped a single check out of her checkbook. She placed the check in front of Ada on the desk.

"You let me be the judge of that, Miss Stinson. I am sure that check will cover your expenses. I need Portia Lee to defend Lela. I just hired you to make that happen."

Ada looked at the check amount with amazement.

"Well, well, let me see what I can do," Ada reluctantly surrendered. "I am not making any promises. I will see what I can do."

Ashley put her sunglasses back on and walked out of Ada's office. She walked passed Keisha's desk and out the front door without a further word.

Keisha raced into Ada's office.

"Oh my God!" Keisha shouted. "What are you going to do Miss Ada? Are you really Portia Lee's aunt?"

"Biologically, yes," Ada admitted.

"Oh my God!"

"We have a big problem," Ada said. "The last time I saw Portia, she was probably twelve years old."

"Oh my God!" Keisha shouted again.

"Portia is my brother Robert's daughter. You know how these men have all these kids by all these different women. I never tried to keep up with all those seeds Robert kept planting around this town. I think I went to a birthday party and that was the last time I saw that child. Her mother finally gave up on Robert and married some other guy. They moved up there to some fancy suburb outside of Cleveland. Lee is my maiden name. Stinson was my third husband's name. I was not married long enough to that last husband to even remember his last name. I don't fault Portia's mother for finally marrying a good man and forgetting all about Robert. Robert never did anything good for that woman or that child. I cannot even remember Portia's mother's first name right now. It'll come back to me."

"What the hell?" Keisha said in amazement. "Why didn't you tell all of this to Miss Powell?"

Ada handed Keisha the check. Keisha looked at the check amount and her eyes revealed the excessive compensation.

"Oh shit! You have got to remember her mother's name before we go see Miss Portia Lee," Keisha advised.

"I know," Ada said. "I know."

six

Unpleasant Surprise

Curtis never really liked Ashley. He simply tolerated her because she was like a child from a previous relationship. If you wanted Lela, you had to accept Ashley.

Curtis didn't really like Lela's other two close friends either. In his opinion, Mavis really needed to charge a monetary fee for the premium-level, sexual services she was providing to the male members of the community. Her standards for providing personal butt-naked, booty-banging activities were extremely low. Any well-hung stud that happened to say hello had a high probability of being allowed to invade her private parts repeatedly.

Curtis could not believe that Mavis had the audacity to vehemently reject him. He tried to ban her nymphomaniac, nasty behind from his home. Lela just laughed at what she called his outrageous demand.

Fran was a crybaby. Curtis tried to leave the house whenever he saw her car pulling into the driveway. He knew it would not be long before she was whining and crying about something. Mainly, she complained about all those bad-ass kids she kept giving birth to or all those bonehead deadbeats who went in and out of her bedroom creating all those bad-ass kids.

He could not understand why Fran would not go to some psych ward for some emotional help instead of coming to his house for therapy.

If he had to choose between Lela's three best friends, he could stomach Ashley the most. He could not understand why Ashley had chosen education and career over a husband and family. There was no doubt that she was book smart, which had led to plenty of money in the bank. However, she had channeled all her excess love and emotions into his wife and children. He felt like he had to constantly compete with Ashley to win over his own family. It was extremely difficult for him because he felt Ashley was sneaky and silently evil. She always avoided any real confrontation with him.

"Hello Curtis," Ashley would say with a dry sarcastic tone and phony smile.

He always tried not to respond. Lela would give him that look that indicated he had better return the greeting. Ashley was like a diamond to Lela. She was precious and untouchable.

Curtis never tried to pretend to anyone that he had any great affection for Ashley. He often wondered if Ashley loved his wife or was she in love with his wife. It didn't really matter. Whatever type of love it was, Curtis knew he would never be able to love Lela as much and as hard as Ashley could and would, forever. That was his explanation to his lawyer.

"Your mother and sister will go up in flames," Mica Goldman had advised. "I'm nervous just talking about this."

Mica Goldman was his mother's personal lawyer for well over twenty years. Over the years, she had become more like his mother's sister than someone on the payroll. This would become the first and only secret between the two women.

"Well, God-willing, you will never have to bring these papers out the vault," Curtis told Mica with confidence.

"Why Ashley Powell and not one of your family members?" Mica asked.

"Mama thinks Lela is mindless and has no respect for her. Tracey hates just about everybody on planet Earth. I wonder sometimes if she even likes me. My brother Charles is so blinded by Lela's looks he can't ever think straight when she is around. She has been making him crazy ever since I married her. He is such a baby. I have never been able to count on him for anything. Ashley is the only one I can trust to take care of my family if something were to happen to me. But, like I said before, I don't really expect anything to happen to me."

Curtis' words echoed through Mica's head as she stood at the center counter in the kitchen adding vodka to her glass of orange juice. She needed a little more kick to this morning beverage to get through the pending conversation.

Mica remembered how she was a young, struggling lawyer when Doris first came into her office. Her very first paid task was to get Curtis out of an auto thief charge when he was a teenager. Curtis claimed he was just joy riding with the fellows. He did not know the car was stolen. It was a lie then and a lie now. The other fellows spent time in a juvenile detention center. Curtis spent time at the church's food bank doing community service.

Guilt was creeping up Mica's spine as she sipped on her improved beverage. She had spent years getting Curtis out of one incident after another. Maybe once she should have let him suffer the consequences of his actions.

Then she remembered it was never really about Curtis. It was always about Doris. She had spent the majority of her law career doing whatever it took to keep Doris Mercer happy.

Doris had been adamant that her babies would never suffer like she had during her childhood. This rule especially applied to Curtis.

Mica drank some more juice. She was finally facing the reality that she had failed Curtis. In the past, she should have just once insisted to Doris that Curtis feel a little pain for his mischievous ways so they all would not be feeling so much pain now.

Doris came into the kitchen. She looked around the room like she was seeing her own kitchen for the very first time. The kitchen was bigger than some people's entire apartments. It was filled with the latest in appliances and gadgets. Sunlight beamed through the glass-enclosed breakfast nook. It filled the kitchen with a heavenly light. The flat screen television mounted on the wall was loudly reminding Doris of her very real tragedy.

Mica hit the button on the remote to turn off the television. Doris smiled with pride at Mica. Mica was living proof that she could turn any woman into a raving beauty. Long, tangled hair was now cut and styled. Uneven and dirty fingernails were now long and polished. Greasy skin filled with pimples was now tan and flawless. Cheap, wrinkled suits were now replaced with tailored, designer outfits. Mica was a sophisticated living sculpture that Doris had chiseled to create.

Mica offered Doris some orange juice.

"My own special mixture."

"I will take you up on that offer this morning."

"Did you sleep?" Mica asked as she fixed another breakfast cocktail.

"I fell asleep for a little while," Doris said. "When I woke up, I thought it was all just a dream. It's not a dream is it. My baby boy is really dead."

Doris began to cry again. Mica rushed over and clutched Doris tight. She kissed her forehead.

"I am so sorry Doris. I am so very sorry."

"It's not your fault," Charles sternly said as he entered the kitchen.

Mica released Doris and went back to fixing breakfast cocktails. Doris looked through tears at her only living son. Charles sat down at the kitchen table across from his mother.

"Have you talked to the funeral director?" Doris wanted to know.

"They have already picked up Curtis' body. They are waiting for me to bring a suit and whatever directions you want," Charles informed her.

"How is Eden?" Mica wanted to know.

"She is fine. The doctor said we are just waiting for the baby to shout let's get this party started. That could be any minute now."

"Are you and Eden ready to be parents?" Doris asked.

"I thought I was until all of this happened, but now..."

Doris had asked a question, but she really didn't care about the answer. Her mind was wandering in every direction. She didn't even realize she had cut off Charles in mid-sentence.

"Where is your sister?" Doris interrupted.

"She should be here any minute now."

"What is happening with Lela?" Doris wanted to know.

"I went this morning," Charles told his mother. "Lela was on some type of video monitor. I had to leave quickly. The news reporters were just terrible."

"It was just an initial arraignment," Mica explained. "They set bond at seven million dollars. They will turn it over to the common pleas court. She will go before the magistrate next week and they will assign the case to a judge. That hearing will also be by video monitor. My sources says that Judge Susan Hoffman is probably going to get the case. That is when they will march Lela out in person. When she first appears before Hoffman, it will be a circus."

"When is that court date?" Doris asked.

"They are going to move fast on this one. I'm told it should be in about two weeks."

"I want to be there."

"No way you should go Doris. I will be there. Tracey, Charles, and, especially you, Doris, do not need to be there. All they are going to do is drag Lela out in front of a bunch of cameras. She will plead not guilty and that will be it. There is no way they are going to reduce that seven million dollar bond. We all know Lela can't post that type of money. It will be an absolute madhouse with all the news reporters."

"How is she going to plead not guilty?"

"Listen Doris, she will probably plead not guilty until, whatever poor soul agrees to be her lawyer, can work out some kind of deal with the prosecutor," Mica continued.

"Deal?"

"I'm sure her lawyer is going to try to keep her out of the electric chair."

"Jesus Christ, they can't kill Lela," Charles cried out.

"Why not? She killed Curtis," Tracey barked as she entered the kitchen and slammed her purse on the kitchen counter.

The sound of Tracey's angry voice startled them all. Tracey marched further toward her brother and folded her arms in disgust with him.

Mica took a huge swallow of juice.

"I have been so out of my mind that I totally forgot about my grandbabies. What about Curtis' children?" Doris asked.

"Yeah Mica, tell her about those children," Tracey said with her usual bitterness. "Come on Mica, tell mother about Curtis' children.

"What is the matter with you?" Charles strongly inquired.

"My brother was murdered. That's what is wrong with me. Tell her Mica," Tracey commanded.

"What is she talking about Mica?" Doris gently asked.

"The children are with Lela's mother, Cheryl, right?"

Mica took a deep breath and continued trying to explain this stressful ordeal.

"Curtis and Lela made wills about three years ago. They have legal instructions that indicate if anything happens to them, Ashley Powell is not only the executor of their estate, but the guardian of their children."

The look on Doris' face reflected her puzzlement.

"What are you saying?"

"I'm saying that I will probably have to go to probate court tomorrow morning. But there is no doubt after all the documents are revealed, temporary custody of those children will be immediately granted to Ashley Powell. All Curtis' financial affairs would have fallen to his wife. But since his wife is in jail for murdering him and, per his own legal instructions, all his financial affairs immediately transferred over to Ashley Powell. Ashley Powell is in charge of Curtis' children and his entire estate."

Doris rose up from her chair.

"What are you saying?" Doris strongly asked again.

"Calm down mother," Charles said as he also rose up from his seat.

"Where are my grandchildren? Who the hell is Ashley Powell?"

Charles rushed to his mother's side and tried to comfort her. He gently stroked her back.

"Mother, mother, Ashley is Lela's best friend. You know Ashley. You just don't remember her right now. The children are safe with her."

"You would say that," Tracey spit out. "Anything that Lela does is fine with you, right Charles? Does that include killing your own brother?"

Charles charged toward Tracey. Mica jumped between the two siblings.

"Everybody just calm down," Mica instructed. "Charles is right. The children are safe with Ashley Powell right now. She would never do anything to hurt those children.

She loves those children and, most of all, Curtis trusted her. She will not interfere with any funeral arrangements. She knows you don't need money from Curtis' estate for any type of funeral expenses."

"Interfere with me burying my own son!" Doris hollered in amazement.

"Ashley Powell is the executor of Curtis' estate. His legal instructions was that if he died, she is totally in charge. However, she has absolutely no interest in the funeral. Her main concern right now is just the mental and physical care of your grand-children. She will probably not even come to the funeral. She will leave all the funeral arrangements to you."

"That is mighty big of her. She's going to let me bury the child I birthed into this world? You have talked to this woman?" Doris asked.

"As Curtis' personal attorney, I spoke to Ashley early this morning," Mica replied. "Ashley is not the enemy. So let's just all calm down and think clearly."

Charles looked into Mica's pleading eyes and retreated back to his seat.

"Why didn't you tell my mother about all of this three years ago, Mica?" Tracey insisted on an answer.

"You already knew about all of this?" Doris asked Mica.

"I just said that I was Curtis' personal attorney too, Doris. Anything he requested me to do legally for him was confidential information."

"You helped turn my grandchildren over to some stranger?"

"I did what your son wanted and legally instructed me to do as his attorney."

"You helped stab my mother in the back," Tracey said.

"I did what Curtis wanted," Mica repeated.

"I want those children," Doris ordered Mica.

"Let's just wait until after the funeral," Charles told his mother.

Mica took another swallow of her juice. Doris slowly sat back down and looked into the sunlight.

"Why would he do that?" Doris asked herself out loud.

"Let's just handle all of that after the funeral," Charles whispered to his mother. "You heard what Mica said. Ashley has no plans to interfere with any funeral arrangements we make. Let's just be a family first and give Curtis back to God properly."

Tears flowed down Charles' face. Doris looked around at her only living son and realized his pain. She smiled at him and grabbed his hand.

"Yes, you're right," Doris agreed. "I trust you Charles. The children are safe for now with this Ashley Powell. Let's just concentrate on Curtis right now."

"Thank you mother," Charles said.

Tracey stormed out of the kitchen. Mica took another deep breath and finished off her breakfast cocktail.

seven

Portia Lee

The elevators opened on the twenty-third floor.

Ada and Keisha stepped out of the elevator facing a wall full of paintings of old dead white men. They turned to the right and started walking toward the big wooden doors with giant golden door handles at the end of the hallway.

When they entered the office, Mrs. Hansberry looked over her reading glasses and greeted them.

"Hello, may I help you?"

Mrs. Hansberry was an African American woman in her late fifties. She looked more like a school teacher than a legal assistant.

"We are here to see Miss Portia Lee," Keisha quickly blurted out.

"And you are?" Mrs. Hansberry asked.

"I'm her aunt, Ada Stinson," Ada proudly announced.

"That is correct," Keisha added. "This is Miss Lee's aunt. I'm Miss Ada's assistant, Keisha Johnson."

Mrs. Hansberry slowly rose from her seat with a look of suspicion in her eyes. She took off her reading glasses and laid them on her desk.

"Have a seat ladies. I will let Miss Lee know you are here."

Mrs. Hansberry disappeared into the back of the office leaving Ada and Keisha sitting alone.

"She doesn't believe us," Keisha told Ada.

"I don't believe it myself," Ada replied. "Look at this office. I knew Pookie was a big time lawyer, but damn!"

"Pookie?" Keisha said with amazement.

Mrs. Hansberry suddenly reappeared.

"Miss Lee will see you now. Just follow me."

Ada and Keisha marched like soldiers behind Mrs. Hansberry back to another huge wooden door with golden handles. Mrs. Hansberry opened the door and ushered them inside.

When they entered the office both Ada and Keisha were in shock. The office was humongous and quite lavish.

Portia Lee rose up from a leather seat behind a magnificent desk. Behind Portia were glass windows that looked out over the endless, turbulent waters of Lake Erie.

Portia Lee was as splendid as her office. She was average height, but not average in looks. The proper adjective for Portia was expensive. Her dress looked exclusive. The jewelry looked like it needed to be insured. The hair seemed professionally styled. The makeup was impeccable.

Keisha stood silent during this brief family reunion. She was able to make an observation that she had not anticipated. The great Portia Lee actually seemed nervous to finally see an aunt she had not seen in years.

Ada's demeanor was unchanged by Portia's larger than life presence. She was temporarily oblivious to all these signs of success. She did not pick up any hint that Portia seemed anxious, but angry. Her loud and unorthodox style sprang forth immediately at the sight of her impressive niece.

"Pookie! Oh my God, Pookie!" Ada yelled. "Look at you, Pookie!"

Portia walked to the front of her desk and extended her hand to greet Ada. Ada bypassed her hand and enclosed Portia in a bear-style hug. She kissed Portia on both cheeks several times.

"Oh my God, Pookie, you look just like Robert."

Portia had been caught off guard by Ada's outburst of affection. However, the sound of her father's name sent up a stone wall around her heart.

"My name is Portia."

The cold in her voice sent a chill through Ada. Ada slowly released her grip and tried to regain her composure.

"Oh yes, that's right. I am sorry, Portia," Ada apologized.

The nervousness had evaporated from Portia. Now it was Ada's turn to be a little uneasy. Portia motioned for Ada and Keisha to sit down. She returned to her seat behind the desk.

"Well, it's been at least twenty years so I'm sure there has got to be a very good reason you came to see me Ada."

"We actually came about a legal matter," Keisha said.

Portia turned and looked at Keisha like she had just realized Keisha was also in the room. Her eyes examined Keisha with a long look of disapproval.

"Who are you?" Portia asked.

"I'm Keisha Johnson. I'm Miss Ada's assistant. Miss Ada has a new client. We actually wanted to consult with you about how to handle a very difficult case."

"Well, my first advice would be to take some type of no-doze medication before you go into court so you won't fall asleep during trial," Portia said with sarcasm.

"I was extremely tired that day," Ada said defensively. "How did you know about that?"

"What do you want Ada?" Portia demanded.

"I have a new client that is a little bit out of my league," Ada explained. "She really is more in your league. Did I say how proud I am of you and all of this? My God, I really have to tell Robert."

The sound of her father's name once again brought back the anger in her tone.

"What do you want Ada?" Portia sternly repeated.

"Miss Ada has been hired to represent Lela Mercer," Keisha abruptly uttered.

There was a brief moment of silence. Portia began to laugh uncontrollably.

"You have got to be kidding? The woman who killed Doris Mercer's son?"

"Sounds hilarious to you too," Ada giggled. "But it is true."

"Why would she hire you Ada?" Portia inquired. "Slicing her husband's throat was not enough? She wants to make sure she gets the death penalty?"

"Now, no need to be rude Pookie," Ada gently scolded.

Portia did not appreciate being reprimanded by this absentee aunt.

"Stop bullshitting me Ada," Portia strongly warned. "I have not seen you in years and now you just show up out of the blue talking about some fool that killed her husband. What exactly do you want from me?"

Ada took a long deep breath.

"Well, I want you to be co-counsel with me on this case."

"Did you walk in here blinded-folded? You want me to assist you?" Portia asked. "Hell must have frozen over and nobody bothered to tell me."

"Now, listen Pookie. I know I'm wrong to be asking you for any type of favors. I can't make up for what Robert has done to you, but we are still family. We are still blood. I really do need your help with this case."

Portia sprang up from her seat like it had caught fire.

"You have got a lot of goddamn nerve. First of all, stop calling me Pookie. My name is Portia. Now, I am not sure what you told that idiot who thought it was a good idea to kill the heir to the Mercer fortune. I don't know how much she is paying you to come up here and beg me to be a fool too. I don't really care. There is nothing I can do for you or her. She killed her goddamn husband. Her husband was not just some Tom, Dick, or Harry off the street. Her husband was Doris Mercer's son. She has no legal case. She really needs to plead guilty and just get this nasty mess over for everyone. Any sense she had left must be gone if she would hire some crack head defender like you. But, let me say it once again, I really don't care. Now you and Miss Ghetto U.S.A. get back on the interstate and head south. Tell your client that she really does need to get a real lawyer. But you make sure you tell her that you don't know me at all. Because that would be the absolute truth. If you were really my blood aunt, it would not have taken you twenty years to come up here and see me. Oh yeah, I forgot. You didn't come here to see me. You came here so that I can help you get your sorry ass paid. Well, the answer is no. So, you can get out of my office right now. And, be sure to tell that motherfucker you call my father that I said he can go straight to hell where I'm sure he will feel right at home."

Portia was exhausted from her rage. Her chest was rapidly going up and down to prevent tears from escaping from her eyes.

Ada realized at that moment that she was no better than her brother, Robert. She had also abdicated her role in this child's life. Her absence as an aunt had caused almost as much pain as the absence of her brother as a father. Ada had under-estimated her importance in Portia's life.

"I apologize for myself as well as Robert. Good people raised you Portia. Do you think you would have all of this if Robert and I had any influence on you."

"Thank God you didn't have any influence on me," Portia answered. "You're an attorney, but I'm a damn good attorney."

Ada was stunned. It had never entered her mind that Portia might have become a lawyer because she was a lawyer. Her disappointment transformed into overwhelming guilt. She slowly rose from her seat. Keisha followed her lead.

"Forget we ever came here," Ada responded. "I was very wrong to come to you in this way. Let's go Keisha."

Portia watched her aunt and Keisha leave her office.

However, within a few seconds, Keisha returned. Portia was still fuming with rage.

"I told Miss Ada that I left my lucky ink pen," Keisha told Portia. "As the reigning Miss Ghetto U.S.A, I really just wanted to make a brief speech. I know you and Miss Ada have some major family issues to work out, but you are absolutely right. Lela Mercer needs a really good lawyer. I love Miss Ada, but you know she is a little rusty on the law. They came to her because she has bragged about being your aunt. She never thought that some of that bragging would come back to bite her in the butt. Nobody truly believed that she was your aunt. That's because everybody knows that you are one of the best. Miss Ada is lucky to still have her license to practice law. Miss Ada needs you right now. What is more important, Lela Mercer needs you."

Keisha started to walk back out of the office. She stopped to add one more comment.

"The FBI went to see a Mrs. Goodman who lives across the street from Curtis and Lela Mercer."

"Why would the FBI be inquiring about a local murder case?" Portia asked.

"I'm just Miss Ghetto U.S.A. You're the damn good attorney. You tell me."

As she left the room, Keisha watched the rage in Portia's eyes turn into pure curiosity.

eight

The Funeral

Calling hours were held between the hours of noon and seven the previous day. That still did not diminished the number of people who attended the funeral.

A sea of mourners dressed in black filled every seat in The House of Mary Baptist Church. Those unable to get inside the church, lined the streets just to get a glimpse of this prominent, local family.

Levi Sutton, director of the Sutton Funeral Home, was overwhelmed by the honor that Doris Mercer had given him the task of preparing her son for heaven. Along with his son, Bradley, Levi had hired extra help to assist with this massive assignment. Levi told Doris two additional hours before the funeral would be needed to try to accommodate more of the known and unknown who wanted to pay their respect to her and her dearly departed son.

Charles was being continuously hugged, kissed and given words of comfort. This was interrupted by Levi's growing concern for Charles' pregnant wife.

"Is Eden alright?" Levi asked Charles. "Does she need some cold water?"

"She's fine," Charles replied.

"When is that baby due?"

"She may have the baby any minute now."

"Lord don't let that happen," Levi laughed. "I have enough to deal with right now. Your mother is holding up pretty good. What about your sister?"

Charles looked around at Tracey who was standing alone by the casket. Tracey was fixated on Curtis' face. They had placed Curtis in a jet black casket with silver trim. The inside of the casket was pure white. A bed of red roses covered the lower end of the casket. Curtis wore a black suit with a white shirt. He had on his favorite red tie and pocket handkerchief that his children had given him for one of his birthdays. Even in death, Curtis was extremely handsome. He could have risen at any moment and walked out the front door of the church. He looked like he was just in a peaceful, deep sleep.

Tracey stood alone trying to blaze a permanent photograph of Curtis' face in her mind.

Charles looked far to the left of the casket and saw his mother standing. She was trying to graciously greet as many as she could that came to offer her their sympathy.

Sister Mary, who was considered mother of the church, was clinging to Doris like a shadow. Charles was a little surprised how concerned Sister Mary was about his mother during this ordeal. He knew that his mother and Sister Mary had a long and complicated past together that periodically resurfaced and brought them clinging back together again. They shared secrets that were not really secrets. Time had just made ugly truths turn into faint memories for everyone except these two women. Their relationship was like hot and cold water that was continuously running.

Sister Mary was prepared today to be a rock to lean on if Doris would suddenly be overcome by grief. Charles knew Sister Mary would not be able to exercise her ability to be a pillar of strength during this funeral. There was no way his mother was going to show any form of weakness in public.

Charles looked out over the church. It was filled with faces that he just could not recognize right now. Church fans waving continuously only circulating the intense heat around the room. The church was filled with the low murmur of disbelief mingled with the sound of church hymns being played on the organ.

"I would like some water," Eden told Levi.

Eden walked up behind Charles and rubbed his back.

She still looked beautiful despite her enormous expansion in size due to pregnancy.

"No problem," Levi said. "I will go get it personally myself. You just sit back down. Girl, please, just sit back down."

Eden was amused by Levi's jittery behavior. She knew that he was more afraid of any sign of displeasure from Doris than any sign of labor that she might give.

Charles smiled at his wife. He was unable to offer her any proper spousal support. Eden looked into her husband's eyes and knew his mind was preoccupied with thoughts of Lela. She fought hard not to make any comments. This was not the time or the place to start another discussion about Charles' endless obsession for Lela.

No one in the church was aware of the events taking place outside. Bradley, the funeral director's son, was struggling, along with the other assistants, to keep all the limousines moving and the crowd outside the church under control. Then Bradley's worst nightmare suddenly started to materialize before his eyes.

At the far end of the street, Curtis' black Cadillac sports utility vehicle came to a stop at the police barricade. Everyone in town knew that vehicle. The license plate simply displayed, "CJM."

The vehicle was being closely followed by a black Lexus with a license plate that displayed "CJM2." Bradley watched the police officer approach and speak to the vehicle driver. A chill shot up Bradley's spine when the police officer motioned for the other officers to remove the barricade. The two vehicles slowly proceeded toward the front of the church.

When the two vehicles stopped, Bradley raced to the driver's side of the Cadillac sports utility vehicle and opened the door.

"Hello Bradley," Ashley said as she emerged. "Leave this truck parked right here. We will not be staying long."

"Are you sure you want to do this?" Bradley nervously asked.

"I don't have any choice," Ashley answered.

Bradley ran around to the other side of the vehicle to help the other passengers. He looked inside and saw Curtis' children. Twelve-year-old Kelly, ten-year-old Junior, eight-year-old Callen and his six-year-old baby girl, Jade, were all looking back at him with fear in their eyes.

"Hello Miss Kelly," Bradley tried to smile as he gently took her hand.

"Hello sir," she politely replied.

Bradley helped Kelly out of the car like she was a princess. Her siblings closely followed behind her like she was the only form of mother they had left.

Mavis and Fran bolted from the Lexus and rushed to Ashley's side.

"You and Fran take the kids and just stay behind me," Mavis instructed. "There is no doubt this heifer is going to make a scene."

"It's her brother's funeral and these are her nieces and nephews," Ashley whispered. "She could not possibly be that crazy."

"You know she is fucked up in the head," Mavis reminded Ashley. "You can believe me. She is getting ready to act a fool in here. If I have to, I will stomp her crazy, black ass right here in the house of the Lord."

"Maybe we should not take these poor children in there," Fran cautioned. "Haven't they been through enough?"

"The almighty Doris Mercer demanded that I bring them. There was no fight. I agreed with Miss Doris. They have to see their father one last time," Ashley reassured her friends that their actions were correct. "They have to see Curtis one last time."

Mavis took the lead. Kelly took Junior's hand and followed. Fran took Callen's hand and Ashley took Jade by her small hand. They began their procession into the church.

The roar of disbelief from the crowd outside had caused a ripple of curiosity inside the church. It also broke Tracey's trance. She instantly knew what that sound meant. Charles and Doris were unable to move as they watched the aisle clear as Tracey marched unstoppable toward the front door of the church.

The funeral assistants opened both front doors of the church and Mavis came through with her head held high and ready for battle. Ashley, Fran, and Curtis's children followed closely behind.

Tracey met Mavis in the front lobby almost nose to nose. Levi quickly came out to the lobby to help his son try to prevent a catastrophe. Levi and Bradley were not sure how to defuse this volatile situation.

"What do you think you are doing?" Tracey demanded to know.

"These are Curtis' children," Mavis told her. "They have a right to see their father."

"You have no right to come in here."

"For once in your life, open your eyes and your heart. These are your brother's children," Mavis pleaded.

"You can leave my brother's children right here with me. We are their family. Not murderers, liars, and thieves disguised as women. You and these two other bitches need to leave this church right now."

"Not everybody is scared of your crazy butt, Tracey. It's going to take more than your skinny ass to stop my big ass from coming into this church. I am taking these children straight to that casket. You better do what you have to do right now."

"Please ladies," Levi pleaded. "This is the house of the Lord for God's sake."

Tracey moved closer toward Mavis and clinched both her fists. Charles' voice stopped his sister from going any further.

"Don't disrespect your mother and your brother's children. Don't disrespect Curtis. Let these children see their father for the last time in peace."

Charles stood behind his sister ready to fight for the right for the children to enter the church. A worried Eden wobbled toward her husband. Levi rushed to Eden and tried to make her return to her seat.

Tracey stood for a moment looking into Mavis' eyes.

Mavis returned the glare of pending battle. It was evident that Mavis had no intention of backing down. After a brief silent moment, Tracey finally moved back. She reluctantly moved to the side to let Mavis and the children proceed into the church.

Mavis did not look around at all the eyes focused on her as she moved up the aisle toward the casket. The church had gone totally silent. Mavis' steady stride was suddenly broken by the loud cry of pain from Junior. She turned around to see Junior had released Kelly's hand. He had fallen to his knees at the sight of his father lying in the casket. Junior could not lift his head as his tears began to flow like a river of pain to the floor.

"No!" Junior hollered. "No!"

Charles tried to rush to his nephew's aid but Kelly's scream stopped him cold.

"Don't you touch him. Don't anybody touch him," Kelly shouted. "Get up Junior! Get up!"

"No!" Junior continued to cry out. "No!"

"Get up Junior! Get up!" Kelly continued to shout.

"No, I can't," Junior cried out. "I can't."

All the adults in the church were frozen. They did not know what to do. Callen stood frozen like a statue looking at his father in the casket. Jade tried to bury her eyes and ears in Ashley's dress.

Suddenly, a pleasant voice flowed through the church like music from heaven.

"Curtis"

The calm in Doris' voice was shocking to everyone.

"I need you to get up Curtis."

Junior stopped crying at the sound of her voice.

His grandmother had never called him Curtis. He had always been Junior. He felt ashamed that he was on his knees. What if his father opened his eyes and saw him like this?

What did his grandmother think about him showing such weakness? He could not cry anymore, but he was afraid to move.

Doris slowly walked down the aisle and held out her hand.

"Get up Curtis. I need you to take my hand."

Junior took a deep breath and slowly rose up. He used the sleeve of his suit to dry his face and wipe his nose. He took his grandmother's hand. His siblings quickly rushed to their grandmother's side. The children slowly walked with Doris to their father's casket.

"Your father is gone," Doris told her oldest grandson. "Now you are my Curtis. You have to be strong."

Doris kissed each of her grandchildren and tried to make them realize they would be fine.

"Your father loved all his children and that will never change. His body is leaving us, but his spirit will be with us forever. His spirit will protect you forever."

Her gentle words and peaceful demeanor gave some comfort to her grandchildren. Doris looked at these children and knew there would be no more crying on her part. She suddenly realized that her beloved oldest son was dead, but the rest of her children were very much alive.

She needed to regain her focus, her strength, and her determination for them. She could not let her sadness cause a distraction. She was still a mother. Her other children needed her as much as she needed them. She had been knocked down hard by Curtis' death. It was time to get back up. The look in her grandchildren's eyes made her know that she could not accept defeat. Her undying love for all of her children had brought her back. She had to begin right now living again for them.

Ashley had given Bradley misinformation. Ashley and her friends stayed for the entire funeral. They heard women and men sing like angels as they musically alerted God that Curtis was on his way to the kingdom of heaven. They laughed as friends and relatives recited stories about their encounters with Curtis. They listened to Pastor Nadine Dandridge preach the goodness of Curtis James Mercer and the hope of eternal life offered by Jesus Christ. They cried when Charles took the podium and gave a final salute to his brother. They were unable to look when Charles walked to the casket and bent down to give his big brother a final kiss.

Curtis had not been a perfect man, but he had been a man. Curtis had done all he could to take care of his family and friends. He had chosen not to follow in his absentee father's footsteps or stand in his powerful mother's shadow. He created his own unique style. For that fact, men respected Curtis. They showed their respect that day by lifting up his casket like he was a king.

Women who loved Curtis and who Curtis had made love to carried the numerous baskets of flowers that would adorn his graveside.

The funeral car procession drove down streets that were lined with mourners. This was a family from their city and their neighborhood that had gone from rags to riches.

People had come out to give honor for what this family had accomplished and for giving them everlasting hope.

At the cemetery, the mourners crowded around the casket to hear Pastor Nadine Dandridge give Curtis permission to return to the earth. As the mourners drove away from the grave site, they watched Doris Mercer stand alone at Curtis's casket. They watched a woman who they thought had infinite power stand powerless.

The news of Curtis' death had been unbelievable. The funeral made it all real for everyone. A family that for years seemed immortal was mortal after all.

nine

Women In Agreement

She had never physically given birth to a child. However, she felt she had spiritually given birth to Portia. The moment Portia stepped into her office, she saw the potential. The realization was instant. She had found someone that could be molded into a professional masterpiece.

Candace Farrell did not care that her skin was white and her hair was blond. She envied Portia's real mother for having a real physical bond. Candace knew that blood and skin color were not necessary ingredients for love.

She loved Portia as if she had felt the labor pains. She was willing to give Portia every drop of her knowledge. It did not matter if Portia was merely using her to gain an advantage in reaching her career goals. Portia, as well as other men and women in their profession, obviously felt she had a talent that they needed to soak up from her aura. If Portia was using her, Candace was flattered to be used.

She was determined to train Portia to reach career heights that time had put totally out of her reach. She would live out her remaining career dreams through Portia.

Candace sat silent and proud as Portia filled the room with wit and charm. She and Portia had been summoned to the home of Betty Endress, one of the founders of Endress, Neal, Tuthill & Cruz, to explain Portia's request to give assistance to Ada Stinson. The other founders of the firm, Martha Neal, Donna Tuthill, and Victoria Cruz, sat absorbing every word and gesture by Portia. Candace could tell they were in awe of her protégé.

The founders of the law firm were women who had paid their dues in both their professional and personal lives.

Together, they had managed to build a respected law firm in between marrying and divorcing several husbands and giving birth to numerous children. Their triumphant accomplishments were reflected in their extravagant attire.

Hair that time had turned gray or white was camouflaged by hair coloring. Their jewelry was costly and excessive.

Although they were senior beauties, a sudden smile or turn of the head gave glimpses of their youthful exquisiteness.

They all no longer actively practiced law, but actively oversaw what took place at the law firm. They were already intrigued by this sensational murder case. They were even more excited by the prospect of the law firm being part of this media bonanza. They sat comfortable with their elegance listening to a young woman who might be the future of the legal firm that they had built.

Portia had come to Candace tormented by Ada's unexpected visit. She had revealed her paternal family tree. She had vividly tried to surmise her conflicting feelings she had for her father and her father's sister.

Portia had also woven into the story her curiosity about some of the unusual facts concerning what should be a routine domestic murder case. Why was there so much trust that she was the right lawyer that could bring about something good out of this horrendous situation?

Candace was not sure if Portia just had a thirst for a legal challenge or if she just needed to reach out and grab anything that was part of her real father. It did not matter. Candace was prepared to step in at any moment and fight with these old women to get what she realized might help give Portia some peace of mind and restore a lost part of her soul.

"I was not aware that Ada Stinson was your aunt," Betty said.

"I believe every woman should have her own unique style," Martha commented. "Ada takes that rule just a little bit too far."

The women all laughed as they thought about their uncommon colleague.

"Ada is totally alone in a category created just for her," Portia admitted. "My father has never been a part of my life. I never really talk about his side of the family."

"You feel compelled to come to her aid?" Donna inquired.

"I really cannot explain why. She has been living just 40 miles down the road, but I have not even seen Ada in years."

"You don't have to try to make sense of your feelings, young lady. We all have family issues," Victoria informed Portia. "But my dear, this seems like a winless case."

"Why should Endress, Neal, Tuthill, & Cruz want to get involved? Betty asked. "Do we really want to go up against Doris Mercer?"

"Doris Mercer is not the prosecutor," Portia reminded the founders of the firm.

"Believe me, Doris will be the driving force," Martha rebutted.

"And Doris is a force not to go against without careful thought," Donna added.

"What could our firm achieve by getting in the middle of this public domestic mess?" Victoria asked.

Portia sat with no reasonable reply. Candace sensed it was time to spring into action.

"There is more to this case than what is visual to the naked eye," Candace responded. "The FBI is snooping around. There is something they are trying to dig up. Whatever it is, it could be something that we can use. I know that Shay Newman is the lead prosecutor. Shay and I went to law school together. She will be sending out her top black female assistant prosecutor to handle this case. They want to cover all the bases. I say we send Portia right back at them."

"This is not a racial case," Betty said. "It's just plain old fashion murder. Some fed up wife killed her husband. It's not black or white. It's just human."

"Shay will make sure no one can bring in race as an issue," Candace clarified. "I don't even anticipate ever going to trial with this case. I say the first good deal they put on the table we take."

"I still don't understand why we should get involved?" Victoria asked again. "Any lawyer worth a grain of salt can take a plea bargain."

"A good deal for Lela Mercer can be a great deal for our law firm," Portia regained her voice. "There is no shame in pulling something good out of adversity. This case, because of Doris Mercer, is getting national media attention."

"Win or lose, the firm will be put on the map with this case," Candace added. "There will not be any woman in any type of legal trouble in this state, maybe even in this country, that will not want the services of a law firm founded by and run by women. The same law firm that came to the rescue of the poor soul that is standing defenseless against the mighty force called Doris Mercer."

Betty had to use a cane to stand and walk around the room. She needed the blood to circulate so that she could think better. The room was a showplace for overpriced artwork and sculptures. The superb taste of well-paid interior designers had made art and furniture come together with perfection. Betty walked aimlessly around the room.

"Candace, make us some drinks," Martha ordered.

"Portia, do you want a drink?" Donna asked.

"No ma'am," Portia politely declined.

"Make Portia a double on the rocks," Victoria said laughing.

Candace quickly went to the bar and began her amateur bartending duties. Betty flopped back down on the couch almost exhausted by her little walk around the room.

"What type of husband was he?" Betty breathlessly asked.

"I used Tavares Investigation Services. Delia Tavares did a little checking for me," Portia revealed. Curtis Mercer was Doris' oldest son. Most people around town don't believe that Mercer was his real father. His real father was probably one of them wham, bam, and thank you ma'am kind of guys. Curtis was a pretty man who needed a pretty wife to make the family pictures look good. He was spoiled, selfish, and self-centered. Women, money, and cars were never an issue for him. Regardless of some of his bad qualities, everybody in the community loved Curtis. He was flashy and flamboyant. A very charming man. Men admired him and women wanted him. He was a gentle giant in the community and at home. This man was a lover, not a fighter. He would never even think to raise his hand or fist to his wife or children. They were like trophies to him. He would not dare think to put any blemish on his trophies. Some men are very mentally cruel and have no idea that they are being cruel. This is what may have been Curtis Mercer's undoing."

Candace passed out drinks to her elderly bosses. The liquor helped to fuel their growing interest in the case.

"What makes you throw out that type of statement?" Martha wanted to know. "I think men know when they are being physically or mentally cruel to women."

Portia used Betty's method and got up from her seat.

She began walking around the room. It helped her think better and put more emphasizes on her spoken words.

"Curtis was the type of man that everyone knows the deal," Portia continued. "Everyone expected him to throw around money. Having lots of women was part of his persona. Everyone accepted his style and justified his behavior, except his wife. He didn't realize he was being mentally cruel. As far as he was concerned, she should have been happy to get him. I'm sure his last emotion was pure genuine shock when his pretty wife sliced open his throat."

"What type of woman would we be defending?" Donna weighted in. "She is an accused murderer. Her prior character will reflect on us."

"An extremely beautiful, accidental murderer," Candace chimed in. "Lela Mercer has a squeaky clean history. Being late to a church service was probably the worst offense she had committed before killing her husband. She didn't mean to kill him. It was just an act of sudden passion."

"Sudden passion against a man that did nothing to provoke that action," Victoria made clear. "By your own investigators admission, this man was well-loved by everyone in the community and never raised a violent hand to his wife or children. How can we defend that?"

"And let us not forget that he is Doris Mercer's son," Betty reiterated. "Doris Mercer who is black, beautiful, and filthy, stinking rich."

"Why is everyone so afraid of this Doris Mercer?" Portia questioned.

"Money honey!" Donna acknowledged. "Doris is full of money. Her dead son might have been a sweetie pie, but his mother is a bitch when necessary. And at all times is when she feels it is necessary. Don't forget about that daughter too. That girl is far worse than her mother. Doris will use every dime she has to put this Lela under the jailhouse. Then she will come after this law firm with whatever she has left in her change purse."

"What kind of money can we make?" Martha wondered. "What do we have to gain? There is no way this Lela is going to wind up with any cash. How do we recoup the time, the effort, and, most of all, our reputation trying to save poor little Lela from the electric chair?"

"The publicity!" Candace joyfully announced. "The national attention brought to this law firm will be priceless."

"You want to use this family tragedy for our own personal gain?" Donna asked.

"As a law firm founded by and run by women, shouldn't this firm be first in line to defend this particular woman?" Portia challenged her bosses. "Which woman in this room has not felt like Lela did that night at some point in time. The difference between Lela and all of us in this room is that Lela actually did what we all at one time wanted to do."

"Amen! I will drink to that," Betty said before gulping down her drink.

"That does not make what she did right," Victoria said. "You cannot just kill men for being men."

"We are not trying to prove she was innocent or morally right," Candace explained. "We are going to just prove that her life should be spared. That is our only goal. Lela was wrong for what she did, but she does not deserve to die. Her children do not need another dead parent."

There was silence in the room for a moment. Both Portia and Candace were not sure if they had convinced the founders of the firm. Their moment of uncertainty was short.

"Make sure that Ada is only a silent fixture in the courtroom," Martha advised. "We cannot afford for Ada to even try being a lawyer at this stage in her life."

"We want to be kept in the immediate loop on this case," Donna warned. "We do not want any surprises."

"Candace, make sure that all the firm's legal weapons are made available to Portia," Victoria instructed. "Going up against Doris Mercer will not be a battle, but a war."

"Portia, the stage will be yours," Betty informed. "Remember, the most important aspect is not your career or this firm. This also is not at all about your relationship with your dear Aunt Ada. The most important point that should be constantly in your mind is that Lela Mercer's life is now in your hands. Her children's future depends on you."

Candace smiled with relief at accomplishing permission for her protégé to tackle this pivotal case. Portia was suddenly overcome by the enormous task that she had actually fought to receive. She had entered that room only wishing to seek permission to publicly embarrass Ada for abandoning her. Betty's statement made her realize this was not about her vindictive need to make Ada pay for her absence. This case was only about Lela's children.

Portia suddenly realized that she was now responsible for saving more than just Lela's life. Just like Ada easily had forgotten about her, Portia had just as easily forgotten about Lela's children.

Candace and the founders of the firm felt more drinks were needed to seal this agreement. Portia did not need any more cold beverages. A chill was already racing down her spine.

ten

Thou Shall Not Kill

"You need to tell her now," Keisha whispered into Ada's ear.

Ada looked over at Ashley who was sitting silent and at attention next to Lela's mother, Cheryl Bishop. It was obvious that Lela's beauty was a heredity trait. However, Cheryl was trying hard not to look unpleasant this morning. She was using all her inner strength to keep any tears from flowing again. She could not stop fidgeting with the tissue in her hand. Cheryl was anxious to see her daughter.

The judge had not even entered the courtroom yet.

There was at least thirty minutes before court proceedings would begin. Lawyers and assistant prosecutors were scurrying into the courtroom. They were quickly reviewing case files, searching the room for clients, and recanting their personal weekend activities to their colleagues. Spectators and the media had already packed the courtroom. There was barely enough room for all the media equipment as well as local and national news reporters.

"I will excuse myself from the case for personal reasons. They will set another court date," Ada whispered in Keisha's ear. "Miss Powell will rip another hole in my big ass. Then we will be done with this mess."

"We'll be done in more ways than one," Keisha concluded.

Keisha looked through the open door leading to the judge's chamber. She could see Mica Goldman talking to the judge's bailiff.

"You see who is back there," Keisha whispered to Ada again.

"I know. I know," Ada acknowledged. "Doris' attack dog, Mica Goldman. It must be a full moon, because all the were-wolves have come out."

Suddenly, news reporters began rushing out of the court-room. There was a low murmur of curiosity.

"I better go see what is happening."

Keisha left the courtroom to investigate further.

Ada walked over and took the case file out of the bin again. In her effort to avoid eye contact with Ashley and Cheryl, Ada turned and was suddenly eye to eye with the assistant prosecu-tor, Marian McNair.

Marian was like a strict schoolteacher that you never forget. She rarely smiled. Everything was always a serious matter. She always dressed her dark brown, incredibly curvaceous figure in tailor-made suits.

Black, brown, and gray were the only choices in her color scheme. It was as though she was making a conscious effort to project an intimidating image to everyone in the courtroom.

"Hello Ada," Marian said with a sour expression.

"Marian, I thought your kind only came out at night?"

"You always have jokes, don't you Ada? I was looking at the docket. I know my eyes must be going bad. It says that you are the lawyer for Lela Mercer."

"Contrary to popular believe, some people actually do hire me to be their legal representative."

"I did not realize Lela Mercer was pleading insanity."

"Now you have jokes," Ada said smiling. "Glad to see you are trying to get a sense of humor."

"No Ada, I'm not trying to get a sense of humor," Marian corrected her. "Let your client know that I don't think what she did is very funny at all. And hiring you will really be no joke when I get done."

"Marian, you don't need to try to be an unlovable person," Ada advised.

Marian walked away from Ada. Ada looked around and saw that Ashley and Cheryl had been watching this chilly encounter. No one inside the courtroom was aware of the legal blizzard that was occurring outside the courtroom doors.

Portia Lee, Candace Farrell, and a platoon of female legal assistants had come out of a high-rise building in downtown Cleveland and got into three black limousines.

Television station helicopters had followed the vehicles forty miles south down the interstate. When the limousines pulled up in front of the courthouse, an avalanche of media reporters descended upon the vehicles.

Numerous sheriff deputies had to come out and provide a pathway for Portia and her associates to get through the sea of media reporters into the courthouse. This high-priced legal team went through the metal detectors and courthouse hallways greeted more like movie stars than lawyers.

When the elevator doors did not open immediately, Portia made the decision to use the stairs to the third floor.

Keisha had managed to get ahead of the legal storm.

Keisha rushed into the courtroom and motioned for Ada.

"Portia Lee and the league of legal bitches are right behind me," Keisha blurted out.

Ada looked around at Marian whose face had turned into a frown of concern caused by the increasing sound approaching.

"Keisha, let this be proof to you that there is a God," Ada said with joy.

"I believe! I believe!" Keisha joyfully agreed.

Portia burst into the courtroom followed by an all female legal team. She threw her briefcase on a chair and walked straight to Ada.

"Hello Auntie."

"Well, if it isn't my favorite niece. What took you so long to get here? I was getting nervous."

"I bet you were," Portia replied. "Who is paying my bill?"

Ada guided Portia over to Ashley. Ashley and Cheryl stood to greet Portia.

"Miss Powell, this is my niece, Portia Lee. Portia this is Ashley Powell, Lela's best friend."

The two woman shook hands.

"And this is Lela's mother, Cheryl Bishop," Ada continued the introduction.

"Can you help my baby?" Cheryl asked with tears streaming down her cheeks.

Portia gently took Cheryl's hands and softly spoke.

"We will do everything we can to help your daughter. I just need you to stay strong Mrs. Bishop."

"I'm trying. I'm really trying."

Ashley never spoke. She and Portia just exchanged long stares. Portia could detect immediately that Lela was not just Curtis' prize procession. She knew that Ashley was not absolutely sure about her legal abilities or her commitment to Lela's case. She saw the fear and uncertainty in Ashley's eyes. Portia did not care at this moment. The real show was about to begin.

Everyone stood when Judge Susan Hoffman finally came into the courtroom. Judge Hoffman had been on the bench for over ten years. She was in her early sixties and had a reputation for being tougher than her male counterparts.

Judge Hoffman's facial expression clearly indicated that she was very surprised to see Portia Lee and her team in the courtroom. The amount of press reporters was also overwhelming. There was no doubt that Lela Mercer would have to be the first case on the docket.

Only the sound of Lela's chains rattling could be heard in the courtroom. Her appearance hypnotized everyone. There was no makeup and her hair had been brushed back away from her face. Even shackled like an animal, Lela was gorgeous.

Ashley had already made Lela aware that Ada and Portia were her lawyers. Portia was seeing her client for the first time. She was amazed at how calm and relaxed she seemed despite her dilemma. Lela searched the room for Ashley. Ashley stood up briefly so that Lela could locate her. Lela seemed even more at ease at the sight of her best friend and mother. She flashed a smile at Portia that made it all clear.

Portia knew exactly why Curtis had married this woman. He did not care about her mind or her feelings. Her outer appearance was just stunning. Lela was a prize that any man would have tried to acquire.

Judge Hoffman immediately wanted a sidebar. Ada, Portia, and Marian went to the side of the bench and met with the judge. Judge Hoffman could barely keep her voice at a whisper.

"What the hell are you pulling Ada?"

"I'm not pulling anything. My niece is going to assist me with this case. Since when can't family help family?"

"And just when did Portia Lee get to be family?"

"Judge Hoffman, I have been Ada's niece since birth," Portia explained. "My aunt wanted my assistance with this case. I am sure you can understand why."

"Did you know this?" Judge Hoffman asked Marian.

"I am just as surprised as you are Judge Hoffman," Marian replied.

"I don't want any television reality show with this case," Judge Hoffman instructed.

"I really do not know the need for Portia to come this far," Marian said. "Ada could have handled this case alone. Everyone in the free world knows your client is guilty."

"I don't know that," Portia told Marian. "As far as I know my client is innocent until you prove she is guilty."

"You cannot be serious?" Marian sternly replied. "You could not possibly be thinking of going to trial with this one?"

"I'm sure you graduated from some type of law school," Portia said. "That is how we establish innocence or guilt in this country. We go to trial."

"Her own children saw her kill this man," Marian almost yelled.

"Are you going to put those children on the stand?" Portia asked. "They won't be on our witness list."

"Okay Miss Lee, you and Marian can fight this out later," Judge Hoffman interrupted. "I am just warning all of you that I will not tolerate any courtroom theatrics. This case is already about to make this city explode. We are going to go by the book on this one. I will need some respect displayed in this courtroom. Now let's get this brief formality done and this circus out of my courtroom."

They resumed their normal courtroom positions. Judge Hoffman conducted standard procedures. However, everyone was anxiously waiting to hear Lela speak. When Judge Hoffman finally asked her directly for her plea, you could hear a pin drop in the courtroom. Lela turned and first looked at Portia and Ada. Then she turned and looked directly at Ashley. Ashley shook her head from side to side. Lela looked back at Judge Susan Hoffman who was waiting patiently for her answer.

"Not guilty."

eleven

Mother Of The Church

When the bond was set at seven million dollars, it was assumed that Lela would have to sit in the county jail until trial. The media madness shifted from the courthouse to the county jail when the news spread like wildfire through the city that the bond had been made.

Mary Dandridge and Mildred Cross, senior executives on the finance committee for The House of Mary Baptist Church, walked into the county clerk's office late afternoon and signed a ten percent signature bond to free Lela from her jail cell.

Several male members of the church were needed to get Lela out of the county jail through a sea of media cameras and into a waiting Lincoln model sports utility vehicle. Lela's home and her mother's home were out of the question. Lela was taken to the home of the mother of the church, Mary Dandridge, also known as Sister Mary.

Sister Mary's home was located at Burning Tree Lane. It was only several streets over from where Doris Mercer resided. The house was a French country manor that sat on about two acres of land that looked more like a French countryside painting than the home of one of the founders of the church.

Lela's mother had already been brought to the home for safety. By the time Lela arrived, it was late evening. She was greeted by her mother, Cheryl, with tearful hugs and kisses.

"Mama, who put up the bond money?"

"They did not tell you?" Cheryl asked. "Mary Dandridge, mother of the church."

"Where are my children? Where is Ashley?"

"Ashley has the children at her house. She will bring them in the morning. We thought it would be best to handle it this way. Sister Mary says we can stay here until this entire ordeal is over."

"You mean until they send me to the electric chair."

Mary Dandridge came strolling into the living room.

"Honey, we have no intention of letting them send you to the electric chair."

"Who is we?" Lela wanted to know.

"Me and almighty God," Sister Mary informed. "Who else do you need beside that?"

Sister Mary sat down on the couch. She looked like she was already prepared to attend Sunday morning church service at this late hour. She had on full makeup, jewelry, and high-heels. She had to be her late sixties and heading into her early seventies. However, she barely had one strand of gray hair. Her perfume lit up the room like it had just been applied. Her unique and sophisticated way of speaking and behaving did not reflect being born several feet from a cotton field or being raised in an urban housing project. For a brief moment, Lela felt the same uneasiness she always felt in Doris Mercer's presence.

"Cheryl, I know your daughter wants a hot bath and something to eat. Why don't you check and see if they have set that up for our girl. I would like to have a moment alone with Lela."

"No problem," Cheryl said. "I will be upstairs baby if you need me."

Cheryl kissed Lela and left her standing alone with Sister Mary.

"Come my dear and sit down. Sister Mary wants to talk with you."

Lela sat down on the couch next to Sister Mary.

"Sister Mary, I really do appreciate what you are doing for me and my family. I have no idea how I will ever be able to pay you back."

"Honey, don't you worry about anything that I do. The Lord will give me my reward."

"Why are you doing this for me?" Lela asked.

Sister Mary took a deep breath and sat back to get more comfortable.

"Let me tell you a few facts about the past. It will make the present more clear to you. I'm sure you do not know that Doris Mercer and I first met in the seventh grade. It seems like a hundred years ago now. Doris and I were inseparable friends. After high school, Doris and I were headed toward a place called nowhere fast. We drank, smoked, and fooled around with more men than the average bad-ass woman."

"You do not have to tell me this," Lela tried to stop the direction of this conversation.

"No, I just need you to listen to me,' Sister Mary continued. "I need you to know about your mother-in-law so you have a better understanding of how to deal with her. I should have told you all this years ago. I have been dealing with Doris Mercer practically all my life. I know people think Doris and I are like night and day, but that is absolutely not true. Doris and I are really just one woman split into two. I am quite sure most people in our church now do not even realize that Doris and I have any past connection to each other. Unless you are from the real old days, folks don't know that Doris is more my sister than my real sisters. When we were very young, Doris and I were just plain crazy together. Then one day, I had the bright idea to marry Nathan Dandridge. I have no idea why he married me. I know why I married him. He had gotten a job at the auto factory. I didn't really love him much. I thought he would be a good financial future. He wasn't that easy on the eyes, but girl, Nathan was built like a man should be. Just like Curtis, women wanted him bad. But Nathan just wanted me, so I thought."

Sister Mary took a moment to laugh to herself before continuing her story.

"I think Doris got a little jealous and felt like I had just abandoned her. Out of the blue, she hooked up with this guy named Hoover. He was light, bright, and damn near white. Hoover was mean and crazy. She tells people now, as well as herself, that she was legally married to Hoover. I'm probably the only person, except for Hoover, the IRS, and the Social Security Administration, that knows that Doris was never legally married to Hoover. They were just sharing a shack. And I truly mean a shack. Then she gave birth to little Curtis James. He was such a pretty baby. After that boy was born, Hoover turned into an absolute living, breathing monster."

Sister Mary paused for a moment. She seemed to be reliving every word. Lela was not sure if she should try to stop her again. Then Sister Mary suddenly started recanting the past.

"Nathan was working at the auto plant and had started a little store-front church. I was now the pastor's wife. I had to stop all that drinking, smoking, and going in and out of bars. I got a steady job. I did day work. You don't know anything about that type of work. Back in those days, black women would go out to the rich white folk's homes and work. You would cook, clean, and take care of their snotty-nose kids. Nathan and I were doing pretty darn good. Doris, on the other hand, was spiraling clean out of control. Doris and Hoover would drink and fight. Then they would fight and drink. Doris called me one night hollering and crying. I went running over to their house. Hoover was beating the living daylights out of Doris. That was my first mistake. Never get in between a man and a woman who are fighting to the death. When I got there, I thought Hoover was going to kill Doris. I don't even remember where I got the gun or pulling the trigger. I shot him three times."

"You killed him?" Lela shouted in shock.

"It would have taken more than three bullets to kill that son-of-a-bitch. He lived, but he let the prosecutor know that he was pretty damn angry about those three holes I put in his pretty, light, bright body. I had to do three years in the pen for them three gunshots."

"Sister Mary, you were in prison?"

"All of us don't come to the dance with Jesus. Some of us only meet Jesus after we have been at the dance for a little while," Sister Mary said laughing again.

"Is that what actually ended your friendship with Doris?"

"Hell no, Doris and I got even closer. Doris came to see me at least once a month while I was in prison. She wrote me letters every week," Sister Mary continued reminiscing.

"When I got out of prison, Hoover was gone and Doris not only had Little Curtis, but two more babies and some legal husband named Mercer. Mercer was meek and mild and black and ugly. He was just the opposite of Hoover. Doris didn't want him. He helped pay the bills and provided a good name for her and her children. She would just run all over poor Mercer. Now at the same time, my Nathan was getting better and better at preaching sermons. I think his sermons about how he and the children suffered while I was in prison actually packed the church pews. When I got out of prison, Nathan went on and on about how Jesus had changed my soul and made me a better wife and mother. The folks in the church loved it and loved him. The church membership numbers got bigger and bigger."

"You and Doris both were doing better," Lela interrupted. "So what happened to your friendship?"

"Doris came to the house late on a Friday night. It was thundering and lightening something terrible. The rain was coming down in buckets. I remember it like it was yesterday. Mercer had left Doris and those babies by then. A man can only live for a short period of time with a woman like Doris. Doris' money was drying up. She had moved those babies into a two-bedroom apartment in the projects. She came in the house soaked from the rain. She told Nathan that she needed three thousand dollars to start Mercer Health and Beauty Supplies so she could get her babies out of those projects. If Nathan did not give her at least fifteen hundred dollars, she was going to stand up in church on Sunday morning and tell everyone that the pastor and founder of the church had been sleeping with his wife's best friend for years. She was going to tell the entire congregation that Nathan Dandridge was the father of all three of her children."

Lela jumped to her feet.

"Reverend Nathan Dandridge was Curtis' father?" Lela shouted.

"Sit down child," Sister Mary sternly instructed.

Lela slowly sat back down to hear the rest of the story.

"Nathan Dandridge is the father of Curtis, Tracey, and Charles. I couldn't believe it either," Sister Mary said shaking her head. "That's why Hoover was beating the crap out of her that night. They fought so much I had never even asked her what they were fighting about that night. Hoover had learned that Doris was sleeping with my husband. She had told him the truth about who was Curtis' real father. I spent three god-damn years in prison because my best friend was fucking my husband. Three long years in the state penitentiary."

"What did you do?" Lela had to know the rest of the story.

"I was not going back to jail. Believe me, prison is one of those places that you can visit, but you don't want to live there. Oops, sorry! I really shouldn't have said that to you," Sister Mary apologized.

"Please, just finish the story Sister Mary," Lela urged her to continue.

"I did not even say a word to Nathan. No yelling, scream-ing, crying, or cussing. I did not say one word to him ever about what happened that night. I didn't sleep one wink that night. I spent the entire night just praying. Then I got up that next morning and put a pistol in my purse. I went to the bank and took out all but fifty dollars from my account. I went to Doris' apartment and put that pistol right to her head. I told her that most women would have wiped the floor with her back-stabbing dirty ass after what she had done to me. But I was not going to do that. I told Doris that she was fucking my husband, she let me go to jail for years, and her children and my children are actually brothers and sisters. Despite all of that, I was not going to blow her damn brains out that day. Then I slammed fifteen hundred dollars down on the kitchen table. I told Doris that if she lost one cent of my money, I would come back and kill her dead."

Sister Mary took a long deep breath as though a weight had been lifted from her shoulders.

"As you can tell by this house and my lifestyle, Doris decided to take my good advice that day. She made us both very rich women. I married Nathan because I thought he would one day have a pension for me to live on. In the end, Nathan only stayed married to me because Doris made me filthy, stinking rich. If he could have found a way, he would have dumped me and swept Doris right off her feet. Nathan loved Doris from the first day he saw her until the day he died. He stayed with me because that was the only way to stay close to Doris. Doris didn't want him at all. If she had to chose between Nathan and me, I was the better investment. Nathan and I kept pretending to everyone that we were a happy couple. All three of us knew the real truth. Doris and I helped him build one of the biggest churches in this city. He became one of the most respected pastors in this city. Most people think Nathan died of a heart attack. He died of a broken heart. He loved Doris more than life itself. I probably would have cared more if I had loved him."

Sister Mary began laughing like she had just told an amusing tale.

Lela was speechless by this revelation. She struggled to finally get some words out.

"You own part of Mercer Health and Beauty Supplies?"

"Fifty percent," Sister Mary proudly proclaimed.

"Did Curtis know about your relationship with his mother?"

"Yeah, he knew. Hoover told him the whole truth when he got grown. Hoover didn't want that boy thinking he was his father. I'm not sure if Curtis ever told Tracey and Charles. I know Doris has never told nobody nothing. Not with her high and mighty attitude. She would not dare tell that story to anybody. I have never actually sat down and told my own children. Their father told Nathan Junior and Nadine. Who knows what version of the story he gave them. For women, anger fades with time. I got over being angry with Doris. For men, anger just intensifies with time. Nathan stayed angry with me and Doris until he dropped dead. I'm sure he told our kids some kind of tainted truth. All those kids should know something by now. They just don't say anything about it out loud to anybody, especially to me and Doris. I had to say something to Curtis myself long before Hoover confirmed it all. Curtis started looking at Nadine the wrong way when they were teenagers. With that Curtis, no woman was safe. I felt his own sister had to be off limits."

"You don't think your children should hear all of this directly from you?"

"All that is personal stuff between me and Doris. It is really nobody's business what Doris and I have done in the past. If you had not killed Curtis, I really would have never told you."

"Your children are brother and sister to Curtis, Tracey, and Charles. You don't feel they have a right to know all the details immediately and from their own mother?"

"You're probably right. I'm sure if they don't know everything by now, they will know pretty soon. Now that you killed Curtis, people are starting to talk again about who really is his daddy. Mercer and Hoover are both still very much alive somewhere. Plenty old folks noticed that neither one was at that funeral. There is still a lot of old geezers in this town, like me and Doris, who are starting to remember the old days. You opened up a mighty big can of worms young lady."

"You are not worried at all about how your children will feel about all of this when they finally have the whole story?"

"I'm their mother. What are they going to say to me? Oh Mama, we're so hurt and mad that we don't want a dime of your money when you drop dead. I'm quite sure they have a few of my good senses. I have learned how to live with the shit done to me and they should know how to live with the shit done to them."

"Curtis never said one word to me about any of this," Lela said in amazement. "Nathan Dandridge was the minister who married us. He knew that Pastor Dandridge was his father and he never told me?"

"Honey, your husband did not marry you because he respected your mind," Sister Mary said with a smile.

Sister Mary's joke was not amusing to Lela. She hated when people tried to insinuate that her beauty was the only worthwhile quality she possessed.

"Why are you telling me all of this now?" Lela bitterly asked.

"I wanted you to know why I'm trying to help you," Sister Mary explained. "I'm sure you of all people know that Doris can be mean and vicious. She is going to go into overdrive on you. Women should not have a favorite child, but they do. Curtis was her favorite. She is going to use all the power she has to put you in the hot seat. I see myself in you. You are just like I was when I was young. I loved Doris. Hell, I still love Doris. I made the mistake of letting Doris disrespect me. I paid a good price for that mistake. You did the exact same thing with her son. You let him start out disrespecting you. Then you wanted him to suddenly start treating you right. I have been there and I have done that. Now honey, don't get me wrong. What you did was horrible. I shot Hoover, but I didn't kill him. But then again, that may have just been some good luck working. Unfortunately, you did kill Curtis. I have been in at least one of your shoes so I do know how you feel. You are going to jail just like I went to jail. You will be staying a lot longer than I did. I can't stop that from happening. But, I'm not going to let Doris make them kill you. You do deserve punishment. I just can't let them give you the death penalty. You are still the mother of Curtis's children. In an indirect way, those are my grandchildren too. I have to look out for their best interest. Doing all I can to save your stupid ass is in the best interest of Curtis' children. Plus, any opportunity I get to put a little knife in Doris' back, I always take. I spent three long years in jail because she was fucking my husband. I still can't believe that myself. The money has soothed the pain over the years, but I still remember."

Cheryl tiptoed back into the room. She was not sure if the conversation was over so she softly asked her question.

"Lela I have fixed you something to eat. Do you want to get a bath first or eat something first?"

Sister Mary got up slowly. She acted like her journey back in time was exhausting.

"I am going to bed now," Sister Mary announced. "Try to get some sleep tonight young lady. You have got a lot to deal with in the morning. Ashley will bring the children tomorrow. Your mother will show you the layout of the house so you can get around this little hut."

Sister Mary began walking toward the staircase. She stopped when Lela blurted out some cautious words.

"She is going to come after you," Lela warned.

"Honey, please!" Sister Mary laughed. "I have been dealing with Doris Mercer for over fifty years. I will be fighting with Doris long after we both are dead and gone. There is no doubt that Doris and I are going straight to hell together."

Sister Mary started slowly leaving the room.

"Did you love Curtis?" Lela asked.

Sister Mary slowly turned around at that question.

Her voice quivered. She took a deep breath to keep from crying.

"I loved Curtis like he was my own son," Sister Mary said. "When I went to prison, I know that my children needed me.

Your children need you. Those children cannot afford to lose both their parents. As far as I am concerned, Doris is my blood sister. What belongs to her, belongs to me. If you were not the mother of Curtis' children, I would kill you myself with my own bare hands."

There was an awkward moment of silence.

"Thank you Sister Mary," Cheryl said nervously. "Thank you for helping our grandchildren."

Sister Mary smiled at Cheryl and shook her head in agreement. She continued slowly walking toward her bedroom. She yelled one last statement.

"Save your thanks. Our Lela has done far more damage than just killing Curtis."

twelve

An Evil Solidarity

Lying naked on the bed, Tommy Dancy had his muscular legs spread wide apart. He was unable to speak any coherent words. He continuously let out baritone moans of pleasure. Tracey, who had mounted herself on top of Tommy, reached out and tried to grip the bed sheets. The pleasure of Tommy's massive manhood within her body caused her to scream out the name of the son of God mixed with various curse words. Tommy cupped his huge hands around Tracey's bare butt cheeks and violently lifted her up and down. In one sudden thrust, Tracey's head went down and she sank her teeth into Tommy's right ear. Their fierce movements caused Tommy's ear to rip and blood to splatter on the bed sheets.

The explosive pain from this sudden savage injury made Tommy grab Tracey's hips and hurl her from his body. He leaped out of the bed and grabbed his ear. Blood rushed down the side of his head.

"What the fuck?" Tommy screamed.

Tracey laid naked and splattered with blood in the bed laughing.

"You're fucking crazy," Tommy continued screaming.

Tommy rushed into the bathroom. Tracey slowly rolled out of the bed. She took tissue and wiped Tommy's blood from her body. She put on a silk bathrobe and sat down in one of the love seats in the bedroom. Tracey did not have to wait long for Tommy to emerge from the bathroom.

Tommy rushed back into the bedroom naked and outraged.

"What the fuck is wrong with you?"

"Oh, stop crying like a baby. It's just a little scratch."

"You tried to bite my goddamn ear off."

Tommy went to the mirror to again survey the damage to his ear. Tracey made an in-depth observation of his body. His buttocks was big, round, and firm. His shoulders were broad and solid. He turned around and came charging toward her. Even in anger, Tommy had a face that was made for magazine photos and movie pictures. His arms were like rocks fused together and his chest seemed chiseled from stone. His male attribute was extensive in length and extremely thick in width. Physically, Tommy was a dream to any woman who craved the masculine gender.

Tracey could never understand why Tommy wanted her. She always had doubts if a man really loved her or if he was really in love with her mother's money and notoriety.

Being Doris Mercer's daughter was always an obstacle in her relationships. However, Tommy had refused to let go despite her early attempts to push him away. His job as a police officer gave him some respect in the community. However, being known as Tracey's man made him a celebrity.

Tommy loved all the attention. He loved escorting Tracey to events. He had no problem stepping back to let the photographers take only her picture. He was content not being the star of the show. Tommy just wanted to be at the show. Tracey loved having something that she had actually acquired all on her own. The feeling was almost orgasmic having someone so physically powerful that she could mentally control and dictate. It didn't matter anymore if Tommy really loved her or not. Tracey just needed him to need her.

Tommy bent over and slammed his huge hands down on the back of the love seat enclosing Tracey. He slightly turned his head so she could see the physical damage she had done to his ear.

"Say you're sorry."

Tracey at first refused to apologize.

"Say you're sorry," Tommy strongly repeated.

Tracey knew she would not be able to bite any more of this magnificent body if she did not give in.

"I'm sorry Tommy. I didn't mean to hurt you."

Tommy slowly stood up straight. He walked over and sat down on the side of the bed. He continued to feel his injured ear.

"She is out on bond," Tommy causally said.

"What? What did you say?"

"Lela got out on bond tonight," Tommy reported.

Tracey sprang up from her seat.

"That bond was seven million dollars. Who could put up that type of money for her?"

"The House of Mary Baptist Church."

Tracey could not believe her own good ears.

"That unholy bitch."

Tommy leaned back on his elbows on the bed.

"Why would Sister Mary put the church on the line like that for Lela?" Tommy asked.

"Because she has some sick love-hate for my mother. I guess we are going through one of her periodic hatred phases right now. Where is Lela?"

"Church members took her to Sister Mary's house. The court put her on an electronic monitoring system. She will be pretty much confined to Sister Mary's house until she goes to trial. Tracey, should we be worried?"

Tracey walked over to the window and parted the drapes. She looked up at the moon and stars. A sudden concern about the new turn of events made Tommy straighten up.

"Tracey, I'm going to ask you again. Should we be worried?"

Tracey turned to face him.

"My brother had made a will several years ago. He made Ashley Powell executor of his estate and guardian of his children if anything happened to him or Lela. I think this situation qualifies. Ashley Powell is in charge of all of his finances."

Tommy jumped up off the bed. He had forgotten about the pain of his ear and was now more focused on the pain of Tracey's words.

"What are we going to do?" Tommy shouted. "Ashley Powell is no dummy. She is going to go through Curtis' business books and realize that two and two don't equal ten."

"Just calm down," Tracey replied. "Curtis' business is hardly on her mind right now. She is concentrating on the main love of her life, Lela."

"It's not going to take them long to throw the book at Lela. She sliced that son-of-a-bitch's throat clean open. Then Ashley is going to have nothing but time to start reading the fine print."

"That son-of-a-bitch was my brother," Tracey said with bitterness.

"Well, Lela may have cut your brother's throat, but, I don't want Ashley Powell cutting off my balls. You better do something."

Tracey stepped up to Tommy and gently laid her hands on his massive chest. She had to stand on her tip-toes to kiss him on his lips.

"Don't worry your pretty little head. I have taken care of bigger problems in the past. I will take care of Ashley Powell," Tracey assured him. "You belong only to me. I would not ever let anything bad happen to you. You just need to trust me."

Tommy smiled with satisfaction from Tracey's reassurance. He grabbed her by the arms and violently threw her on the bed. He spread her legs as wide apart as he could and thrust his hardened manhood within her again.

The abrupt feeling of pleasure made Tracey holler Tommy's name.

She pulled his head down and whispered in his bleeding ear.

"Make it hurt."

thirteen

The Executive Committee

"Why do you need us? You've already made all the decisions."

"The church has to stand united," Sister Mary commanded.

"We are united in knowing that this is an executive committee of one," Colette Bailey angrily responded. "Our opinions do not matter."

The five members of the executive committee had assembled in the sanctuary of The House of Mary Baptist Church for an emergency meeting.

Virginia Anderson agreed with her colleague, Colette.

"Shouldn't we have all met and had a discussion first before putting up the bond for Lela Mercer. You have put the church on the line for a large amount of money. Putting up a bond for a church member accused of any crime is highly unusual and puts the church in a questionable light. Lela is accused of killing her husband."

"I have never made any financial decision for this church that caused a loss in money or members," Sister Mary defended her actions. "If anything happens, I am more than prepared to cover the bond and absolve the church from any financial responsibility."

"So that makes everything okay?" Colette said with disgust. "Just because you're rich enough to make this type of financial gamble, we should sanction your decision to gamble with the church's honor and reputation?"

"Lela killed Curtis," Virginia emphasized. "When did the church start bailing out members for any type of crime, especially murder?"

"Lela is a valued member of this church," Mildred Cross reminded the committee members. "Mercer Auto Body and Repair sponsors numerous youth programs. Lela and Curtis have made extremely large tithes to the church."

"Our decisions should be based on bible principles and not who gave the most money, Colette scolded.

"The electric, water, and gas companies don't take prayer for payment," Mildred stated. "We need to hold on to our faith when making decisions, but we can't be naïve. It takes a lot to run this church and all the programs this church sponsors."

"So you don't think we need to be worried about Doris Mercer?" Virginia reminded everyone. "After Sister Mary, Doris is our largest contributor. Once she discovers the church put up the bond for Lela, she will come burn this building down with us inside."

"Don't worry about Doris," Sister Mary assured. "Doris has always been and will always be my problem alone to handle."

"You are the church's problem," Colette acknowledged. "We respect that you are one of the founders and the mother of this church, but you have let your money and influence elevate you above this church and the entire city. You no longer answer to anyone, including almighty God."

Nathan Junior had sat quiet as he normally did during executive committee meetings. However, the continuous attack on his mother had finally caused him to stand and bellow out a thunderous ultimatum to the group.

"Helping Lela through this horrible ordeal will eventually be beneficial to the church," Nathan Junior advised. "I trust my mother. She has never led us in a wrong direction. I don't believe now is an exception. Nothing seems to make sense right now. You all know in your hearts that my mother would never do anything to put this church in moral or financial jeopardy. This entire mess threatens to break the church family apart. That will not happen if we unite behind my mother, Sister Mary. Are we united?"

There was silence within the church walls.

Nathan Junior reiterated his call for a vote of confidence.

"Are we united?"

Mildred Cross, Colette Bailey, and Virginia Anderson took another long moment of silence to formulate their responses. However, each woman eventually verbally signaled their approval to unite behind Sister Mary.

Sister Mary was more than elated with the victory.

fourteen

In The House Of The Lord

The House of Mary Baptist Church sat in the middle of an enormous Christian campus. The former store-front church was now a cathedral of worship. The church provided a day-care, elementary school, and a community center. The sanctuary was surrounded by numerous satellite buildings and beautiful landscaping. Statues of various religious figures were scattered throughout the property.

When Portia walked into the church with Ada, she was impressed with the craftsmanship of the building. The stained glass images were spectacular. However, the image of Jesus with jet black skin nailed to the cross located behind the pulpit was breathtaking.

Members of the church executive committee sat in the front pews waiting for their invited guest. Portia's eyes shifted from the back of their heads to the eyes of Mary Dandridge.

Sister Mary was sitting on the stage just below the image of a crucifixion. She was smiling and waiting for Portia and Ada to get close enough to deliver her greeting.

Sister Mary rose from her throne and began ascending down from the podium.

"Ada, I have been trying to get you in this church for years."

"I can't afford Jesus," Ada laughed. "I have to settle for home-based religious services."

"Miss Portia Lee, your reputation is far greater than you know," Sister Mary complimented. "We welcome you into the house of the Lord."

"It is an honor to meet you Sister Mary," Portia returned the compliment. "We are extremely grateful for what you have done for our client."

Sister Mary laughed out loud.

"I didn't do anything for your client. I only acted in the best interest of innocent children. I'm sure Ashley Powell has a little cash, but we thought that bond might be a little out of her range. I felt it was best if the church took over the responsibility of handling Lela's legal expenses."

The members of the executive committee stood to be introduced. Sister Mary made the introduction.

"This is our church executive committee, Mildred Cross, Colette Bailey, Virginia Anderson, and my son, Nathan Dandridge Junior."

A young, light brown woman came rushing into the church from a side door. She was petite and extremely neat in appearance. She extended her hand to Portia. Sister Mary continued with the introductions.

"Miss Lee, this is the current pastor of our church, Nadine Dandridge. Most important, Nadine is my daughter."

"I am sure my mother has already given you a proper welcome. I too wish to extend a welcome into The House of Mary Baptist Church," Nadine said. "We only regret that it is due to such an unpleasant circumstance that brings you and Ada into this house that has been built to worship our Lord and Savior. Let's all sit."

Nathan Junior retrieved a chair so that Nadine could sit facing the participants of this meeting. He put the chair at the bottom of the pulpit and right in the aisle dividing the left and right rows of seats in the church. Sister Mary returned to her seat in the pulpit like a queen waiting for her subjects to inform and advise.

"Well, I don't mean to be blunt," Ada began. "But why did the church bail out Lela Mercer?"

"Lela is more like family to us than you know," Nadine explained. "Her children are like my own flesh and blood. My mother and I want to try to lessen the mental weight that this awful tragedy has no doubt put on those children's hearts and minds."

"Don't you think it is highly unusual for a church to bail out an accused murderer?" Portia asked.

"Both Lela and her children are members of this church," Nadine clarified. "This church was built to be the foundation for our families to stand on during a storm. It is not our way to abandon families in their time of need."

"The bond was seven million dollars," Portia reminded Nadine.

"And my mother will make sure that the church does not lose one dime. We have put our faith and trust in your abilities. We know that you are not the Savior, but we are investing our money in the belief that you can save those children's mother from the angel of death."

"I would not call the state of Ohio the angel death," Portia said. "However, we intend to do everything humanly possible to get the death penalty off the table. I'm still not clear on why the church is so vested in Lela's fate."

The meeting participants were startled by a voice from the back of the church.

"Because that is how Mary makes her money. She turns someone else's bad situation into a financial gain for herself."

They all turned to see Doris Mercer charging up the center aisle of the church. Portia had seen Doris in newspapers and magazines, but never in person. She understood why Doris made such an impression on everyone. Doris was not really the most beautiful woman to ever live. However, she had an aura that most women do not possess. She had a presence that demanded attention. Unique was not the right word Portia was searching. Extraordinary was the adjective that best suited Doris Mercer.

Doris' lawyer, Mica Goldman, was closely following behind her boss. They all sprang up from their seats like a hurricane had struck the sanctuary. Sister Mary, however, rose from her seat like a cobra unleashed. She started slowly walking back down off the podium and down the aisle toward Doris.

"If you didn't keep creating such bad situations, I would have nothing to gain from," Sister Mary roared back at Doris.

"You think it's my fault that my own son is dead," Doris shouted.

"If you had raised him right, Lela would not have had to kill him," Sister Mary shouted back. "If she didn't kill him, somebody else would have sooner or later. He was domed the first time he called you Mother."

Both Doris and Sister Mary increased their movement up the aisle toward one another. Mica grabbed Doris from behind.

Nathan Junior leaped between the two elderly women.

"I should have never taken that money from you," Doris said with continuing regret.

"You should be grateful I didn't blow your brains out that night," Sister Mary answered.

"That is what this is all about," Doris screamed. "You're still whining about something I did forty years ago."

"No, I'm whining about the mess you have made for all of us right now," Sister Mary corrected her.

Portia whispered in Ada's ear.

"Did I miss a part of this conversation?"

Ada whispered back.

"I missed the same part you did."

Nathan Junior gently guided Sister Mary back toward the pulpit. Mica managed to get in front of Doris. Mica directed her comments to opposing counsel.

"Miss Lee, I'm Mica Goldman. I represent Doris Mercer and I was the personal lawyer for Curtis Mercer. I am not sure what you and Mary Dandridge are trying to do. It really does not matter. Your client is more than guilty. We will be doing everything in our power to make sure she is prosecuted to the fullest extent of the law.

"We are both honorable women of the law, Miss Goldman," Portia stated. "You do what you have to do for your client and I will do the same."

"So be it," Mica responded.

Mica began gently pushing Doris back out of the church.

"I am standing in the house of the Lord," Doris shouted. "Let the Lord be my witness that I will make you pay, Mary Dandridge, for trying to help that bitch get away with killing my son."

"I'm the best friend you will ever have Doris," Sister Mary calmly informed. "You'll realize that very soon."

Mica continued gently urging Doris out of the church.

After Doris was gone, the participants of the meeting breathed a sigh of relief.

"I'm not sure what that was," Portia told them.

"That was a distraction to the Lord's work," Nadine declared. "We need you to look pass the obvious grief and pain that a mother would normally have for a fallen son and do what is right. We wanted you to know, Miss Lee, that the church is willing to spare no expense to keep Lela out of the electric chair. Do not let money be an obstacle in this fight. We want you to be free to give Lela the best defense possible. We do not want and cannot have Lela Mercer get the death penalty."

"It is always good to see when clients have support," Portia said. "I'm a little surprised that the church would take such an active role in this case. Ada and I won't refuse any help no matter what the source."

Sister Mary pushed away Nathan Junior who still had her in his loose grip. She walked up to Portia and looked her directly in the eyes.

"Don't let Doris Mercer intimidate you. Remember, God is on your side. And more important, I'm on your side."

Sister Mary gave Portia a sinful grin.

"I will keep that in mind Sister Mary," Portia told her. "Ada and I have to go now. We have a legal defense to prepare."

Only the echo created from the sound made by their high-heel shoes filled the church as Portia and Ada walked out.

When they got in the church parking lot, Portia slammed her briefcase on the hood of her luxury vehicle and lit verbally into Ada.

"What the hell was that?"

"I have no idea," Ada yelled. "I think me and you were the only ones in there standing in a holy fog. They were all talking about something, but I'll be damned if I knew what?"

"I thought Ashley Powell was paying our salary?"

"That is who hired you. I mean us. Looks like Sister Mary and the church are taking over."

"Why are they trying to take control? Why would any church be trying to take on a murder case?"

"That's why I needed you. I am totally out of my league on this case."

Portia looked at Ada and realized she was telling the truth. Ada was clueless.

"Okay, I'm calling Delia Tavares, my investigator. She has got to get me out of this cloud. Those people in there know something that we don't know. All that talk about helping poor children is bullshit. Doris Mercer is right. Those people sitting in that church want something, but what?"

"This is not going to be a routine murder case is it?" Ada asked.

"Hell no, Ada!" Portia said with anguish. "I should have known when I saw you that you were bringing me a royal god-damn mess."

"Oh Pookie," Ada purred. "Aren't you glad we're working together? It's giving us an opportunity to sort of bond. Don't you think?"

"Stop calling me Pookie," Portia said grinding her teeth. "Just get in the car. Just get in the goddamn car, now!"

fifteen

Representing The State

The inbox was overflowing. Case files were piled high in chairs on both sides of the desk. Papers were scattered in the middle of the desk between manuals and law books.

Shay Newman sat, not bothered by the disorder of her office. She peered down through reading glasses to review a case file. She did not even acknowledge Marian when she entered her office and shut the door. Marian sat down in one of the chairs facing Shay's desk. She silently watched her boss continue going over a case file.

Marian never understood how Shay could find anything in the disorganized clutter that filled her office. Shay had been the county prosecutor for eight years. She had won each re-election with ease. Shay had gained a reputation for bashing the good book of law as hard as she possibly could against the heads of those who dared to break laws in her county. She was known to personally handle high-profile trials. Everyone was surprised when she handed off the Lela Mercer case to Marian McNair.

Marian was now working on her fourth year with the county prosecutor's office. She had rejected a lucrative offer to work in a less stressful private practice. She had come to the prosecutor's office draped in a blanket of delusion. Marian had convinced herself that she would be some crusader for true law. As an African American, she had seen so many people of color and poverty who were constant victims of crime and system abuse. She had decided to personally try to right a continuing wrong.

She thought with her expertise she would slip into her civil service armor and fight for the less advantaged. She soon realized that her career goals were fueled more by drunken idealism and unrealistic perceptions about people in general. Cases like Lela Mercer also challenged her clear cut outlook on criminal cases. She had learned that the line between victim and perpetrator was not always clearly defined. She knew her case against Lela should be effortless. Lela had committed a heinous murder. Marian was not sure if she would be committing an equally heinous deed by pursuing the death penalty.

"You gave me the Mercer case because I'm black."

Marian's words pulled Shay out of her trance. She put the case file down on the desk and took off her reading glasses. She leaned back in her chair and took a deep breath.

Shay's skin was like porcelain. Her blonde hair had been pulled back in a loose bun. When she removed her reading glasses, you were upset that she would ever dare cover those hypnotic blue eyes.

"Of course you have the case because you're black," Shay admitted. "You also have the case because you are a black woman. Did you think I would not tell you the truth?"

"I didn't expect you to be so blunt," Marian acknowledged.

"If this goes to trial, I cannot afford for one juror to be a sympathy holdout for poor, beautiful, and black Lela Mercer. Killing your lying, cheating husband is not a foreign idea to any women. I cannot afford for anyone on a jury to bring race to the table too. I will not tolerate just blatantly killing a man without provocation on my watch. People in this town already believe I go hard on men that commit crimes against women. Well, they will see that my brand of justice goes both ways. We are going to throw the good book of law at our Mrs. Mercer. That is why you are handling the case."

"I'm your form of black face."

"You can make all the little racial jabs you want at me," Shay told Marian. "If I got up in front of that jury, there might be just one juror that will see a white, blond, blue-eyed woman stomping on the soul of a poor black female. But if that same juror looks at you, they only see equal justice. I need that one problem juror to see Lela Mercer not as pretty and pitiful, but cold and heartless."

"You think just because a juror is black and I am black that is all that will come into play in their mind?"

"Not all the black jurors," Shay clarified. "Just that one juror that may be black or white that needs to know in their mind that the system is being fair to people of color. I need that one juror to see you as the color of justice."

"I'm not sure all that is necessary. I think people of any color know you should not kill your husband in cold blood."

"You don't think you have enough guts to go up against all show and no substance, Portia Lee. Just be blunt too and say it. You're afraid of her."

This accusation caused Marian to sit up straight in her chair.

"You think I am afraid of Portia Lee?"

"Why did you come in here crying about being born black? You never seemed to care about color in any of your other cases."

"You're using one black woman to destroy another black woman."

"I'm using one good lawyer to prosecute a criminal."

Marian got up and walked around for a bit. Then she was ready to argue again.

"Should we really be going after the death penalty?"

"Doris Mercer will not rest good at night until a bolt of electricity is rushing through Lela Mercer's body."

"What about those children? We can't call them to the witness stand."

"I'm quite sure that Lela will not have her lawyer put her children through that type of ordeal," Shay said with confidence. "Portia Lee is a protégé of Candace Farrell. She is being mentored by a social club of old bitches called Endress, Neal, Tuthill, and Cruz. She is definitely going to plea bargain. She has not earned her reputation by going to trial. She is more famous for avoiding trial. She is more of a negotiator than a lawyer."

"You want me to offer a plea bargain?" Marian asked in shock.

"Hell yeah!" Shay answered strongly. "Nothing less than life in prison."

"You just said Doris Mercer wants the death penalty."

"I run this office. I make the final decisions. Doris Mercer is a female dog, but she is still a female. She is not going to put her own grandchildren through even more trauma. She will accept the deal we make and like it. The case will be off my desk. You become a legal hero in the white community and a respected prosecutor in the black community. Ammunition to use when you decide to run for my job. Portia Lee gets her high-priced, fancy ass right back on the interstate heading north with reputation intact and more money for those old bags that own that law firm. Everybody lives happily ever after, including Lela Mercer. Well, she may not be happy, but she will continue to live."

"You think it will be that easy?" Marian asked.

"Why would it not be that easy?" Shay questioned. "She took a kitchen knife and sliced open his throat in front of her own children for God's sake. She had the presence of mind to take a shower to wash away all the blood off her body and throw her bloody clothes in the trash. She sat in that house with her friends and children looking all pretty and sweet with a gun in her hand contemplating suicide. She knew what she did was wrong. This is an open and shut case."

"Mary Dandridge put up the bond for Lela. I just have a hard time thinking Sister Mary put up that type of money just because she is a good Christian."

Shay had to think about that one herself. She stood up and walked around to the front of her desk.

"What else could there be? Is there anything we don't know?" Shay wondered. "What about Curtis' business life?"

"He owned those three auto shops, Mercer Auto Body and Repair Shop. He didn't directly have anything to do with the day to day affairs at his mother's business, Mercer Health and Beauty. As far as I know, those auto shops did extremely good financial business. I still have to investigate his finances a little deeper. I really don't think money will be an issue."

"Money is always an issue. What about women?"

"He had plenty before and after marriage. It's a well-known fact that Curtis was a ladies' man."

"Now you do have me thinking," Shay admitted. "Why would Sister Mary input herself in such a messy situation?

She has to be taking a lot of heat from her parishioners."

"Sister Mary has Lela, as well as Lela's mother, and Lela's children all staying at her house. The House of Mary Baptist

Church has had other members who turned out to be crooks, thieves, and murderers throughout the years. Sister Mary has never put up any bond for them. Why the personal interest in Lela?"

Shay walked back around her desk and sat back down.

"If this is all crossing your mind, it is going through the mind of Portia Lee too. I suggest you do a little more leg work than I thought was needed. Find out what is the connection between Sister Mary, Lela Mercer, and Doris Mercer? Do it fast, but be accurate. We cannot have any mistakes. We need this case over and done with as soon as possible. I still think it will be a piece of cake. We still have to remember that Portia Lee is not Ada Stinson. We will have to stay one step ahead of Miss Lee."

Marian had begun walking out of the office when Shay stopped her.

"Marian, keep me informed daily. And most of all, have your watchdogs keep an eye on Lela. Don't let her out of your sight. We can't afford for Lela Mercer to try to run."

"I don't think that is a concern," Marian said. "It would be hard to run with four children."

"Just keep an eye on Lela. Keep two eyes on Portia Lee. If Sister Mary has gotten involved, Portia has more money than the economic budget for this entire city. She has plenty of cash to work this case. Don't let her start manufacturing the truth. I'm putting my bet all in on you, Marian. You have to crush that Portia Lee. Don't let the media make Portia Lee the bigger star of this show than Lela Mercer."

sixteen

The Eyes Of Children

"They may have a hard time forgiving you. They will never stop loving you. You are their mother."

"I killed their father."

"Their need for you to love them far outweighs their need to hate you. It will take a lot of time. It won't all happen today. Pastor Nadine and I are going to set up some type of counseling with a professional. We have to start somewhere. We can start today."

"They are afraid of me."

"They were afraid that night. That night is over. Callen and Jade don't really understand everything that is happening. Junior is just hurt and scared. Kelly is very angry. Even though she is angry, she is still very concerned about you. Now that Curtis is dead, Kelly thinks she needs to take his place. She feels she has to take care of you and those children. They all don't want to lose you too."

"I can't believe this is happening," Lela expressed out loud. "I can't believe he is dead. What did I do? I think I'm losing my mind."

Lela collapsed on the bed. She pulled out the pillow from under the bedspread and buried her face and tears.

Ashley collapsed on the bed beside her and began gently rubbing her back. She kissed the back of Lela's head.

"We can wait if you don't think you are able to face them now," Ashley said ignoring Lela's words. "I can take them back home. They can stay with me at my house."

Lela realized Ashley did not want to hear any remorse about killing Curtis. She knew Ashley was glad he was dead. She was glad to finally be totally in charge.

Lela got up off the bed and walked to the window. She looked out over the grounds. The flowers and trees were in full blossom.

Ashley continued sitting on the bed trying to come up with more convincing words that this horrible situation would eventually end. She was not sure how to reunite Curtis' broken family that was now her family.

Ashley had brought the children to Sister Mary's house to be with their mother. She had left them out on the back terrace with Sister Mary, Pastor Nadine, and Lela's mother, Cheryl.

The women were sitting in white mesh-pattern lawn chairs at a glass patio table. There was a tray filled with slices of cake and cookies on the table. Nadine carefully poured glasses of lemonade.

The stone terrace led to steps that went down to a large rectangular swimming pool. Beyond the swimming pool was an endless well-groomed lawn that was surrounded by a floral garden.

"Where is my mother?" Kelly demanded to know.

"She will be down soon," Sister Mary assured her. "Eat some of those cookies."

"I don't want any goddamn cookies," Kelly roared.

"Kelly!" Cheryl cried out.

"Don't you blaspheme in this house young lady," Sister Mary roared back. I'm the only one that can cuss in this goddamn house."

"Mother!" Pastor Nadine scolded.

"Sorry," Sister Mary apologized.

Kelly looked off into space and waited. She had no desire to speak to her mother. However, she needed to see Lela. She needed to know that her mother was safe.

Kelly refused to eat any of the cookies or drink any lemonade that Sister Mary had provided. Her siblings had no problem devouring her share. Jade sat in Cheryl's lap and Callen sat close by. They both were comforted by the endless hugs and kisses that their grandmother was providing. Junior sat close to his sister Kelly. He was trying to be as strong as she was about this entire situation. He felt it was his duty to stand by his older sister's side and provide her moral support.

Sister Mary was impressed with Kelly. She admired her innate inability to shrink from adversity. Sister Mary was overjoyed that there was possibly a lump of clay sitting before her that needed to be molded. A potential candidate for mentoring that she had not noticed until now.

"Mommy!" Jade shouted as she jumped out of Cheryl's lap.

Jade ran to her mother with Callen following close behind. Lela fell to her knees and swallowed her two youngest children in her arms. Junior wanted to move but could not. He watched Kelly for a signal on what he should do. Only anger beamed from Kelly's eyes. She was mad over the awful deed her mother had done. Yet, she was mad that she might lose her mother forever too.

Lela picked up Jade and took Callen by the hand. She walked to the table. She looked Kelly directly in the eyes.

"I love you," Lela softly announced to her oldest child.

Kelly sprang up from her seat. Junior followed her lead.

"We need to leave. We need to leave now," Kelly demanded.

"Where do you want us to go," Lela asked. "There is nowhere that we can run. We have to stay right here."

"They will kill you," Kelly bluntly told her mother.

"There is nowhere for us to run," Lela reiterated to her daughter. "I did something very wrong and I have to accept whatever punishment I am given. I apologize for putting you and your brothers and sister through all of this. We can't run from what has happened."

Kelly was outraged that her mother had rejected her advice. She stomped out into the floral gardens. Junior hesitated. He wanted to hug his mother tight, but could not betray his sister. He was afraid his sister may be all he had left soon. He remained loyal to Kelly and silently followed her to the floral gardens.

Jade hugged Lela tighter trying to stop the tears running down her mother's face. Ashley walked up behind Lela and whispered in her ear.

"Just give them some time. It will take lots of time."

Sister Mary seemed delighted with this first attempt.

"Put that big girl down," Sister Mary told Lela. "You kids go on out there with foul-mouth Kelly and your deaf-mute brother. Let grown folks talk. Sit down Lela. Sit down Ashley. We need to take a little time to relax. We can worry about our shitty situation later. It's too nice out here not to just sit and drink some lemonade."

Lela could not take her eyes off her children who were walking and whispering among themselves out on the grounds. She wondered what was going through their minds. How much damage had she caused? Would she ever be able to repair her relationship with her children, especially Kelly?

"I need us all to hold hands around this table," Pastor Nadine instructed.

All the women held hands around the table and bowed their heads. Pastor Nadine began her prayer.

"Look what God has given us, another beautiful day. My mother has given Lela a history lesson on this family. I'm sure Lela has shared this information with her mother and Ashley. We now all know that we have a common bond and a common interest in those children that play together within our sight. No one at this table can afford to lose faith. We don't condone what Lela has done. Clearly, there was another way to resolve her problems. We cannot go back and undo the deed, but we can clean up the mess and rebuild. We are not here to pass judgment on Lela. We all answer to a greater power than any man or woman. We women who sit around this table must embrace one another during this crisis. We must look into the eyes of those children and create an island of calm in these troubled waters. We must let Lela know that God has not turned away from her. She must not turn away from her children or us. It is a beautiful day today and we must make sure every day is beautiful again for those children, our children. In Jesus name, we offer this prayer."

The response was the same for every woman at the table.

"Amen."

Sister Mary sat back and got more comfortable in her chair. She didn't seem worried at all about the tragic circumstances they all were facing. She barked out a command as she enjoyed the sunshine.

"Pour me some lemonade."

seventeen

A Good Neighbor

"You are Mrs. Goodman?"

Mrs. Goodman was down on her knees trimming the edges of her immaculate front lawn.

"Whose asking?"

"I'm Delia Tavares, Mrs. Goodman. I am a private investigator. I work for attorney Portia Lee. Miss Lee is representing your neighbor, Lela Mercer."

Mrs. Goodman squinted her eyes. She was a short African American woman whose small frame had expanded with time. Beads of sweat littered her dark brown forehead. She put up her hand to try to shield her eyes from the glare of the sun. She still could not make out the details of Delia's face. She looked down at the ground and wondered how she was going to get to her feet.

"Help me up off this ground."

Delia quickly positioned her right arm down low so that Mrs. Goodman could use it for support. Mrs. Goodman tossed her lawn shears into the grass. She gripped Delia's arm and struggled to her feet. As she slowly rose, there were grunts and groans that emphasized the pain associated with rising to a standing position.

"Oh Lord! I'm not sure how I would have gotten back up if you had not come along."

Mrs. Goodman shook her body trying to wiggle out the arthritic kinks. She suddenly grabbed Delia by the arm and started leading her to the backyard.

In the backyard, a lawn table set with umbrella and chairs decorated the beautiful landscape. It was more than obvious that Mrs. Goodman took great pride and care of her home.

"Mrs. Goodman, I need to ask you a few questions about the unfortunate incident at the Mercer home."

Mrs. Goodman flopped down into one of the lawn chairs.

"Sit, sit," Mrs. Goodman instructed. "Unfortunate incident? Is that what you call killing your husband on a hot, summer evening?"

Delia smiled and sat down also.

"You called the police ma'am?"

"I saw Ashley Powell running to the house. That woman has two expensive cars in her garage and she was running to Lela's house. Then little Junior was in the window crying and signaling for me to get help. So that is exactly what I did. The police had already been at the house earlier, so I knew something bad was going on in there. I really thought Curtis had killed Lela. Never in a million years would I have guessed she killed him. I thought she worshiped the ground that dog walked on. I guess I was wrong."

Delia was startled by the revelation that the police had been at the house before the murder.

"Are you sure the police was at the house before the murder?"

"What did you say your name was?"

"Delia, Delia Tavares."

Delia handed Mrs. Goodman her business card.

Mrs. Goodman looked at the business card and took a more long, in-depth look at Delia. She was comfortable with the gorgeous facial features, long, brown hair, and caramel color skin. However, she was a little uncomfortable with the Caribbean sound in the voice.

"Where are you from? That voice doesn't sound like any part of Ohio."

"I started out in Puerto Rico, but a strong wind blew me into Cleveland."

Mrs. Goodman was amused.

"A stronger wind blew me right out the cotton fields of Alabama. I landed right out there on the front lawn."

Both women laughed.

"Were you good friends to Lela?" Delia asked.

"Hell no!" Mrs. Goodman quickly replied. "She is a pretty woman, but not friendly at all. She would say hi and bye to you. That was about all you were going to get out of her. She has those three friends that come all the time. Fran is a very nice woman. You would not believe she has some hardcore bad-ass little boys. I have to run them little gangsters out of my yard all the time. She is always apologizing for them knuckleheads stepping on my flowers. Now that other friend, Mavis, is a chain-smoking witch. She has a stanky attitude problem. She will look dead in my face, turn up her nose, and go right in that house without any kind of Christian hello. The real prize is Ashley. That is my girl. She is just as sweet as sweet potato pie. Lela just loves her. When Ashley comes, Lela is a whole different person. I can't fault her. I love that Ashley myself. Curtis hated every last one of Lela's friends with a passion."

"You liked Curtis?"

"Double hell no!" Mrs. Goodman quickly replied. "Now don't get me wrong. Most people in this town loved them some Curtis. He was a charming, rich, spoiled brat. There are only a few of us that were not a member of his fan club. Curtis was just too flirty and too arrogant for me. He was as fake and phony as they come. I would be fake and phony right back at him. He did all the talking all the time. He was zapping all the life right out of poor Lela. He was never at a loss for words. And was he nosey too? Honey, he wanted to know everybody's business and was not afraid to ask. I felt sorry for Lela. I might have had to kill him myself if I had to live with him day in and day out."

"Most women would have considered Curtis Mercer the ultimate catch," Delia tried to explain. "He was very handsome. He had plenty of money and his family is very powerful in this town."

"You don't have to tell me," Mrs. Goodman said. "I have lived across the street from the bastard for years. He kept Lela like a trophy in that house, but he was out in those streets doing his thing. If you're asking me, he was just a male whore. That man was definitely not gay. He was one hundred percent het-erosexual. He would sleep with anything born with a uterus. Women loved Curtis and Curtis loved women. He was good to women too. He spent money like it was running water. I know his mother has a lot of homemade dough, but even she has to have a limit. Curtis didn't seem to have no limits. He was a flashy bastard. But, I have to admit that I actually miss him. He really didn't have to live in this neighborhood. We aren't poor in this neighborhood. Don't get me wrong, we all have some very nice houses that we paid good money to buy. We don't have Doris Mercer type of money. Curtis lived in this neighbor-hood because he wanted to and not because he had to. Curtis was his own man. He wasn't trying to let his mother control his life. He tried to run his own business, his own home, and his own life. He did look out for everybody he knew. He used his clout to make sure the neighborhood was safe. He was actually a bad husband with a good heart. Does that make sense?"

"How can you say he had a good heart in the same breath you say he constantly lied and cheated on his wife?"

"That was Lela's fault," Mrs. Goodman said. "She knew what she had when she married that dog. Don't marry a dog and except him to act like a kitty cat. When she stood at the altar and said the words I and do, she agreed to let Curtis drag her through the mud. Pretty shouldn't make you stupid. Every woman should know that for a man like Curtis, once he gets a taste of pretty ass, it's time to move on to the next pretty ass. It ain't nothing personal. That's the way some men just are."

Although they were alone in the back yard, Mrs. Goodman leaned in to whisper her next opinion.

"I don't have personal knowledge. I have heard he knew how to work that package in his pants too. And, I was told that it was a mighty big package. There are plenty women around here that can give you some testimonials."

Delia tried to restrain her laughter before speaking.

"You said the police were at the house before the murder," Delia reminded Mrs. Goodman. "Do you know why the police were at the house earlier that day?"

"Just like I told those FBI agents, I have no idea why the police came to their house that afternoon."

Delia paused for a moment at hearing the FBI had intensely interrogated Mrs. Goodman. She did not want her facial expression to reveal that she was unaware the FBI's involvement in this case was much more serious than she had suspected.

"Just one police officer came to the house?" Delia asked.

"A tall white guy with sunglasses on. He stayed in the house about 20 or 30 minutes and then left. Let me tell you like I told the FBI, I don't remember the police car number. If I had known Lela was going to kill Curtis about an hour later, I would have tried to memorize the entire day."

"Which FBI agents came to see you?" Delia wanted to know.

"I can't remember their names. I put their card in the house on the kitchen counter. They told me to call if I remember anything that might help with the case."

"Did they ask you a lot of questions?"

"You would have thought I killed Curtis. They seemed more interested in that police officer that came to the house that afternoon than about Lela. I told them to go ask the police department who did they send to the house that day. They should have a record of who went to that house and why. They kept acting like I keep the books for the police department. They wanted a full description of that police officer. I told them they needed to stay focused. Lela killed Curtis, not that white police officer."

Mrs. Goodman sat up and examined her yard.

"I'll have to finish my yard work tomorrow morning," she continued. "The sun is way too hot now. I'm tired now anyway. You have killed my mojo for today. I'm going to have to get up and get me something to eat pretty soon. You can't help her you know. Poor pretty Lela is done. Women should not let emotional pain build up inside. Sooner or later it will explode and you'll have a private detective snooping around asking about your dead husband that you killed."

Delia smiled and stood up to leave.

"Thank you Mrs. Goodman. I really appreciate your honesty. I hope I'm free to come back and ask you some more questions if necessary."

"I'm sure you will be back," Mrs. Goodman acknowledged as she sat up and braced herself on the lawn table preparing to try to raise from her seat.

"I'm not senile. And like I said before, pretty don't make me stupid. The FBI don't come calling when you kill your husband. That son-of-a-bitch was doing something crooked."

"You're right Mrs. Goodman," Delia admitted. "There does seem to be a fly in the buttermilk."

"There is a bunch flies in the buttermilk," Mrs. Goodman agreed. "Lela probably didn't know half of what Curtis was doing out there in the streets. It'll all come out now. It's not shocking that he got killed. It's shocking that pretty little Lela is the one that killed him. Now you and the FBI are going to dig him up and kill him again. It is so damn hot out here. I should have asked you earlier did you want something to drink?"

"I believe I will take something cool to drink," Delia accepted.

"Good!" Mrs. Goodman was delighted. "You're standing up already. Go right in that back door to the kitchen. There are some clean glasses in the dish rack by the sink. Soda and ice are in the fridge. I have been telling you everything I know. You can come back and sit down and tell me everything you know. Get that card from the FBI off the counter while you're in that kitchen too."

Delia observed Mrs. Goodman sit back in the lawn chair. She began to relax and wait for something cool to drink on a hot summer day.

"What type of soda would you like Mrs. Goodman?" Delia asked.

"Ginger ale baby," Mrs. Goodman requested. "A poor woman's champagne."

Delia smiled as she started walking to the house, but stopped and turned to ask one more question.

"Do you think Curtis loved Lela?"

Mrs. Goodman paused to think before she answered.

"Curtis was raised to have everything and anything he wanted. He would go out in those streets and sample everything and anything. When he came home, all he wanted was his precious Lela."

eighteen

The Price Of Silence

Mavis gripped the edge of the kitchen table and held on tight. The force of each thrust, from behind that Andre made, went harder and deeper inside of her. Her huge breasts swung back and forth against the kitchen table causing the salt and pepper containers to fly across the kitchen floor. Her right hand came loose from the tight hold on the edge of the table and hit the napkin holder.

Napkins went floating like white clouds throughout the room. After each thrust, Andre made a loud caveman-like grunt. Mavis' howls of ecstasy could have easily been confused with screams for real help.

"Oh God, help me!" Mavis hollered. "Oh shit!

Fran was paralyzed by the observation she was making through the glass outer kitchen door. Her four small sons who were standing with her tried to verbally communicate what they all were observing.

"What they doing?"

"Ooh wee, they naked!"

"They doing something really nasty!"

"They are doing the nasty, stupid."

Fran was finally able to break free from her temporary paralysis. She began rushing her four small sons back to the car.

"Shut up! Shut up! Close your eyes!" Fran shouted. "Get back in the car right now!"

Fran frantically tried to use her auto remote control to unlock the doors and put all the windows down in the car.

"Get in this car right now!" Fran continued strongly commanding her children.

Fran's four sons could not stop giggling as they scurried into the backseat of the car.

"Do not get out of this car," Fran resumed shouting out commands. "Stop all that laughing! I will be right back."

"Are you going to stop them from doing the nasty."

"Shut up! Shut up! Shut up!"

The four little boys found their mother's embarrassment tremendously amusing. They continued giggling despite her demands for them to be more serious.

They watched her try to collect herself and march back into the house.

When Fran came charging through the kitchen door, Mavis and Andre had concluded their act of pleasure. Fran slammed the inside door closed hard enough to make the windows rattle. Mavis was still leaning on top of the kitchen table naked, exhausted, and breathless. Andre did not even try to cover his bare body from Fran's eyes as he slowly approached her. His massive male asset was pointed directly at her.

"You came back to get some of this," Andre offered.

Fran took her purse strap and started winding it up in her hand. She was prepared to use her well-stuffed purse as a weapon if necessary.

"You better back up brother," Fran warned. "Don't make me have to give you an old-fashion sex change right here in this kitchen."

"You know you want to ride on top of this," Andre said pointing downward.

"You better try to keep that thing attached if you plan on ever riding somebody else's backside again," Fran warned.

Andre just laughed and slowly moved closer toward Fran. Mavis finally gathered her composure. She rushed in front of Andre and gently pushed on his huge, hairy chest.

"Stop messing with Fran," Mavis instructed. "Go upstairs and wait for me. Since that thing is still attached, we need to work it out some more a little later."

Mavis softly kissed Andre's chest. She gently pushed him backward again.

"We can all be good friends," Andre informed. "There is enough of me to handle both of you ladies."

"You better make him stop," Fran cautioned.

"Go upstairs Andre," Mavis insisted. "I will be right up. Let me and Fran have a little sister time."

Andre smiled and surrendered to Mavis' request. He blew a kiss at Fran. Andre proudly marched out of the kitchen. Mavis grabbed her bathrobe off the kitchen floor and put it back on. She sat down at the kitchen table and lit up a cigarette.

"I will never eat off that kitchen table again," Fran said.

"Good, that means I won't have to offer you nothing to eat when you come over," Mavis replied.

"How old is he?" Fran asked.

Mavis slowly blew smoke at Fran from her cigarette.

"The government says he can drink, drive, and go to the Army. If he is old enough for the government, he's old enough for me."

Fran threw her purse on the kitchen counter with enough force to cause a loud thumping sound. She paced back and forth fuming in silence. She finally found the appropriate scolding words.

"You are so damn nasty! You couldn't close the inside door. Anybody could have walked up and saw your naked butt."

"What's your point?"

"Do you have to fuck every man that says hello?"

"Just the ones that say it with a smile."

"You're not funny."

"Fran, every time some man you think you might love darkens your door, you have them legs lifted up in the air and spread wide apart. Those brats locked up in that hot car outside are proof positive. Stop acting like I invented getting freaky. I still have a long way to catch up with you."

"You are so damn nasty!" Fran repeated.

"What did you come here for?" Mavis asked still puffing on her cigarette.

Fran pulled out a chair from the kitchen table and sat down.

"We need to tell them what we know."

"What we know about what?"

"Mavis, Lela killed Curtis, remember? We need to tell Lela's lawyers about everything we know about Curtis."

Mavis continued savoring her cigarette and looking at Fran with confusion about her concern.

"Ashley is handling the situation," Mavis assured her friend. "Stop worrying. Ashley will take care of everything."

"This is very serious Mavis," Fran hollered. "Ashley may not be able to handle everything. We might need to give Ash a little help. They will try to give Lela the chair for killing Curtis."

Mavis held her cigarette and leaned over the table to emphasize her words.

"Ashley would burn down the courthouse if they tried to mess up one hair on Lela's head," Mavis said with confidence. "I would not ever tell Ashley, but if I ever get in any type of legal trouble, Ashley will be the only person I use my one phone call on. Listen Fran, Ash already has hired that pit bull, Portia Lee. I'm still a little baffled myself on how she pulled that one off. Ashley already had a few dollars herself. Now she is in control of all of Curtis' money. And who would have ever thought scary Mary would get her sanctified self involved in this mess. Sister Mary has enough money and power to go toe to toe with Doris Mercer and the state of Ohio. There is nothing to worry about."

"Doris Mercer is not going to prosecute Lela."

"Oh yes she is," Mavis laughed. "Those flunkies downtown are just doing Doris' bidding. But they are going to think twice now that Sister Mary and Jesus Christ are working for the defense."

Mavis laughing cause her to choke on her cigarette smoke.

"This is not funny Mavis."

"What do you want us to do Fran?"

Fran got back up and began to pace again before stating her intentions.

"We need to tell Portia Lee about Roni Paige and about those twins?"

Mavis sat back and began puffing harder on her cigarette.

"Everybody in this town knows that Curtis was a husband and a whore. Roni Paige was just one of many. That is all going to come out. A good lawyer like Portia Lee don't need us to help her do her job."

"What about the twins?" Fran asked.

"Curtis always said those boys were not his sons. He has been denying them since they were born. Why should we be the ones to tell it? We will catch hell if it comes out that we knew anything. Plus, we can't prove Curtis is those twins' daddy. All we know is what everybody else on the street has heard and said. Street talk is not always the gospel."

"Lela will be upset, but she won't give us hell if we told her what we know."

"Lela is not who I'm worried about," Mavis informed. "Ashley will go up in flames if she finds out we have been silent all this time. She will get that knife Lela used on Curtis and cut our throats."

"Roni Paige is not no warm and fuzzy woman," Fran replied. She will be trying to get some money for those twins pretty soon. They will think Lela killed Curtis about Roni."

"They don't need Roni Paige just to get a good motive for killing Curtis," Mavis said. "Roni is in prison anyway."

"What!" Fran shouted. "In prison for what?"

"You know that heifer has been selling drugs since she probably was in the sixth grade," Mavis said laughing again. "I bought some leaves from her myself a long time ago."

"Oh my God!"

"Fran, we don't know for sure if Curtis is the father to those twins. We just need to stay on the sideline and let Ash quarterback this game."

Both women were startled by the deep voice in the room.

"Mavis!"

Fran and Mavis turned to see a naked Andre standing in the kitchen doorway.

"Not this nasty bastard again," Fran said with disgust.

Mavis smashed out her cigarette and stood up. She tried to keep her bathrobe from flying open.

"Fran go see about your kids before Children Services comes and takes them out of that hot car. We can talk about all of this later."

"Later!" Fran ranted. "We don't have later. Lela needs us now!"

"I got something that might help relax you," Andre purred as he strutted toward Fran again.

Andre took his hand to playfully shake his extensive male appendage at Fran.

Mavis stepped in front of Andre's path to block him from getting any closer to her friend.

"Go put the air conditioning on in that hot car before those babies suffocate," Mavis again instructed. "Sister Mary, Portia Lee, and Ashley have bigger balls than my Andre. They are the last three women on earth that need any help from us."

"Balls bigger than mine? I don't think so," Andre joked as he playfully pushed Mavis forward toward Fran.

"They're going to save Lela some kind of way," Mavis reassured her friend. "Trust me Fran. Just trust me."

"Trust this," Andre said making more obscene gestures at Fran.

Fran grabbed her purse and stomped back out of the kitchen door.

Mavis dropped her bathrobe back on the kitchen floor. She turned around and faced a delighted Andre. She purred back at him.

"Ooh wee, let's do the nasty again."

nineteen

Survival Strategy

"Who is Roni Paige?"

"I have no idea."

"I am your lawyer. You have got to tell me everything. Now let me say this again, who is Roni Paige?"

"I have absolutely no idea."

Portia Lee walked across Sister Mary's kitchen to the center counter where Ada was sitting on one of the counter stools. She snatched a manila folder filled with papers out of Ada's hands. Ada's face showed she was nervous and frightened by a furious Portia.

The kitchen seemed to be transplanted from a real French colonial manor. The ceilings were high, several arches, detailed woodwork, and numerous green plants all gave a touch of elegance to this room used for preparing meals.

The enormous kitchen opened up to a sitting area. Two love seats were positioned sideways in front of a fireplace.

Portia marched in anger from the kitchen counter to the sitting area where Sister Mary, Cheryl, Ashley, and Lela had assembled for this defense strategy meeting. She threw the folder on the coffee table between the love seats. The weight of all the paper contained in the folder caused a loud thumping noise when it landed in front of Lela on the table. Lela refused to even touch the folder. It showed on her face that she was annoyed by Portia's theatrics.

Lela was not in a traumatic daze like they all believed. She was taking a little time to thoroughly examine her lawyer. She didn't know if she really liked Portia. Portia seemed too much like a female version of Curtis. She was extremely flamboyant and outspoken.

Money had made her physically far more attractive than nature had actually meant for her to be. She was a sneaky flirt, but could be explosively evil. Whenever she was around, there was always lots of strutting, yelling and drama. Portia barely spoke to Lela directly. Lela was sure that Portia was mainly working hard to give this legal performance to an audience of one.

Ada was oblivious to how hard her niece was trying to impress her. Portia didn't seem to realize she could do just about anything and still not be offensive to Ada. She just needed to breathe and her aunt would cry tears of pride.

Lela realized Portia didn't care anything about her or her family. She didn't care if she was guilty or innocent. She was just using legal skills to manage this horrible tragedy to impress and gain Ada's respect.

Ashley tried to ease the mounting tension in the room.

"You all know that I'm the executor of Curtis's estate," Ashley explained. "I have been going through his business dealings. There are a number of items that need some major clarification."

"Like what?" Lela curiously inquired.

"Like who is Roni Paige?" Portia strongly reiterated.

Lela ignored Portia's question and continued listening to Ashley.

"Curtis co-owned your house with you. The house totally reverted to you upon his death. He had one car and one truck in his name. He had one savings account and one checking account that he shared with you. He had one joint credit card with you and two credit cards that were only in his name. He had a few stocks and bonds. His biggest asset was a life insurance policy that is valued at one million dollars. The beneficiaries on the policy are you and the children. That is all of Curtis Mercer's assets."

Portia paced the room ready to explode. Cheryl quickly grabbed the folder to examine for herself.

"This is impossible," Cheryl blurted out. "Curtis had three auto body and repair shops. Curtis had rental property. Curtis had plenty money."

"Curtis was just an employee of those auto shops," Ada informed. "He did not own any of those auto shops. The only house he owned was the one he lived in."

"This is impossible," Cheryl repeated.

Sister Mary had sat silently until this information was revealed.

"Who was Curtis working for?" Sister Mary wanted to know. "Who owned those auto shops?"

"Lela Marie Mercer," Portia shouted.

Lela looked around at Portia with confusion in her eyes.

"All three auto shops were transferred into your name three years ago," Ashley reported to a stunned Lela.

"How could he do that without me knowing?" Lela asked her friend.

"That is not all of it," Portia bellowed out. "Tell her the rest."

Ashley took a deep breath before revealing the rest of her findings.

"There are three business accounts at three different banks in the name of Mercer Auto Body and Repair Shop."

"How much is in those accounts?" Sister Mary quickly asked.

"Combined, well over five million dollars," Ashley replied.

"Oh my God!" Cheryl shouted.

Cheryl kept leafing through the folder and shaking her head in amazement. Lela just continued to sit silent almost in a catatonic state.

"You didn't need Sister Mary," Portia hollered. "You could have bailed yourself out. You are a very rich woman, Mrs. Lela Mercer."

"Lela, not Curtis, also owns three rental houses," Ashley continued with her explanation. "The houses are located at 202 Sugar Lane, 51 East Street, and 1357 Copley Boulevard."

"The house on Copley is empty," Ada added to the explanation. "The house on East Street, some senior citizen lady and her three cats are living there. The house on Sugar Lane was rented by a Veronica Paige. Most people, including myself, know her as Roni Paige. Roni's mother and her seven-year old twin sons are living in that house right now."

"Where is this Roni Paige?" Cheryl asked.

"In the federal penitentiary, doing the third year of a six year sentence for narcotics distribution," Portia vehemently blurted out. "Her mother and two sons are living rent-free in the house on Sugar Lane. What do you think about that landlord Lela?"

"How did Lela get these houses?" Sister Mary calmly asked.

"All three were owned by a Wallace Penny," Ashley explained. "Three years ago he sold the houses to Lela."

"Lela, you don't remember ever buying and signing for any rental houses?" Sister Mary wanted to know.

"I don't know any Wallace Penny. I have only signed for one house in my whole entire life. That is the house that Curtis and I bought to be our home after we got married," Lela confessed. "Curtis called those rental houses his money shacks. He said it was rental property that he was going to get rid of soon. He said he was sick of the tenants calling him with their maintenance problems. I didn't even know where they were located. He said he was getting rid of them. He didn't even own those houses?"

"No he didn't," Portia strongly reminded her client. "His wife owned those houses."

"How could any of this happen without my knowledge? There has to be bank statements for these accounts. Where were they being mailed? How about taxes? I would have had to pay taxes on all this stuff. I'm sure the IRS would have come after me by now."

"Everything was being mailed to the main office for the auto shops," Ashley said. "The office manager was handling most of your business affairs. City, state, and federal taxes were being signed, sealed, and delivered every year."

"That little white girl that was Curtis's secretary?" Lela questioned. "Amber something is her name. I can't believe she is smart enough to have done all of what you say. What has she said about all of this?"

"If you know where she is, please tell me," Portia said. "I have Delia out there right now trying to track down little Miss Amber Gail. She has suddenly disappeared."

"Have you talked to this Wallace Penny?" Cheryl asked.

"I represented Wallace a couple of times on some minor misdemeanor charges," Ada revealed. "He's a street punk. I have a hard time believing he ever owned a good pair of decent underwear to put on his nasty behind, let alone own some houses. He has got to be a front man for somebody."

"Where is Wallace Penny now," Cheryl again inquired.

"In the state penitentiary," Portia announced. "Doing a life sentence for murdering police officer, Terrell Monroe, about three years ago. Right after he sold the houses to Lela. Terrell was killed in the house on Copley."

"Police officers, Thomas Dancy and Terrell Monroe, went to Lela's house on Copley Boulevard for a routine domestic violence complaint from a neighbor," Ada explained. "The house was a known drug house and the police officers apparently walked in on more than they bargained."

"You're talking about that rookie cop who got killed with Tommy?" Lela asked.

Portia was baffled by Lela's question.

"You know Thomas Dancy?" Portia asked.

"Everybody knows Tommy," Ada admitted.

"Tommy is Tracey Mercer's boyfriend," Ashley acknowledged.

"Bingo," Portia told Ada. "That's why the feds are snooping around. Rookie cop coincidently killed at a drug house owned by the same person who owns those auto shops who just killed her husband. The feds smell a rat."

"What are you thinking?" Ada asked anxiously.

"Over five million dollars in bank accounts, but Sister Mary bails her out of jail," Portia said. "I bet the amount of money in those bank accounts is far more than all the car repairs that got done at Mercer Auto Body and Repair."

"Unless you're laundering drug money through those auto shop bank accounts," Sister Mary concluded.

"They never counted on Lela killing Curtis," Portia included.

"They?" Cheryl wondered. "Who is they?"

"Ashley, what bank handled the sale of those houses from this joker, Wallace Penny, to our Lela?" Sister Mary asked.

Ashley looked at Sister Mary and suddenly had the same suspicions shoot through her mind. She took the thick folder from Cheryl and quickly shuffled through the countless number of papers.

"Every transaction was handled by a Meghan Reilly at Crestview Savings and Trust."

"Where Tracey Mercer is a vice-president," Ada realized out loud.

"The paper trail shows that Curtis did own all three of those houses before they were sold to Wallace Penny. Penny then promptly sold the houses back to Lela. Tracey does not just look like her mother," Portia admitted. "She has the same good business sense. However, it may have gone in the wrong direction."

"You think Tracey Mercer is behind all of this? We have to let the prosecutor know all this information," Cheryl shouted. "This can help Lela."

"How does any of this help Lela?" Sister Mary asked. "Tracey may be laundering drug money for Roni Paige. So what! Lela still killed Curtis. Nothing changes that fact."

"You're right Sister Mary," Portia calmly agreed. "If anything, the prosecutor will use all this as a motive for Lela to kill Curtis. They will try to say Lela killed Curtis to cover up her involvement in a drug ring operating in that house on Copley that she owns."

"You really believe that Tracey Mercer could be involved with people who are dealing drugs?" Cheryl asked. "Doris is beyond rich. Her kids just have to ask and she would give them the world."

"Tommy Dancy," Ashley softly said with disappointment in her tone. "Maybe Tracey is trying to help her man."

"You would be surprised at what stupid things smart women will do for a man," Sister Mary informed the group.

"I can't keep Lela out of jail," Portia bluntly admitted. "But, I can keep her alive."

Lela slowly got up from her seat. She walked up to Portia and looked directly in her eyes for the truth.

"You think my own husband was setting me up to take the fall for some type of drug-dealing scheme?"

"I'm working on theory not facts right now," Portia gently told her client. "I need to know what police officer came to your house before you killed Curtis?"

"It was that white guy. I don't know him at all. He talked to Curtis in the backyard and then he left. He has come to the house many times before. He's really Tommy's friend. I don't think Curtis actually liked him that well. He was always very polite to me. He would try to make small talk all the time. I was half listening to anything he said. He's a tall, muscular guy. He's not bad looking, but he is a little creepy and scary. Curtis told me his name several times. I never tried to remember it."

"Hunter"

Everyone in the kitchen was startled by the tiny voice that suddenly invaded their intense conversation. All the women turned around to observe Kelly standing in the kitchen doorway. The child elaborated on her revelation.

"Daddy called him Hunter."

There was a moment of silence as no one knew how to respond to this actual witness to the crime. Portia finally regained her speaking ability and addressed her client.

"I have to admit Lela that I had no clue on how to defend you. Now I think the survival strategy Curtis was setting up for himself is inadvertently turning into a survival strategy for you. Your husband may have gotten in over his head with some mighty rough characters. The worse one may be his own sister. I think he suspected whatever shit he was in was about to hit the fan pretty soon. You suddenly killing Curtis was not in the equation for anyone, especially Curtis."

"Why didn't all this come out when Terrell Monroe got killed," Lela asked. "If he got killed in a house I supposedly owned, why did the police never come question me?"

"Good point," Portia admitted. "Who insulated you from that whole fiasco? Somebody was running interference when Terrell got killed. Was it Curtis or somebody else?"

"Lela, honey, it sounds like Curtis was not trying to hurt you. In fact he may have been trying to protect you and save his own skin at the same time. It may turn out that everything he was putting in place to save himself from doing a little time in prison will actually save your pretty little head from the guillotine," Ada added.

"Funny how what goes around comes right back around." Sister Mary snickered.

Portia looked at Sister Mary and wondered about her extremely calm reaction to all these revelations. Sister Mary showed absolutely no sign of being shocked by all this information. Portia really needed to investigate further Sister Mary's motives for such an intense involvement in this case.

Sister Mary probably knew even more dirt than what had just been put out on the table. Portia had a suspicion that the person running interference in Lela's life in the past and right now was Sister Mary. Portia would have to figure out how to deal with Sister Mary later. Right now, Portia felt it was more important at the moment to give her client a glimmer of hope.

"Curtis may have actually not been thinking of himself. He actually could have been trying to protect you from his sister." Portia said with confidence. "The husband you killed may actually be your savior."

Lela suddenly realized her oldest daughter had heard every word that had been spoken in that kitchen. She looked back at the doorway for Kelly. Kelly had disappeared.

twenty

Missing Witness

"My kids don't need no trifling whore for a mother."

"Can you please wait until our kids leave the room before you start expressing your hatred for me."

Meghan Reilly looked at her son and daughter and saw the fear in their eyes. They looked back into their mother's eyes and saw the pain and frustration.

"Go get in the car," Trevor Reilly yelled. "Did you kids hear me?"

"You have to go with him," Meghan told her children.

The children rushed to their mother and gave her one last hug and kiss before going out the kitchen door to their father's car.

"If the court did not order visitation, my babies would never see your psycho butt ever in life," Meghan informed her ex-husband.

"Tell it to the judge," Trevor advised. "Don't think this is over. You just won round one."

"You call this winning," Meghan replied.

Trevor stormed out the kitchen door and got into his car with the two children.

Meghan walked out the kitchen door and watched the car whip out of the driveway. She walked out to the middle of the street to continue waving to her children as Trevor's car drove down the street. She pulled her long red hair back and folded her arms tight across her chest to stop herself from crying. Her children took off their seat belts and looked out the rear car window. The children waved to their mother until distance made her image fade from their sight.

***

Sherry Ferguson, Meghan's assistant, tried to visualize that same image of her boss.

"I'm sure something bad has happened to her."

"The police have been questioning her ex-husband," Tracey said. "I was told that they had a very ugly divorce. The rumor is that he was really angry when he did not win full custody of the children."

"They had a rocky relationship and he is not the kindest man to ever live," Sherry admitted. "I still never took him to be capable of that type of violence towards Meghan. I think something else may have happened to her."

"Exactly what do you think might have happened?" Tracey asked.

Sherry's eyes were red from crying. She took a balled up tissue and tried to dry her running nose. She was not sure it was wise to confide in Tracey Mercer. She knew that Tracey could really care less if anyone that worked at the bank fell off the edge of the earth. However, her brother Curtis, had been Meghan's biggest client. She also knew Tracey had enough clout, with the company and in this town, to make everyone search a little harder for her missing boss, Meghan Reilly.

Sherry started to open her mouth to give her theory on why her boss had been classified as missing for the last five days. Her words were stopped from rolling off her tongue by the sight suddenly standing behind Tracey Mercer.

"Hello ladies."

Tracey turned around to see Tommy standing behind her. It was his off day, so instead of his police uniform, he was dressed in an expensive light gray suit. He gave Tracey a quick kiss on the lips. His sinister smile made Sherry's plea for help from Tracey freeze in the back of her throat.

"Hi Tommy. Is it lunchtime already?" Tracey wondered. "Oh my goodness, let me not be rude. Tommy this is Sherry Ferguson. Sherry was Meghan Reilly's administrative assistant. I'm sorry, I should say Sherry is Meghan Reilly's administrative assistant. God forbid that anything horrible has happened to our Meghan."

"That's the young lady that is missing?"

Tommy asked the question, but already knew the answer.

"Meghan is a personal banker here at Crestview," Tracey replied.

"Well, none of you at Crestview Savings and Trust need to worry. The entire police department has been put on alert to find her. Something like this makes the community nervous and women afraid to venture out. She was a mother too. It's always terrible when kids loose a mother. Everything possible is being done to get this case resolved very soon."

Tommy looked Sherry directly in the eyes and gave her another uncomfortable smile. The look in his eyes kept Sherry from responding at all. Tracey did not even seem to notice that Sherry had stopped speaking.

"Let's think positive," Tracey tried to reassure. "There is still a good chance that Meghan will be found safe and sound."

"You are absolutely correct, my sweet love," Tommy agreed. "This may actually have a happy ending."

"Sherry, just take the rest of the day off," Tracey instructed. "I will let everyone know that I authorized it. Just go home and relax. I know those police detectives have put you through the grinder. This entire situation is very stressful. I'm sure they will find Meghan safe and sound real soon. Just go home for the day."

Tracey did not even wait for any type of reply from Sherry before marching away. Tommy gave Sherry another sinful smile before turning and arrogantly strolling toward Tracey's office.

Sherry felt Tommy's tone of voice and facial expressions were warning gestures to her rather than gestures to assure her that Meghan would possibly be found.

When Tracey got into her office, she could barely wait to chastise Tommy.

"Close that goddamn door!" Tracey commanded. "Lock it."

Tommy closed and locked the office door. He turned around slowly with a broad smile on his face.

"How is my boo-boo today."

"What have you done?"

"I don't know what you're talking about."

"I told you that I would take care of everything."

"What do you mean?"

"Meghan Reilly."

Tommy walked closer and got more serious.

"Did you know that Delia Tavares works for Portia Lee?"

"I don't know any Delia Tavares."

"She used to be a police detective. She was a very good police detective. She has her law degree now, but, she makes more money doing private investigation work for high price attorneys like Portia Lee. There is a reason she makes so much money doing private investigations. It's because she is good. She is damn good. Sniffing around constantly like a dog looking for a bone. She won't rest until she finds the truth."

"You're panicking. I told you there was nothing to worry about. You're going to make them start looking for pieces of a puzzle that they didn't even know existed. You're going to make them take their focus off of Lela. Don't make Lela a victim. She killed my brother and that is what needs to be the only thought in anybody's mind. My brother Curtis was the victim."

Tommy walked around the desk and grabbed Tracey around the waist and pulled her close.

"Meghan Reilly had a very mean, controlling, and abusive husband," Tommy informed his lover. "I'm sure no one in this entire town will question his ability to do something awful to his young and beautiful wife who had just gained custody of his children against his wishes."

"I told you that I would take care of everything," Tracey reiterated.

"You and your mother are the only two women in the world who don't realize that sometimes you do need a man to take care of things. Just let me be your man, Tracey. Let me take care of you for a change."

"Tommy..."

Tracey tried to continue her grievance. Tommy slipped his tongue into Tracey's mouth. Tommy's kisses were truly mouth to mouth resuscitation for Tracey. She had been dead inside before Tommy made her feel alive again. She was always questioning if the feelings she had for Tommy were true love or just insane lust. If he was not so handsome, would she care what happened to him? If the sex was not so good, would she take such risks for him?

She responded to his warm, wet tongue like it was a baby's bottle. While his kiss seemed to go on endlessly, Tracey pulled down the zipper of Tommy's pants and slipped her hand inside.

twenty one

Misperception

"You need to hear this."

Marian was puzzled by the visitor sitting in Shay's office.

"Sit down Marian," Shay instructed. "This is Sherry Ferguson."

Marian shook Sherry's hand before sitting. Sherry seemed more like a teenager than a full-grown woman. She had long brown hair and a thin, undeveloped frame. Marian could tell that fresh tears had just been swiped from Sherry's blood-shot eyes.

"Miss Ferguson just left Crestview Savings and Trust," Shay continued. "She was given the day off and told to get some rest. Miss Ferguson is the administrative assistant for Meghan Reilly. I'm sure you know that Meghan Reilly is the young mother that has been missing for the last five days. Miss Ferguson came to tell me that she believes Meghan Reilly has met with foul play. She also has informed me that she is afraid that if she goes home, her life will be in serious danger also. And after hearing her story, I tend to agree."

"Well, that is a lot to digest," Marian said.

"Miss Ferguson, Marian is the assistant prosecutor handling the Lela Mercer case," Shay explained. "Would you be so kind and tell Marian why your visit today relates to her case."

Sherry cleared her throat and took a deep breath before launching into her deadly hypothesis.

"My boss, Meghan Reilly, is a personal banker at Crestview Savings and Trust. One of our biggest clients was Mr. Curtis Mercer. We handled a lot of real estate and business deals for Mr. Mercer. We transferred a lot of his holdings into his wife's name just a few years ago."

Marian's interest began to peak. She sat up in her chair to give better attention to Sherry's information.

"What type of holdings?"

"All the auto repair shops that he owned. There were also several houses that were once solely in Mr. Mercer's name that had been sold to a man by the name of Penny. I never once saw Mr. Penny. I'm not even sure what was the purpose of selling the houses to Mr. Penny. The houses were rental property that Mr. Penny sold almost immediately right back to just Mrs. Lela Mercer only. Mr. Mercer wanted all the auto shops and all the rental property put solely in his wife's name."

"Why is that so alarming? She was his legal wife."

"You are absolutely correct. Lela Mercer was his legal wife," Shay agreed.

"I was never present when Mr. and Mrs. Mercer did business with Meghan," Sherry continued. "I always saw Mr. Mercer. He was always there for business or to see his sister, Tracey Mercer, who is a vice-president at our bank. The majority of the time, Meghan went to Mr. Mercer's office at one of the auto shops to do business. I had never seen his wife, except for one time."

"Pay attention Marian," Shay instructed smiling.

"On one rare occasion, Mr. Mercer and his wife were coming to Meghan's office late in the evening to sign some papers. I had a class at the university that evening, but I had left my notebook at work. I went back to the office to get my schoolwork. They were all surprised to see me. Meghan introduced them to me as Curtis and Lela Mercer. After Mrs. Mercer killed Mr. Mercer, her picture was all over the television and in the newspapers."

Shay sat up in her seat and waited for Marian's reaction.

"I'm assuming there is a punch line coming soon?" Marian asked.

"The Lela Mercer that you arrested has light brown skin, but she is clearly an African American," Sherry informed. "The Lela Mercer that I was introduced to that evening and that was signing all those business transactions with Mr. Curtis Mercer was one hundred percent pure white."

Marian looked at Shay whose face revealed that she was just as amazed by this revelation.

"Miss Ferguson, this is a murder case that is causing a heat wave in this city," Marian emphasized. "I cannot afford for you to be guessing, mistaken, or unclear. Are you trying to tell me that some white woman came into that bank impersonating Lela Mercer."

"I would not be here if I was not sure," Sherry replied.

"That does not make a bit of damn sense," Marian strongly responded. "Curtis Mercer would go behind his wife's back and use a surrogate to put his fortune in her name. What woman in her right mind would not come running into that bank to put her name on every piece of paper he put in front of her? Why would he have to give everything he owned to his wife fraudulently? That makes no damn sense."

"I'm just telling you what I know," Sherry said. "Mr. Curtis Mercer is dead and now Meghan is missing. I just don't want to be dead or missing next."

"Curtis Mercer had a young white girl working as his assistant in the auto shops," Marian remembered.

"I showed a picture of Amber Gail to Miss Ferguson," Shay quickly responded.

"That was not her," Sherry confirmed. "The woman was older and looked very sophisticated."

"What do you know about Meghan Reilly's husband?" Shay asked.

"I can't imagine there was ever a time when he had any kind of love for Meghan," Sherry said. "He just detested her. Don't get me wrong, he was always very cordial to me. He hated Meghan exclusively. When she won custody of the two children, he was just furious. Then she seemed to be dating someone and he really lost it."

"Who was she dating?" Marian inquired.

"Meghan said it was too soon to reveal," Sherry reported.

She said she didn't want to jinx the relationship, so she was not giving any details. She definitely hadn't brought him around her children yet. She said it was someone that had been in plain sight that she had not ever noticed before."

"You don't think her husband is responsible for Meghan Reilly's disappearance?" Shay wanted to know.

"No, I don't," Sherry confirmed. "I think Trevor Reilly was extremely angry that his marriage ended and he lost custody of his kids. I think he is a mean jerk, but not mean enough and not a big enough jerk to murder Meghan."

"You hear that Marian," Shay announced. "Trevor Reilly is a monster. However, he is not the type of monster that kills. Imagine that?"

***

Marian looked at Trevor Reilly through the observation window of the police interrogation room. She wondered if a young girl like Sherry Ferguson had acquired enough woman's intuition to have a good feel for the true soul of a man like Trevor Reilly. If Lela Mercer could kill her husband, why wouldn't Trevor Reilly be capable of killing his wife?

"Why have you dragged me back in here again," Trevor shouted.

"Listen Trevor, you better tell us everything that you know," Detective Barry Becton advised.

"Right now you are the main suspect in the disappearance of your wife,' Detective Vernon Hammel added.

Trevor sat back in his seat fuming at the thought that anyone would think he had killed his ex-wife. He wore a Cleveland Indian baseball cap to cover his thinning hair. He was already naturally tall and slender. Now, he looked like he might not have eaten in days. His face was dark and sunken. He had not shaved since Meghan had disappeared.

Becton and Hammel both had excessive weight and gray hairs that clearly indicated the many years they had been working on the police force. They both seemed as annoyed with Trevor's answers as he was upset by their accusations.

"We need to go over this one more time," Becton told Trevor. "You went to the house to pick up the kids."

"She was alive when I left that house," Trevor hollered. "She made me sick to my stomach sometimes, but she was my children's mother. You think I could do anything to my own children's mother?"

"According to your own children, you didn't talk to her like you wouldn't do anything to her," Hammel recalled for Trevor.

"I have a lawyer that does all my dirty work," Trevor screamed.

The door of the interrogation room flew open and Joe Bellamy stormed into the little room.

"And your lawyer is here to handle that dirty work."

Joe Bellamy was a well-paid, well-dressed lawyer that was more than happy to break-up this informal meeting.

"Now, you boys know better than to speak to my client without me being present," Joe Bellamy continued. "We have been cooperating fully, so why are you being so rude now."

"The wife that your client called a trifling whore in front of his son and daughter is still missing," Hammel reminded the attorney.

"That is why you need to be out on the streets finding those children's mother," Joe Bellamy informed the detectives.

"Yeah," Trevor blurted out. "Stop harassing me. Go find that new boyfriend she had. He probably killed her."

"You think Meghan is dead?" Detective Hammel asked.

"Get up Reilly," Joe Bellamy told his client.

"What new boyfriend?" Becton asked. "You never mentioned any boyfriend before."

Joe Bellamy took two business cards out of the pocket inside his suit jacket and threw them on the table. He once again instructed his client.

"Enough has been said. Let's go Mr. Reilly."

"What's this boyfriend's name?" Hammel requested.

Joe Bellamy grabbed Trevor by the arm and started pulling him out of the door. Just before the door closed in his face, Trevor shouted one last bit of information against his counselor's wishes.

"I heard her call him some name like Howard or Harold."

Marian had carefully watched alone and in silence through the observation window at the only known suspect in the disappearance of Meghan Reilly. As Marian continued standing in the darkness, she whispered to herself.

"Who was Meghan's mystery boyfriend?"

twenty two

Wrong Confession

"Where is Charles?"

"He held him, kissed him, named him Charles Curtis Mercer, and then said he had to go. He said there was something very important he had to do."

"What is more important than being with his wife and newborn son?"

"Lela"

Doris stood at the end of the hospital bed looking at the hurt in her daughter-in-law's eyes. She knew Eden's words were true. She tried to continue her denial of the truth. Unfortunately for Doris, Lela had become the most important asset in both her sons' lives years ago. She could not understand how Charles could still be so in love with Lela after what she had done to their family. However, just like Eden, she realized now that there was nothing Lela could ever do that would be unacceptable for Charles. She stood scanning her mind to find the right words to give an explanation for Charles' deplorable behavior.

"I'm sure there was something urgent that made it necessary for him to leave," Doris said.

"Lela," Eden repeated. "Anything important or wonderful in his life, he always needs to share with her first. It has been that way since I met him. I have been fooling myself since the beginning to believe that it would change one day. That I could one day make him love me. That I would ever be the most important thing in his life. That I could make him love our family more than Lela."

"I have a hard time believing Charles went to see Lela," Doris said. "She did just kill his brother."

"You really think he cares that she killed Curtis?" Eden asked. "He couldn't stand Curtis."

"You just gave birth to my grandson. I'm going to hold my temper and not snatch you out of that bed and beat you back into some good sense," Doris sternly replied.

"That's your answer all the time to the truth," Eden informed. "Denial, threats, and violence."

"I understand that you're angry Eden. I would be angry too if I just had a baby and my man was nowhere to be found. Oh, I almost forgot. I've been there and done that three times. Stop being angry about your lack of a husband and be grateful for a healthy, beautiful child."

"Angry, I stopped being angry years ago," Eden explained. "I first thought sex would stop Charles' obsession with Lela. I gave it to him whenever he wanted it and in every way possible. I didn't even say a word when he would slip and sometimes call out her name during lovemaking. Then I thought marriage would stop it, but it just got worse. Then she killed his brother and I was sure it was over. I was so wrong. Now I have given him a son and it still won't end. Nothing can stop him from loving Lela. I'm am not sure now if it is true love or just some sick obsession."

"Well, if it makes you feel better, she doesn't love him," Doris offered.

"That doesn't matter to Charles," Eden told Doris. "Lela is no different than you. He has always wanted you to love him as much as you loved Curtis. Now he just wants Lela to love him as much as she loved Curtis. You and Lela are the exact same person to Charles."

"What the hell are you talking about?" Doris yelled with outrage. "Having a baby has made you absolutely crazy. I love all of my children equally. Charles has never had to question how much I love him."

"Bullshit," Eden yelled back with outrage. "There are only two things you worship on this earth and that is Curtis and yourself."

The tears in Eden's eyes flowed down her face uncontrollably. She sent more words hurling out of her mouth along with bitterness, jealousy, and anger like daggers aimed right at Doris.

"You have always loved Curtis more. You slobbered all over him. Curtis is so handsome. Curtis is so smart. Curtis is so everything. It has turned Tracey into a pit bull that everybody, including you, should worry whenever she growls. Charles has turned into a self-doubting fool. He lives in continuous fear of disappointing you. He believes that he is just nothing to you. He is just as obsessed with you as he is with Lela. That's why he treats Lela just like he treats you, begging constantly for love and attention. Sometimes, I don't even think it actually has anything personally to do with Lela. I think he would have been crazy about any woman that Curtis married. He just wants to defeat Curtis at something. It doesn't even matter that Curtis is dead now. Everybody knows that Lela was and still is Curtis' trophy wife. Charles wants that trophy no matter what the consequences. If he can get it, he thinks he can win over the real woman he is in love with, you. Your children are all a bunch of sick puppies."

Doris was left momentarily speechless by this unexpected venomous outpouring by Eden. She was already mentally drained from everything that was happening in her life. Uncharacteristic of her past behavior, Doris had no strength this evening to put up a good defense against this unprovoked verbal attack from her daughter-in-law. She was unusually calm giving her reply.

"Despite what you or anyone else may think, I love my children equally. I may have showed more attention to Curtis, but it was because he required more attention. Curtis was always finding himself in some type of trouble that I had to clean up. My other two children are strong and good. Curtis was weak and bad. I did not have to do as much for them as I did for Curtis."

"Only in your mind," Eden enlightened her mother-in-law.

"He is a beautiful baby," Doris serenely said. "Regardless of what may or may not happen between you and Charles, I'm the baby's grandmother. I will always be there for my grandchild. I will always be there for you also, because you are my grandchild's mother."

"Just like Lela."

Eden's response felt like a punch in the gut.

"Get some sleep Eden," Doris strongly advised. "Charles will eventually come back to you and the baby."

"Are you sure?" Eden asked.

"Lela will send him back," Doris said. "You're absolutely right. Lela is more like me than I sometimes want to believe. I'm not sure if you want him back, but you don't have to worry. I know for sure that Lela will send Charles right back to you. Don't you ever underestimate Lela. That is what Curtis did wrong. Don't you ever make that same mistake with me again or you may end up just like my oldest son."

Doris walked out of the hospital room and left Eden all alone. As Doris slowly walked out of the hospital, she silently prayed her youngest child was not betraying her and his family.

***

"You need to leave now."

"I had to see you. I just had to see you."

"Who let you in here?"

"Sister Mary let me in. I told her I just needed a moment alone with you."

"I can't believe she let you in here."

"Sister Mary is like family. She has trust in me. She knows I would never do anything to hurt you."

"What do you want Charles?"

Charles was not sure how to begin. How could he finally tell Lela how much he loved her. How could he finally say it out loud and make it all real.

"I know you didn't mean to hurt Curtis," Charles said.

"I didn't hurt Curtis," Lela clarified. "I killed Curtis. Curtis is dead and you need to leave now."

Lela went to show Charles to the door. He grabbed her by the arms and pulled her close to his body. He decided to forget fancy words or graceful ways to express his feelings. He just blurted out what he had wanted to say to Lela for years.

"I love you. Don't you understand? I have always loved you. I love you even more now. I can fix all of this. I can make this all better."

"Have you lost your mind?"

"You have to trust me too. I can make this all better. We can take the kids and go somewhere far from here and start all over."

"And what about Eden? She is having your baby."

Charles released his grip on Lela. She backed away from him.

"He was born today," Charles revealed. "A healthy boy. I named him Charles Curtis Mercer. I have a son."

"What is wrong with you Charles?" Lela asked in amazement. "Eden just had the baby and you are here? Why Charles? There is no us. There will never be an us. I am Mrs. Curtis Mercer. I'm your brother's wife. I will always be your brother's wife. Nothing can change that. Not even the awful deed I did. Charles, go back to your wife and child now."

Charles charged toward Lela trying to touch her.

Lela rapidly backed away from him.

"Don't you understand?" he pleaded. "I can't live without you. Just the thought that I won't have you in my life is suffocating me."

"Charles, please go," Lela begged.

"You can't make me go," Charles informed her.

"I can."

The stern commanding voice froze both Lela and Charles. Charles knew immediately whose voice could echo through a room with such force. He slowly turned to face his biggest adversary.

"You get your wimpy ass out of here right now," Ashley roared.

Lela was afraid of what might happen next. She became nervous and uneasy. She began to fidget and almost lost her voice.

"Charles, please just go," Lela begged again.

"You're worse than Curtis," Charles laughed. "You think that Lela is your property. She does not belong to you either."

"It doesn't matter if Lela belongs to me or Curtis," Ashley bellowed. "We all know for sure that she will never belong to you. So you can just get the fuck out of this house now."

Charles suddenly charged toward Ashley and wrapped his hands around her throat. The two crashed hard into the wall. They knocked paintings off the walls and chairs tumbled over. Vases shattered on the floor as the two struggled around the room. Charles was determined to finally choke the life out of Ashley. Another task he had wished he had done years ago.

Lela was unable to move. She did not want to make the same mistake twice. She regained a more powerful voice and screamed out.

"Charles please! Stop it!"

When the two crashed into the wall again, Ashley frantically reached out for any type of object to make into a weapon. She grabbed a nearby lamp.

Charles slammed her repeatedly against the wall as he increased the pressure of his grip on her throat. Ashley pulled the lamp right out of the electrical socket and raised it up like a weapon. She smashed the lamp against the side of Charles's head. The pain and blood made him release Ashley and stagger backward. He was only temporarily stopped. He wiped the blood and glass from his face. Ashley and Charles were both sweating and breathing hard with anger. After a brief moment, they both charged at one another resuming their mutual combat.

Their need to badly hurt each other was stopped by the sound of a new voice in the room.

"Charles, stop it! Stop it right now!"

The new voice instantly made Charles release his grip on Ashley. Ashley grabbed another lamp and raised it toward Charles.

"Ashley!" Lela shouted.

The pleading tone in Lela's voice made Ashley freeze.

She let the lamp slowly drop down to her side.

Charles walked to Sister Mary and waited for her to scold him. However, she hugged and kissed him like he was a bruised and battered child.

"Don't let this destroy you," Sister Mary pulled him toward her and whispered in his ear. "You have to be stronger than this."

Charles pulled away from Sister Mary.

"Why do you love me so much?" he asked.

"Because I love your mother and you are part of your mother. I will never stop loving Doris and I will never stop loving you."

Shame and embarrassment flowed through Charles' entire body. He closed his eyes for a moment and took a deep breath. He turned around and just stared at Lela. He tried to capture every inch of her face and body in his mind.

"I'm sorry," he said. "I'm very sorry."

"No Charles," Lela corrected him. "The blame for everything that has happened is on me. I apologize for what I have done to your brother and all the hurt I have caused you and your family. I do love you Charles. But, I love you only as Curtis' brother."

"That is all I am and all I ever will be," Charles snickered. "Curtis' brother and Doris' other son."

Charles slowly walked out of the house.

Sister Mary looked at Lela and Ashley. She did not say a word to either. They looked too much like her past. She worried about what would be their future. Sister Mary turned silently and left the room.

Ashley dropped the lamp on the floor and collapsed on to the couch. Lela sank down on the couch by her side. She rested her head on Ashley's shoulder.

"I love you," Lela told her friend.

"I understand how he feels," Ashley confessed. "I will never be able to live without you. I don't know what I will do if you are sent to prison. If they try to give you the death penalty, they might as well kill me too."

"Nothing can break us up," Lela assured her friend. "We're friends forever."

Lela took Ashley's hand and squeezed it tight.

twenty three

A Higher Law

I'm Asia Wang and this is my partner, Lorenzo Flores.

Helen Monroe examined the identification badges thoroughly before she let the two FBI agents enter her home. They followed her to the living room where she instructed them to sit on the sofa. She sat down in a chair across from the two agents. She crossed her legs and waited for the real reason for their visit to unfold.

Helen seemed annoyed by their presence and did not show any eagerness to be hospitable or answer any of their questions.

The two FBI special agents carefully examined their surroundings. There was a large photo of Officer Terrell Monroe in full police uniform on the fireplace mantel. There were smaller photos also on the fireplace mantel that gave a retrospect of Terrell's short, but outstanding life.

His smile in the large photo was upsetting. It showcased how the police rookie was so young and handsome at the time of his untimely death. The brightness in his eyes reflected a promising future that was cut short.

Asia started with a question that she already knew the answer.

"Mrs. Monroe, your son was Officer Terrell Monroe?"

"Terrell was my only child," Helen answered bitterly.

Asia thought Helen looked younger than a woman who had lived more than fifty years. You could tell looking in her eyes and heard it in her voice that grief for her son's death had fermented into anger. As an Asian American, Asia thought she may have trouble connecting with Helen, who was African American. However, Asia felt instantly the weight of losing a child when she walked into Helen's home. She suddenly realized that womanhood had no racial barriers and motherhood had no color. She stuttered as she tried to ask the next question. Her partner, Lorenzo, came to her aid. Lorenzo spoke clear and to the point.

"Mrs. Monroe, do you know if your son had any type of connection to Curtis Mercer?"

Helen smiled at the handsome Latino federal agent.

She knew immediately that this was more about Curtis Mercer than about her son, Terrell.

"My son has been dead for three years," Helen calmly replied. "And you are just now coming to ask me some questions. It took Lela killing her no good husband for you to care about who killed my son, an officer of the law?"

"Wallace Penny was tried and convicted for your son's murder," Lorenzo reminded Helen.

"You really think that street punk had enough sense to ambush my son like that?"

Asia regained her questioning skills and interjected.

"You don't think Wallace Penny was responsible for your son's death?"

"He may have pulled the trigger, but I think someone set him up to pull that trigger. How did my son come out of that house dead and Tommy Dancy waltzed out of that same house laughing and joking?"

"You think it was all a set up?" Lorenzo asked.

Helen uncrossed her legs and leaned forward.

"You know damn well it was a setup," Helen spit out. "That is why you are here. Why didn't you come ask me all this three years ago. Who are you trying to pin this on now? Lela Mercer killed a husband who she couldn't keep out of other women's beds. She isn't responsible for my son's death too. Is that what this is all about? Doris Mercer wants to make sure that poor girl is held responsible for every bad thing that has ever happened in this town?"

"Lela Mercer owned the house where your son was murdered," Lorenzo said.

"The landlord is responsible for what the tenants do in the their rental houses?" Helen asked.

"If the landlord knows exactly what is going on in those rental houses," Asia replied.

"Lela Mercer didn't know what was going on in her own house," Helen said with confidence. "That is why my son and her husband are both dead. Can they charge her with ignorance too?"

"What do you mean Mrs. Monroe?" Lorenzo pressed for more information.

"Roni Paige was selling drugs out of that house," Helen told the agents. "Everybody in town knew about Roni Paige's business activities. Wallace Penny is a big scary-looking dude, but he'll never be more frightening than Roni Paige. Roni was running a drug supermarket."

"She was selling to drug addicts?" Asia wanted clarification.

"No way," Helen continued. "Roni was a big time wholesaler. She was selling to drug dealers only. She was supplying almost every drug dealer in this area. The question you need to be asking is who was Roni's boss?"

"Lela Mercer?" Lorenzo inquired.

Helen laughed and set back in her chair.

"You must be kidding," Helen said. "That pretty pampered fool. I told you already that Lela barely ran her own house, let alone a well-stocked drug house. You go ask Officer Thomas Dancy for his opinion on this whole matter. He's the one that walked out of that house alive and well."

"How do you know all of this information?" Asia asked.

"Terrell had high respect for the law. That is why he joined the police force. He wanted to make a difference in his own community. He wanted to get people like Roni Paige out of our neighborhoods. My son was one of those young dreamers that believed justice will always prevail. He prided himself on being one of the good guys. He didn't trust that anything he said about his suspicions concerning Roni Paige would not get back to dirty Dancy. He suspected from the start that Dancy was a bad cop. He just could not link him to Roni Paige. Many people think those twin boys that Roni has are Tommy's kids. Other people believe their real father is Curtis Mercer. Terrell had not been able yet to verify anything about those twins. He was still trying. That is why he told me things that he really should have kept confidential. Terrell always justified what he told me by saying that I could ask any crackhead on the street and they probably could tell me more than what he knew about Roni and exactly what was happening in that house. Why don't you know all this information? Crackheads know more than the FBI?"

Lorenzo was offended and seemed bothered by Helen's bitter attitude. His tone was harsh when he asked his next question.

"You didn't feel any need to tell all of this to the police when your son was killed in the line of duty? This outpouring of facts is only coming out now?"

Helen leaped from her seat with outrage. She stopped short of laying her hands on this young, naïve agent.

"You have got a lot of damn nerve. Where were you three years ago? Were you sitting in kindergarten when a bunch of drug thugs gunned down my son? Where was the FBI when my son figured out how them leeches were washing all that drug money clean? Terrell did your job for you. I'm sure he finally figured out exactly how Tommy Dancy, Roni Paige, and Curtis Mercer were all connected together. That is why he is dead. You didn't care then, so why do you care now? You really think the police wanted to hear what I had to say back then? They just soothed their souls by believing that I was a grieving mother with an ax to grind against dirty Dancy because he lived and my son died. They were not about to go down that road. Everybody knows that Dancy is a flunky for Tracey Mercer by day and a piranha by night. He is worse than the street punks he is suppose to be arresting. The police department in this town just wrote my son's life off as a causality of the war on drugs. They stood like an iron curtain in front of their most prized possession."

Asia slowly rose from her seat to address Helen.

"Tommy Dancy?"

"Are you joking? They could care less about that weasel. They would kill him tomorrow if they could. Doris Mercer is like a queen in this town. Tommy just has had the good luck and good looks to have her daughter, Tracey, licking his ass for entertainment. Tommy better keep fucking Tracey until she is blue in the butt. That is the only thing saving his stupid, greedy ass. If they had went after Tommy, there was no way they would not have caught Tracey or Curtis up in the net. Nobody in this town is willing to make Doris Mercer upset. Do you know how many people are employed by Doris Mercer in this town. Do you know how much money she gives to local charities and the school system. Nobody has enough guts to cause one frown in her pretty forehead. And nobody really has enough nerve to go up against Lucifer, who is better known in this town as Sister Mary."

"Sister Mary?" Lorenzo asked in shock.

"Do you know how much money goes through that church Mary runs? They should call it the Bank of Jesus rather than The House of Mary Baptist Church. That church practically owns all the land on the west side of town. Sister Mary has got some holy shit on just about everybody with any type of position of power in this little city. Sister Mary has got more people in her pocket than you can count with all the fingers on both hands along with all the toes on both feet."

"Why Sister Mary?" Lorenzo asked again.

"Most people in this town right now don't know the strong bond between Doris and Mary. I'm old enough to remember. Those women go back years. Mary has been worshiping Doris from the top of her head to the bottom of her feet long before anybody in this town ever even knew the name Doris Mercer. Those women started out in the housing projects with nothing but the spit in their mouths. Sister Mary will never let Doris suffer any type of heartbreak if she can help it. Mary has been cleaning up some type of mess for Doris and her children for years. Sister Mary knows all about Tommy Dancy. She lets him just run wild because he keeps mean-ass Tracey happy. Now that pretty Lela has killed Curtis, the shit has finally hit the fan. Shit is blowing up all over this town. That's why you're sitting here in my living room."

Helen fell back into her chair. The pain from the loss of her son suddenly over took her again.

"They killed my baby! They killed my baby!"

Helen continued crying out as an avalanche of tears began streaming down her face.

"Nobody cares that they killed my baby. Now that Lela Mercer has had the audacity to murder the prince of this city, you want to put this all on her head too. They are trying to bury my baby in the same casket with Curtis. They want to sweep his death under the rug for good!"

Asia felt ashamed that their investigation had taken so long to get to this point.

"We care," Asia apologized. "Terrell Monroe was a fellow law officer. We're not going to stop until we get justice for Terrell."

Lorenzo rose from the sofa. He had watched Helen relive the pain of her son's death. He was ashamed for having so much attitude in his questioning. His harsh tone of voice transformed into comforting words for a broken mother.

"We will definitely get you some real justice Mrs. Monroe," he said. "I promise."

twenty four

Betrayal

Her long sharp fingernails caught the corner of his mouth as her hand glided across his face with the force of vengeance.

He didn't realize blood was filling up his mouth and spilling down his chin. He had always been taught never to retaliate against his big sister. His mother constantly preached to her sons that their only sister was a precious commodity of one. It was a lesson that Curtis had never learned. When Tracey tried to physically abuse her brothers, it was Curtis who knocked her back into compromise mood.

Charles felt the absence of his big brother and it was a stinging sensation. Her open left hand turned his head in the opposite direction with even more force than her right hand.

"How dare you beg that bitch. You think Ashley wouldn't take an opportunity to stick another dagger in my back. She called me demanding I keep you away from her precious Lela. Lela slaughtered your brother and you went there begging her like a hungry, wet dog. You pathetic fool."

Tracey started to launch into another violent attack.

Nathan Junior grabbed both of Tracey's wrists and drove her backward. Eden tried to get out of her hospital bed to help her defenseless husband. Nadine stopped Eden before she could get both feet completely on the floor.

A nurse came rushing into the room.

"Is everything okay in here?"

The nurse was visibly upset and speechless by what was happening in this maternity ward room.

Nadine was struggling to get Eden back into her hospital bed. Nathan Junior was still trying to keep an angry Tracey from attacking her baby brother again. Charles stood straight and silent. He seemed almost in a hypnotic trance with blood streaming from his lip.

Nadine turned her attention from Eden to address the concerns of the nurse.

"Everything is fine," Nadine insisted. "We don't need anything right now."

The nurse looked from a smiling Nadine to a bloody, unresponsive Charles.

"I should help him?"

"No, you should leave," Nadine insisted again. "Please close the door."

The nurse slowly backed out of the room and closed the door.

Tracey finally managed to pull away from Nathan Junior.

"Let go of me, you big horse."

"He's your brother," Nathan Junior reminded Tracey. "I'm your brother."

"Both you and him are nothing to me," Tracey hollered. "My only brother is dead."

"We all need to stop pretending," Nadine instructed. "We are all brothers and sisters. Now that Curtis is dead. We need to start supporting each other like family."

Tracey tried to charge toward Charles again, but Nathan Junior grabbed her around the waist.

"You hear that you whining weasel," Tracey said to Charles. "Your other sister says we need to be supporting each other."

Tracey's words mixed with spit flew into Charles face.

"Charles, we all still love you no matter what Tracey says," Nadine said trying to ease the tension in the room.

"Yeah man, we understand," Nathan Junior included.

Tracey broke away from Nathan Junior's strong hold again. "Understand!"

There was a knock on the door and the door slowly started to open. Another nurse began wheeling into the room a glass bassinet containing Charles and Eden's firstborn son.

They all froze as Tracey walked over to the infant and carefully lifted him up. She walked over to Charles with the child in her arms. The baby began to cry.

"Nadine is absolutely correct," Tracey agreed. We all need to stick together and be a surrogate father, since our new nephew doesn't have a real man for a father."

Charles looked over at Eden. She wanted to, but was unable to defend him this time. She felt the same as Tracey. Charles had betrayed his family. Most of all, he had betrayed her and their child. She could not say anything in his defense.

He never spoke a word. Charles simply walked out of the room.

Nadine and Nathan Junior were relieved that Charles had finally left without any type of confrontation. Nadine plumped down in the chair next to Eden's bed. Nathan Junior took the baby from Tracey's arms. The baby immediately stopped crying.

Tracey walked over and sat down in the chair on the other side of the room in front of Eden's bed.

Out of habit and out of undying love, Eden began trying to formulate an explanation for Charles' behavior. She thought she could soothe everyone's anger if she could just make some sense of the entire situation.

"Tracey, Charles loves you and your mother more than anything," Eden tried to explain. "And, he really loved Curtis."

"Shut up!" Tracey stopped her. "Just shut up!"

Nathan Junior paced the floor gently shaking Charles' son.

He was overjoyed to have the newborn cradled in his big, strong arms. The baby looked up at his uncle and smiled back.

twenty five

Previous Convictions

A temporary loss of freedom can permanently alter your outlook on life.

Keisha knew numerous people, including family members, that were currently incarcerated. It never crossed her mind to venture to any penitentiary to visit. Despite her vast street knowledge, a visit to any state prison was not something she could brag about until now.

When Delia extended the invitation to serve as her assistant during this special arranged visitation, Keisha jumped at the opportunity. She realized that Delia was already walking down the path she wanted to take for her career. Working for Miss Ada was nice, but it didn't really pay all the bills. Delia's occupation seemed exciting as well as lucrative. Just the conversation during the ride to the prison was a priceless lesson in private criminal investigation.

They entered the all-male facility during the early morning hours. Keisha was greeted by the clang of steel gates locking, prison guards watching for any sign to use their weapons, the search and seizure of her body and personal property. All of this contributed to the feeling that her freedom had been left parked and waiting on the other side of these prison walls. Keisha actually felt as trapped inside as the inmates.

Keisha and Delia were taken to a large empty room. The four walls were white and a large conference table was in the center of the room. Two chairs had been placed on one side of the table and just one chair on the other side.

Keisha and Delia sat down and waited.

"You told me not to bring in a purse. I didn't think I had to get so plain," Keisha whispered. "I feel naked without some jewelry. I guess we should do our best not to be too tempting to all these locked up men, but damn."

Delia did not respond. She was listening to the intensifying sound of chains rattling. She could hear him getting closer. When Delia did not answer her, Keisha began to listen too. She heard the eerie distant sound suddenly be right outside the door. It caused a strange feeling to shoot up Keisha's spine and settle in her stomach.

The door flew open and prison guards in full protective gear, with weapons in hands, entered and surrounded the room. Then he slowly shuffled into the room followed by more armed guards.

The chains that connected his legs together had a chain that ran up the back and connected handcuffs that held his hands tightly behind his body. There was another chain that led from the handcuffs to a steel collar around his neck.

He was about six feet tall and wearing a bright orange jumpsuit. His skin was light brown. Razor bumps made his face look like rugged terrain. Hair that had not been cut in months was braided in neat cornrows that flowed down his back. Tattoos with various meanings littered his body and make parts of his skin blue in color.

When he dropped down in the chair, his smile indicated a sense of satisfaction in the ability to get to his destination despite the restrictions caused by his shackled body.

"If I had some baby oil, we could use these chains for some real fun."

Wallace Penny laughed at his own sexual innuendo. He leaned forward and made an even more sexual gesture with his tongue toward Keisha.

"Hello Wallace," Delia greeted the prisoner.

He slowly turned his head toward Delia and returned the greeting.

"Buenos Dias"

"I'm sure they told you that I'm Delia Tavares. I'm a lawyer and a private investigator working for Portia Lee.

This is one of our legal assistants, Keisha Johnson. We represent Lela Mercer."

"News even gets through these walls. We all heard how Lela tried to cut off Curtis' head. She cut the wrong head on that pussy-chasing bastard."

Wallace's laughter came deep from within the belly and seemed to have no end. His eyes were filled with water when he asked about Portia Lee.

"Why didn't Portia Lee come and talk to me herself?"

"Miss Lee is a very busy woman," Delia explained. "That is why she hires me to help with some of her cases."

Wallace smiled and addressed his reply to Keisha.

"Portia sent this Spanish-sounding flunky because she thinks she is too damn good to come talk to a hood-rat like me."

Unveiled insults did not endear Wallace to Delia. Her tone of voice grew dark and serious. She decided to get right to the point. She wanted to get this prison visit over as soon as possible.

"Why did you kill Terrell Monroe?"

"I don't know any Terrell Monroe?

"You don't remember why you're in that jail cell?"

"Oh yeah, that guy. I didn't kill him. I'm in that jail cell because it's easier to lock up poor black guys like me than real guilty people."

"You took a plea deal," Delia reminded him.

"You can live in here the rest of your life or we can kill you," Wallace said. "That's what you call a deal?"

"If you had not killed Terrell Monroe, there would have been no choice to make."

"You hear that baby," Wallace told Keisha. "She knows I didn't kill that cop. I'm an innocent man. Now that pretty little Lela Mercer that you came here to try to keep out of prison, that's a real killer. She really should be locked up in here. And you came here for me to help her stay free. Ain't that a real bitch."

Wallace laughed out loud.

"Tommy Dancy laughed when we asked him about you too,"

Keisha informed Wallace. "He said stupid street Negroes like you belong back in slavery and this is as close as it gets."

Keisha's statement turned the smile and laughter Wallace had into frowns of anger.

"Really, that's what Tommy Dancy said?"

"Yeah, Tommy said circus monkeys always should be kept locked up."

The chains made an explosive clanging sound that seemed to echo throughout the prison as Wallace suddenly sprang up from his seat.

The prison guards all suddenly aimed their weapons at Wallace and were prepared to end his life if he made one more unexpected move.

One of the prison guards shouted just one command.

"Sit down Wallace!"

Wallace thought for a moment if he should let this be his final curtain call. The same command was repeated.

"Sit down Wallace!"

It was not time yet for his life to end. He had visitors who had not come for his blood, but for the blood of someone else. He didn't get any visitors. He realized he should not be rude to such beautiful women who wanted to spend time with him. He smiled and slowly slid back down in his seat.

"You ladies came for my help. I have been most impolite. What can I do for you? What can I do for poor pretty Lela?"

Delia could not believe how quick her young student had been able to get Wallace in the right frame of mind.

They had never ever talked to Tommy Dancy. However, Keisha's quick lies had made Wallace ready to seek revenge and talk to them. Delia was so delighted by the inmate's change of attitude, she stuttered as she unleashed her first real question.

"Did... Did you know Lela Mercer?"

"Who don't know Lela Mercer in that town? There isn't a man who ever saw her that didn't dream about getting in those panties. That's why Curtis married her. He knew every man in town wanted that piece of ass."

"You didn't know her personally?" Delia inquired.

"Women like Lela don't look at guys like me," Wallace clarified. "I'm like an invisible man to a woman like her."

"Didn't you sell her three houses?" Keisha asked.

"Sell three houses?" Wallace asked. "I've never owned a house in my life. The only steady employment I had was doing odd and end jobs for Roni Paige. She paid me mainly in crack, not cash. Can you buy a house with crack?"

"You're so funny," Keisha said smiling.

Wallace thought Keisha's smile was beautiful. He softened his voice even more when he spoke to her.

"Listen baby girl, there were times I lived in other people's cars. I sure as hell wouldn't have been peeing in the streets if I had a house to pee in."

Delia looked directly in Wallace's eyes and realized he was actually telling the truth. He really did not know what they were talking about.

"The houses on Sugar Lane, East Street, and Copley,"

Delia said. "You didn't sell those houses to Lela Mercer?"

"Those were Tracey and Roni's houses," Wallace responded. "I thought they owned those houses."

"Tracey Mercer and Veronica Paige?"

"That's right," Wallace calmly said. "Roni was living in the house on Sugar Lane with her kids. They were renting out the one house. Roni had her candy store in the other house."

"Tracey Mercer and Veronica Paige owned those three houses together?"

"Everybody calls her Roni, but yeah. I guess they owned them houses. Maybe Curtis owned them. Somebody named Mercer owned them houses. How the hell would I know anyway. I'm not no real estate agent."

"We need to look further at the complete history of the houses before they were owned by Wallace," Delia told Keisha.

Wallace was confused by what they were saying.

"Before Wallace? What are you talking about?" he asked. "Before Wallace what?"

"Documents show you owned those three houses and you sold the houses to Lela Mercer," Delia enlightened the prisoner.

There was a moment of silence as Wallace absorbed this information.

"It was a goddamn set up from the very start," Wallace said with despair. "That bitch Tommy."

"Why would Tracey Mercer and Roni Paige own houses together?" Keisha questioned.

"Tracey probably thought, like everybody else in town, that those twins were Curtis' children," Wallace responded.

"You don't believe Curtis was the father to Roni's twin boys?" Delia requested to know.

"Curtis wouldn't have screwed Roni. That was just too easy," Wallace revealed. "Curtis liked a challenge. Plus, he knew that Tommy had already tapped that ass. He didn't want Tommy's leftovers. Curtis was such a fucker that when he said he didn't sleep with a woman, nobody ever believed him."

"Wait a minute!" Keisha almost shouted. "Tommy Dancy had a thing with Roni Paige?"

"Yeah, probably child support," Wallace disclosed. "I'm pretty sure those twins are Tommy's children."

"That's the glue that binds Tommy and Roni," Delia said. "But why would Tracey Mercer be buying houses with Roni Paige if Roni was having children with her boyfriend? Everybody else might not believe Curtis, but his own sister would believe him. Tracey knew those twins were not his children. What is the link between Roni and Tracey?"

"I'm sure Tracey was tapping that ass right along with Tommy," Wallace revealed. "It was no doubt Roni wanted Tracey more than Tommy. Curtis wasn't fucking no chick his sister was banging too."

"Tracey and Roni were lovers?" Delia asked.

"I didn't get into that jumping back and forth across the fence like Tracey," Wallace said. "Now that I live in here, I can kind of understand it more. I'm willing to stay on the right side of the fence for you, baby girl."

Wallace made another obscene gesture with his tongue toward Keisha.

Keisha made eye contact with Wallace and asked him point blank.

"Did you kill Terrell Monroe?"

"Terrell was a good man," Wallace admitted. "I feel really bad about what happened to that brother. An honest cop trying to do good got put down that night. I have to be honest. I was so drunk on booze and high on crack, I wouldn't know if I shot my own mama that night. Your guess is as good as mine on who killed Terrell Monroe."

"Did you ever meet Tracey Mercer?" Delia inquired.

"Roni would not let you get ten feet near her when she came to the house. Tracey is like precious gold to Roni."

"Who else was in that house that night?" Keisha asked.

"It was just me, Roni, and, who I thought was my buddy, Hector Alonzo. That rat agreed to testify against me. What was he going to say. Even if I did kill that cop, Hector was suppose to be my buddy. He was suppose to have my back."

"Was Roni and Hector drunk and high too?" Delia asked.

"Hell no," Wallace replied. "We had a deadline to meet that night. They were bagging up the product to sell. I was the only one doing my best to test all the products we had in the house. Roni will barely take an aspirin for a headache. Hector was too scared to death of Roni to be high around her. It was not a good idea to make Roni mad. She would unleash those attack dogs, Tommy and Hunter."

"Hunter?" Delia questioned

"Hunter Lynch," Wallace confirmed. "He's a police officer too. He and Tommy are bosom buddies."

Keisha turned to address Delia.

"Hector Alonzo knows what really happened in that house that night."

"We better find Hector before Tommy and Hunter find out we were here," Delia warned.

***

When they got to the airport in Connecticut, Portia rented a car for her and Ada to make the scenic drive to the federal penitentiary for women.

Ada was astounded that Roni Paige was housed at this particular federal penitentiary. Roni's biography seemed to indicate she was a more violent offender than the inmates housed at this particular institution. The female facility seemed more like a vacation house tucked away in the countryside.

There did not seem to be many restrictions for the minimum security facility. It was obvious that the inmates were accustomed to the finer things in life and this had not changed just because they were incarcerated.

Portia expected the signs of a rough street life to be visible on her face when Veronica Paige walked out to the visitation area. However, Roni may have actually looked better as a prisoner than she did as a free citizen. Her hair was shiny dark brown and flowed down her back like a water fall. Her very light skin was flawless. A broad, bright smile was the result of extensive dental work.

She was much thinner and far younger than Portia had anticipated.

Ada greeted Roni like she was visiting an old friend.

"Hey Roni!"

"Hey Ada!"

The two women hugged like they were relatives.

"This is my niece, Portia Lee," Ada proudly introduced.

"The famous Portia Lee came to see little old me,"
Roni said bashfully. "Sit down. Make yourself at home."

The women all sat down at a visitor table.

"I really don't want to make myself feel at home, but I
appreciate the offer," Portia sarcastically said.

Roni laughed and asked for an update on their prominent
legal case.

"Well, what is going to happen to that Lela Mercer?

I was in total shock when I found out she killed Curtis. You
better not get her off. Tracey will kill you with her bare hands
if Lela don't get the electric chair."

"You ought to know," Portia said. "You know Tracey better
than anyone."

Roni ignored Portia's sly remark and turned to Ada to
clarify her relationship with Portia.

"Ada, how did she get to be your niece?"

"Pookie is my brother Robert's child."

"Pookie!" Roni shouted with laughter. "Who the hell is
Pookie?"

"Miss Paige, we didn't come all this way to go over my family tree," Portia sternly interrupted.

"Now don't get testy, Pookie," Roni joked.

Ada tried not to show her amusement. Portia's voice was
filled with fury.

"Miss Paige....."

"Call me Roni."

"Roni, I need to know why you owned houses with Tracey
Mercer and then fraudulently used Wallace Penny to sell them

to Lela Mercer? Why is Tracy Mercer bringing your sons here to see you once a month. Why is she paying for your twins to attend private school? And exactly why is no rent being paid to Lela Mercer for the house your mother and your children live in now?"

"That's a whole lot of questions."

"Can you answer one?"

"My relationship with Tracey is a private matter."

Portia leaped up from her seat in preparation to leave. Ada was startled by the sudden need to depart.

"Ada and I can go now. I didn't come this far for you to waste my time, Miss Paige. We will be heading straight to the FBI and see if they think your relationship with Tracey Mercer is a private matter. The FBI might be interested in tacking on some more time to your sentence. This looks like quite a lovely place. I'm not sure if you want to stay here twenty more years."

"Curtis was not my cup of tea, but he didn't deserve to die that way. You come here trying to save Lela's pretty ass. She killed him in cold blood. Tracey may not come off as a sweet, caring person, but she loved her brother. She loved him more than anybody. Can't you respect the love Tracey had for her brother?"

"I work for Lela Mercer."

There was a moment of silence. Ada didn't know whether to stay seated or get up. Finally, Roni concluded it was best to work with and not against Portia.

"What do you want to know?"

Portia slowly sat back down.

"How did you and Tracey get together?"

"I was doing sexual favors for Tommy to keep the police from breathing down my back. I wasn't doing nothing big at the beginning. Just mainly a little medical marijuana for the folks in the neighborhood that felt an illness that might be coming on."

Both Roni and Ada started giggling. Portia gave them both a stern look. Roni composed herself and continued with the story.

"I'm sure you have seen Tommy by now. It was no big deal. Tommy is eye candy and even better candy in bed. It seemed like a small price to pay not to be hassled or go to jail."

"Those twins are Tommy's children?" Ada eagerly wanted to know.

"No way," Roni revealed. "There was a fifty/fifty chance between Tommy and my husband. Tommy lost the coin toss. Everybody in town thinks they are Curtis's children. I do everything I can to keep everybody believing that too, especially Tracey. I don't want my boys to ever know their real father, who is an absolute monster."

"Back up," Ada said stunned. "You have a husband?"

"In paper only," Roni admitted.

"Who is this monster?" Portia wanted to know.

"Hunter Lynch."

"You're married to that white guy?" Ada blurted out.

Roni was amused by Ada's shock. She continued her explanation to Portia.

"Hunter Lynch and Tommy Dancy have been buddies since they joined the police force together. Hunter is a white guy, but he loves Tommy like a brother. I can honestly say that Hunter is far worse than Tommy. Tommy mainly talks a bunch of bullshit. Hunter won't ever say a whole lot of words to you. He gets tremendous joy in hassling street folks. The sight of blood has never bothered him, especially when he causes the bloodshed. He is just a heartless monster who thrives on inflicting physical pain on human beings. There was never any type of feelings between us. It was mainly a sex and cash payment arrangement with both Tommy and Hunter for street protection."

"But he is your legal husband?" Portia asked.

"When you are very young and filled to the brim with drugs and liquor, you do a lot of stupid things. Sometimes you forget to go back and correct those errors you made years ago. We just never got around to going to the courthouse and getting a divorce. Hunter is actually how I first met Tommy."

"Hunter didn't mind Tommy sleeping with his wife?" Ada asked.

"I'm very sure I'm not the only woman those two men have shared."

"There was nothing in the newspapers about you being married to Hunter Lynch. He's a police officer."

"There was a lot that didn't go in the newspapers and in the police reports about that entire incident," Roni revealed. "Hunter actually arrested me that night. You won't find that fact in any paperwork. "Did your husband kill Terrell Monroe?" Portia asked.

"Probably," Roni casually admitted.

Portia and Ada were both surprised that Roni so quickly admitted who she suspected actually killed the young police officer. They both also knew that this was not Roni's educated guess. They knew Roni knew the whole truth and nothing but the truth.

"You knew Tracey through Tommy?" Portia asked.

"Tommy is a freak and Tracey is just as freaky as he is. It started with Tommy and me. Then it went to Tommy, Tracey, and me. Finally, Tracey decided I was a delicacy just for her alone. No way Tommy is ever going to object to whatever Tracey wants and she wanted me. She is Tommy's bread and butter. The first house was bought just for me and the kids to have a place to live. The other two houses were bought to fix up and rent out. We paid for the houses, but our names were never on any house deeds. Tracey had all the houses actually in Curtis's name. She had some personal banker at that bank she works at handle all the paperwork. It made Tracey look good at the bank and helped Curtis with all that bad credit that was mounting up. It all started out righteous."

"Did she know about the drugs you were dealing?" Ada inquired.

"I wasn't doing enough business in the beginning to pay the paperboy. It really was nothing for her to be concerned about. After the other two houses were bought, Tracey let me live on the rent money. I didn't really need to risk selling drugs anymore. I had stopped dealing. As long as I had Tracey, I didn't need to do anything illegal anymore."

"Then why are you here?" Portia asked.

"Her brother, Curtis, started losing those auto shops. He was in debt up to his eyeballs. He owed all his vendors and the banks too. He didn't take after his mother not one bit. He was a terrible businessman. The only one that actually has any real legitimate business sense in that family, besides their mother, is Charles. He's too depressed to realize it. Curtis went directly to Tracey for help. It was suppose to be a one-time deal that I set up to get the money to get those auto shops back on track. It went so smooth and easy. It was just so much money. Tracey and I just got all caught up and couldn't stop. One smooth deal led to another and another and another. We developed a distribution and customer service system based on the same model Doris Mercer uses at Mercer Health and Beauty Supplies. I must admit it was just great. Tracey was brilliant the way she was funneling that money through those auto shops. We were making money like you would not believe."

Portia and Ada could not believe what they were hearing. Ada was able to get out the one word they both were thinking first.

"Why?"

"Doris Mercer has enough money to have saved those auto shops ten times over," Portia added.

Roni gave a one word answer.

"Pride."

"You have got to be kidding," Ada almost shouted.

"Their mother started with nothing," Roni explained. "Curtis didn't want to admit he had failed at something else again. Tracey worshiped Curtis. She was not going to let him have to hang his head and admit to another failure to the great Doris Mercer. Tracey thought about going to Charles, but they all treat Charles like a little baby. Plus, Charles is terrified of Doris and obsessed with Lela. He would have pushed Curtis' head under the water and held him down so he could have Lela."

"Tracey would do something that dangerous?" Portia questioned.

"When Doris Mercer is your mother, nothing is dangerous. Doris always makes any wrong right for her children. She just can't undo what Lela did to Curtis. Even Doris has limitations."

"Okay, I'm still not clear on why Terrell Monroe was killed," Portia continued interrogating.

"Terrell knew I was selling drugs big time by then. He told folks that he was going to get rats like me out of the neighborhood. I didn't pay any attention to all that superhero talk. Terrell started snooping around. He found out that Curtis owned the houses. He knew I was not smart enough to be the mastermind of the elaborate operation we had going. The bad part is that he suspected the money was flowing through the auto shops, so he thought that it was all Curtis. He thought Curtis Mercer was the big rat he needed to exterminate. He never ever once suspected Tracey."

"How did Tommy realize Terrell was fishing," Ada asked.

"Terrell went to the wrong person with lots of questions and plenty of suspicions about Curtis," Roni revealed. "His pastor."

"Nadine!" Portia roared.

Roni smiled as she finished putting the frosting on the cake.

"My husband is not the only person who believes in sharing.

Sister Mary and Doris Mercer have a lot more in common than most people know. Terrell told Pastor Nadine about all his suspicions regarding Curtis Mercer. His fatal mistake."

"Do you think Tracey ordered Terrell's murder," Ada solemnly asked. "You think she called in that phony domestic violence complaint to the police?"

"No," Roni firmly replied. "Tommy could have gotten any of his flunkies to make that call. I know it may be hard for you to believe, but Tracey is not an unfeeling pit bull. I'm very sure she doesn't feel as strongly about me. She probably would not care at all if I didn't keep convincing her that my twins are really Curtis' children. I love her with all my heart."

"Curtis never told his own sister the truth about your twins?" Portia asked.

"When you lie and cheat like Curtis did, it's hard for even your own family to believe anything you say. I've worked hard convincing Tracey that the twins are her nephews. I needed her to believe it so that I can keep her loving me. I have never loved anyone as much as I love her. I'm probably the only one that Tracey lets her guard down with and shows her real soul. She is a very hurt soul that uses that tough exterior to keep from being hurt any further. Everybody just looks at her as a mean, difficult woman who is hard to deal with. She may be all of that, but she is definitely not a murderer. I'm sure Nadine told Tracey about Terrell's suspicions. When Tommy found out about Terrell snooping around and getting closer to the truth, his greedy butt panicked. He put the setup in motion and blood-thirsty Hunter did the rest."

"What happened that night?" Portia asked.

"Wallace Penny was passed out in the middle of the living room floor. Hector Alonzo and I were in the basement getting a big order ready. I had everything in that house. It was a super-market for drug dealers. All the marijuana, cocaine, crack, heroin, and assortment of pills that you can imagine. There was enough cash stacked in that basement to start a small bank. I had to have some guns. You can't run that type of business without guns. I used them for protection along with Tommy and Hunter. I didn't really need the guns. Tommy and Hunter were my primary protection. When Tommy and Terrell came waltzing into the house late that night, I was nervous as hell. Tommy told me not to worry. He said he had gotten Terrell straight on how much money he could make and that Terrell was cool. Tommy told me to get them some cold drinks. It was hot and raining like cats and dogs that night. I went to the kitchen and Hunter was slipping inside the back door. He went right down into the basement from the kitchen. He never said a word to me. Tommy and Terrell were still in the living room. Terrell never knew Hunter come into the house. I instantly knew something wrong was about to go down. Terrell came in that house looking like a deer staring in headlights. I can just kick myself. I should have known they were setting him up.

Hell, they were setting me up too. I remember Tommy took Terrell downstairs where Hector was still working. Hunter was already waiting. Gunshots started going off. When the smoke cleared, Wallace was still passed out on the living room floor. He never heard or saw one thing. Terrell was dead in the base-ment. Hector was shot three times. I took off running out of that house and straight down the street. Hunter chased me in all that rain behind houses, cars, stores and through back alleys. He chased me down like a bloodhound. I ran out of breath and fell down trying to get away. Hunter caught up to me and stood right over me. I could barely see him with all that rain coming down in my eyes. I felt that gun barrel pressed point blank to my forehead. If those backup police officers had been one second slower arriving, there is no doubt Hunter would have killed me. My own husband would have killed me dead."

"What was Tommy's explanation," Portia inquired.

"He said they had a report of domestic violence and when they entered the house they suspected drugs. They said a drug-crazed Wallace shot Terrell and Hector. The big surprise to everybody was that Hector didn't die. When he regained con-sciousness, Hector said anything they wanted him to say and signed any piece of paper they put in front of him. They put everything on poor Wallace and Hector walked free."

"You are sitting in a federal prison," Portia reminded Roni. "Murder is a crime against the state."

"Sister Mary got me this fancy white lady lawyer named, Paula Drake. She washed both Tracey and Curtis' name right out of everybody's mouth and mind. The name Mercer never even came up in the whole mess. Sister Mary had already made Tracey put all the houses in Wallace's name and then they quickly switched them into Lela's name. Curtis had no say in the matter. Tracey said it had to be done or Sister Mary would crush us. After Lela killed him, Tracey told me that Curtis had already put the auto shops in Lela's name. We think Sister Mary was behind that too. Maybe God had told her that the shit was about to hit the fan. I'm not going to say much bad about Sister Mary. With all those drugs in the house and a rookie police officer dead, I was looking at a minimum of life in prison. That lawyer that Sister Mary got for me, Paula Drake, she worked out some type of compromise that turned me over to the feds for some type of drug dealing conspiracy. I don't even understand it all right now. I got six years sitting around this fancy joint. I've already done three years, so three more will be easy."

"Sister Mary!" Ada blurted out in shock. "Sister Mary knows everything?"

"Did Doris know all of this too?" Portia asked.

"Doris just needed to know that Sister Mary made any problems go away and here I sit."

***

There was mostly silence as Portia and Ada drove through the countryside back to the airport. Then Ada had to satisfy her curiosity.

"Why didn't Wallace and Roni tell all of this when Terrell was killed?"

"They probably did tell everything they just told us at the very beginning. They didn't have a chance in hell back then. It didn't matter what they said," Portia explained. "Sister Mary is more powerful than even I suspected."

"Can you believe that?" Ada asked. "Sister Mary and Doris Mercer have children by the same man and that man was the honorable Pastor Nathan Dandridge. I always thought he was such a nice man."

"That fight in the church between Sister Mary and Doris makes a lot more sense now."

"Nadine probably went straight to Tracey after Terrell Monroe told her everything," Ada concluded.

"No, I think Nadine went straight to her mother, Sister Mary. Everybody thinks that they should worry about Doris Mercer and it's really Sister Mary that is the one to fear. She made sure that Wallace and Roni when down without Tracey or Curtis."

"You don't think Sister Mary is that ruthless? Ada wondered.

"I think that Sister Mary will do anything for her family and Doris Mercer and her children are her family. Lela killing Curtis was the best think that could have ever happened for both Wallace and Roni."

"Why?"

"Because I agreed to represent both of them before they would consent to speaking with us. It doesn't matter who was listening in on the conversations. Everything Wallace and Roni said to us is attorney/client privileged information. We are going to use that privileged information to get them both out of prison a little earlier than anticipated."

"We are going to get a convicted cop killer and a notorious drug dealer in the federal pen sprung? And exactly how will we do that and how will any of that help Lela?"

"I just need a few more pieces to this puzzle. I need to get it all pieced together before the FBI. That is why the local police is taking a step back on all of this one. They already know Tommy and Hunter are bad cops."

"You think it's just the FBI?" Ada asked.

"It's probably the FBI, DEA, and IRS. The brass downtown never bought that story about Wallace Penny. They are afraid of Sister Mary so they are going to let the FBI do their dirty work. They are trying to get to who they really think is behind the Terrell Monroe murder. They know there was more money than what was found in that house the night Terrell got shot. Where is the real money? That's what the feds are looking for. Right now they think it was Curtis, Lela, or both that was the silent partner in Roni's little operation. All that money in those bank accounts for the auto shops is dirty money made clean. The FBI thinks Lela was part of that drug operation. They're trying to get a piece of Lela, but we know better now."

"You heard what Roni said, Sister Mary has known everything from the very start. She will not let you go after Tracey. If anything, she is trying to protect Tracey more than Lela."

"We just need to get to Hector Alonzo. I think I can make it all make perfect sense. Then I'm going full blast after Tracey to save Lela."

"Do you realize that we are actually being paid by Sister Mary," Ada cried out. "You're going to get us killed too."

Ada was confused by the expression of joy that lit up on Portia's face. Portia's beautiful smile evaporated into a joyless expression when she gave Ada an immediate command for the future.

"Don't you ever call me Pookie again in front of our clients!"

twenty six

Clear Warning

Tommy could not stop his laughter. However, it was impossible to determine if her screams were due to pain or pleasure.

Tommy was totally relaxed as he laid back on the leather sofa supporting her dark brown, full-sized body.

It was effortless for him to hold her in his lap and use his giant hands to spread her legs as wide apart as possible. She leaned back against his muscular body and gripped the back of the sofa with both hands. Her warm skin pressed up against Tommy's smooth face. He would occasionally kiss or lick her cheek. Tommy would periodically inhale deeply the sweet smell of her body.

An outburst of laughter from Tommy would accompany every forceful ram Hunter made inside. Hunter was trying to go as deep as possible within her. He had put one leg up on the sofa and put his huge hands over her small hands to trap her between the two men. He leaned low so that the hard nipples of her large breasts mashed tight against his sweaty, bare chest. Hunter closed his eyes as his determination to reach total satisfaction grew faster and stronger.

Both men didn't care if her continuous screaming indicated their simultaneous presence within her body was intolerable or if she also was experiencing the same tremendous joyous sensation.

The two men barely remembered her name. She was just some young, fresh girl they picked up off the street that couldn't afford to do any jail time right now. Tommy had promised to make her illegal activities that he and Hunter had observed disappear from their law enforcement minds. She simply had to provide an evening of intense sexual gratification for the two men.

Hunter pulled himself from the threesome. He stood up straight, exhausted and sweating. He was naked and felt very relieved as he walked into the kitchen. He took a can of beer out of the refrigerator and sat down at the kitchen table. The cold beverage cooled down his overheated body as it rushed down his throat.

From the kitchen, Hunter saw Tommy playfully chase this big brown beauty into the bedroom. He knew Tommy would continue exploring every part of her body with every part of his body.

Hunter continued slowly drinking his cold beer. He began to rehash in his mind how he mishandled approaching Lela. He couldn't understand how he could end a man's life with his bare hands, but he could barely speak in Lela's presence. He knew that Curtis was making her life miserable. He should have been blunt in telling her that he could have made Curtis as well as her pain disappear.

He was more than willing to do anything to make her notice him. He should have followed his instincts and crushed Curtis like a bug. He had tried to warn Tommy that Curtis was going to do something stupid to mess with their money, and he was right. He hated that spoiled mama's boy.

Curtis never ever realized the best thing he ever did in his whole life was create that beautiful family. Hunter envied every moment Curtis had spent with Lela. A woman like Lela could have made a big difference in the direction of his life. His only violent passion would have been to keep her happy. If only Lela had just asked him once, he would have taken that knife and peeled Curtis down to the bone.

Playful screams and giggles came from the bedroom.

Hunter thought about joining the fun. Lela once again interrupted his thoughts. He knew she had ignored him because he was a white man. Being Tommy's best friend was not enough to convince her that skin color was not a factor. He had been raised in a racially mixed environment. He had never been taught to look at other races as the enemy. His biggest battles had been trying to escape poverty and a dysfunctional family. He should have told her that many times black households were the only places of sanctuary for him from his abusive family. When he looked at her, he didn't see a black woman. She was a beautiful queen in his eyes. He was willing and ready to treat her like royalty.

When she sliced Curtis' throat, any opportunity Hunter had to finally approach Lela was sliced away too. He had to forget about Lela and concentrate now on survival. What Lela had done had actually put his career, his finances, and his freedom in jeopardy. Tommy and Tracey had better figure out soon how to get his money out of Ashley Powell's control. There were millions in those accounts for Curtis' auto shops that he had risked everything to acquire. Once he had at least some of that money back, he was not taking any more chances. He was going to liquidate everything and take his twin sons and leave town.

That low-life bitch, Roni, had let the rumor spread far and wide that Curtis was the twins' father. Even his own sons believed Curtis Mercer was their father. The skin color of his sons was very light. However, Hunter knew African Americans whose parents were both black that were far lighter in skin tone than his sons. It didn't really matter how they looked. They were his biological sons. How dare she encourage people to think that scum, Curtis, was responsible for his children. He should have shot Roni the night he killed Terrell Monroe. He chased her all through that rain for nothing. When she fell down, he stood over her and had the barrel of his gun pointed right at her big head. He heard his fellow cops shouting not to shoot her. He should have done it anyway. He could have come up with some bullshit lie to cover himself.

Damn that filthy whore, Roni, for letting everyone believe his flesh and blood belonged to Curtis Mercer. Roni knew Curtis had never touched her rusty butt. She would do or say anything to keep Tracey in love with her. Roni knew Tracey would not care one minute more about her or her children if she discovered Curtis was not the twins' real father.

His sons were handsome and smart. They were the best thing he had ever done in his life. Hunter realized he just needed to clean up some loose ends and get back at least some of his money. Then he would take his sons and get on the road to California. He would make a fresh start.

He would find a woman that could make him forget about Lela. He would sit back and relax with his new love and watch his sons grow into amazing men.

Tommy and his street meat were both moaning and groaning loud enough to wake the dead. Their sounds of pleasure shook Hunter from his deep thoughts. He finished off his beer and stood up. He decided to go into the bedroom for a little more adult entertainment. Then he and Tommy would have to handle business.

Hector Alonzo needed to be silenced before Delia Tavares or Portia Lee made him start singing the wrong song. Hector always warned that he had some type of evidence that he would use if they tried to hurt him. Tommy was sure that it was all just a bluff. Now that Lela had sliced open a can full of worms, one worm named Hector finally had to be dealt with tonight. Hector never came out of his worm hole before midnight. Therefore, there was still time for play.

Hunter walked nude from the kitchen into the bedroom so that he could turn the twosome back into a threesome once again.

***

"This is not the girl you promised me."

"Sweet is just as pretty and bigger boobs."

"Yeah," Butter laughed. "A lot more booty too. You're absolutely right. These bozos won't care as long as she was actually born a woman. Hell, they'll be so drunk they won't care if she is a man-made woman."

Butter had to be well over three hundred pounds. His skin tone was darker than night and his jet black hair had been straighten and pulled back into a long ponytail. He always dressed like he was permanently stuck in the nineteen sixties.

He was known as a gentle giant in the neighborhood.

Butter had owned Zanzibar for many years. It was a little neighborhood drinking hole. It actually looked like a hole in the wall. Zanzibar was located at the end of a dead-end street on the west side of town. Butter also owned two illegal gambling houses in the neighborhood. Although he handled business above and below the table, he was fair and never attracted any attention or trouble from the street law or the real law.

Hector felt this little gig at Zanzibar would be safe and easy money. He needed just a little bit more cash in his pocket to get out of town. With Curtis Mercer dead, too many questions were being asked about the past. He knew it was only a matter of time before Tommy and Hunter came calling again.

Rita could have really made them more money tonight. She was a younger piece of honey. However, she thought there was a possibility that she might be pregnant. Rita had stood her ground with Hector. She refused to do any more stripping or pornographic videos if she was going to be a mother. She especially did not want to do a private show. She didn't feel good and was not interested in fighting off a bunch of drunk, horny men tonight.

Hector was actually excited also at the thought of being a father. After drug dealing didn't work out very well, Hector served as a manager for women who did numerous types of sexual jobs to earn a living. He had been immune to any feelings toward any of his girls until Rita Foxx came along.

She was a lot younger, but seemed to really love him. If they really were going to have a baby, Hector had to get Rita out of the sex for sale business and out of this town. However, he insisted to Rita that they had to score some big cash just one more time if they were going to start life over clean. She still had refused to work the bachelor party tonight.

Sweet had agreed to be Rita's replacement. Sweet had some serious drug addiction issues and was always in need of some fast cash. She was extremely happy for the opportunity. Sweet and Hector had done several sex videos together in the past. She knew working with Hector and Butter would be safe.

Hector told Sweet to only go down to the G-string. No total nudity and no extra services. Butter had a shotgun behind the bar to guarantee none of the party participants would be allowed to try to force her to do more than just dance.

"Only the joker getting married and six of his silly friends," Butter informed Hector. "I closed the bar tonight for the bachelor party. I'll probably make more money off just these few chumps. These guys got real jobs. They already paid for the entertainment up front. This little bitch better shake that ass. The more they drink, the more dollar bills they'll stick up her butt and drop for drinks. The three of us split everything and I mean everything."

"Don't worry," Hector said. "Sweet is an old pro. A nice payday for easy work."

***

Tommy parked the car he borrowed from one of his street snitches about five blocks back from Zanzibar. He and Hunter got out and walked up the middle of the street.

They were both dressed in plain, dark street clothes. Large, untrimmed trees nearly covered the street lights. The two men looked more like moving shadows as they approached the small, raggedy building.

When the two off-duty police officers entered Zanzibar, the party was in full swing. The music was blaring loud enough to break your eardrums. The future groom had on a fake crown and his eyes were bloodshot red.

Everyone had drinks in their hands. The party goers were sweating, laughing, and spitting when they tried to talk.

Sweet was already down to her red G-string as she shook everything she naturally possessed on a small platform in the middle of the bar. Her breast where like large melons flopping up and down. Her big brown buttocks shook like jelly as she pranced around the platform teasing these lusting men. Dollars bills nearly covered her midriff and was filling up a drink jar on the bar counter.

Butter had a face filled with joy until Tommy and Hunter walked through the front door. He nervously greeted the two off-duty officers as they approached the bar counter.

"Hey Tommy. Hey Hunter."

"Let me have a beer," Tommy requested. "One for Hunter too."

"No thank you," Hunter politely refused.

Butter quickly obliged Tommy's request. The drunken party friends never even noticed the arrival of the two off-duty police officers. They were too captivated by Sweet's giggling body parts. Butter was growing concerned by the minute. He knew Tommy and Hunter well. He had many encounters with them in the past that were both good and bad. He knew what they were capable of doing.

Tommy took a long gulp of his cold beer and then made an additional request.

"Where is Hector?"

"We're just having a little fun tonight. I don't want no trouble Tommy," Butter pleaded.

Hunter leaned over the bar closer to emphasize the request his friend had just made.

"Where is Hector?"

"He's in the backroom."

Tommy and Hunter walked slowly passed the bachelor party participants to the back poolroom. Hector was sitting on the pool table with his mobile cell phone pressed tightly to his ear reassuring Rita.

"Sweet is almost done. She has got these guys totally worked up into a frenzy. It should be a good pay day. These guys are pretty tame fellows. They're family men. They're just perpetrating to be thugs. They'll all need to get back to their good wives pretty damn soon."

Hector looked up to see Tommy and Hunter come through the doorway. His expression of satisfaction quickly turned to crippling fear.

"Tommy and Hunter just walked in. Don't worry. Just don't worry. Remember, we have an ace in our hands. Make sure you keep it safe for protection."

Hector looked at the smirk on Tommy's face and the anger in Hunter's eyes. He had a gut feeling that this meeting was not going to be a routine harassment opportunity for these police officers. Hector whispered to Rita before quickly closing his mobile cell phone and putting it in his pocket.

"Rita, I will always love you and the baby forever."

"Hey Hector," Tommy greeted his former business associate. "It's been a while."

Hector jumped off the pool table and tried to leave the room. Hunter put up his arm to block his passage.

"Listen, I have always done everything you guys wanted. I have never been no snitch. I didn't tell nothing then and I'm not telling anything now. What's in the past is still in the past. Wallace took the rap for us all and we all should be grateful."

"See Hector, you're talking too loud and too much already," Tommy advised. "I can't afford for you and your little stripper girlfriend to be bringing up my name in any conversations with the wrong people."

"I don't know what you're talking about. And Sweet is not my girlfriend," Hector informed. "We're just here together trying to make a little money. Then I'll be out of this town for good."

"I never understand why stupid little punks like you have such a hard time leaving," Tommy wondered out loud. "You should have left this rinky dink town three years ago. Then you wouldn't have to put me and Hunter in this awful position. We actually now might be forced to put your little girlfriend in several bad positions."

Tommy and Hunter chuckled at the thought.

"You nasty bastards keep on dreaming. Me and Sweet are leaving right now," Hector announced. "And you better stop sweating me. Remember, I have a little insurance policy from that night tucked away. Don't come in here doing the bad cop, bad cop comedy routine. If you hurt me, you hurt yourself."

Hector brushed hard against Hunter's shoulder as he stormed passed the two police officers. He grabbed Sweet by the hand and tugged at her to get off the platform.

"Come on down Sweet. The show is over."

"Not yet," the future groom hollered. "She needs to take off that little string thing. We need butt naked. We'll pay extra for butt naked."

The other men yelled in agreement. Hector pulled Sweet off the platform and toward the bar.

"We need our cut so we can go."

Butter was more than ready for the party to be over also. He took the money jar off the counter. The party participants wanted just one more drink for the road. Butter thought that was a fair compromise for ending early. He put the money jar back down on the counter and began making drinks.

Hector was too nervous and scared to wait any longer.

"I trust you man. I'll come back for our cut later. Get your stuff Sweet."

Hector started rapidly walking toward the front door.

He was suddenly stopped by a loud popping sound. He looked down to see blood spreading rapidly across the front of his shirt.

Sweet screamed and the drunken, bachelor party members froze in place. Hector fell to his knees and then face down on the floor in front of the bar entrance. His blood began rapidly spreading across the floor. Hunter walked over to Hector and pointed the gun down at his head.

"You won't wake up this time," Hunter announced before firing several more gunshots into Hector's already lifeless body.

Butter reached for his shotgun under the bar counter.

Tommy shot him several times before he could raise it above the counter. Butter fell back hard against glass shelves. Bottles of liquor came crashing down with the massive bartender's body.

The future groom begged for his life. He promised silence in exchange for a future with his waiting bride. Hunter did not accept the plea bargain. Hunter and Tommy fired their weapons until they were the only two men left standing in Zanzibar.

Sweet took off running to the back of the building. Hunter slowly followed. He was correct in believing this fire trap had a locked and bolted back door. Sweet desperately tried to open the back door. She cried helplessly as her fate approached.

Tommy and Hunter planted cash, guns, and drugs to stage a drug deal gone bad execution scene. Tommy was not satisfied. He decided to test just how flammable was good liquor when he lit a match.

As Tommy and Hunter walked back to the car, the flames within Zanzibar began to burst through the windows.

The street was completely illuminated. No one dared to come out of their nearby houses until the unidentifiable automobile and the unidentifiable males had driven away.

twenty seven

Blood Relatives
Lela, Kelly, Cheryl

"You hated him."

Lela was surprised to see Kelly in her bedroom. She was standing looking out the window. The sunlight hit her in a way that made her look like a mirror reflection.

Since they had been living with Sister Mary, Kelly had done everything in her power to avoid any direct verbal or non-verbal contact with Lela. Lela's other three children were the exact opposite. Junior, Callen, and Jade went about their daily lives like nothing had ever happened. They never brought up the incident or their father's name. They tried to spend every moment they could beg, borrow, or steal with their mother.

Kelly stayed mainly in her room and tried not to speak to anyone. Her attitude was bitter and her voice was always filled with anger. She always seemed to be trapped in deep thoughts. Lela was afraid she had caused mental and emotional damage that could never be repaired.

"I love your father more now than ever," Lela explained. "When you lose your temper, you lose control of all your emotions. For a split second, I forgot how much I loved him. I forgot how much I love you. I did a horrible thing that took away my husband and your father. I hurt us all. I wish to God that I could take it back."

"We need to leave here," Kelly commanded. "They will kill you for what you did to Daddy."

"Any punishment I receive will not be enough."

Kelly whirled around from the window to directly address her mother.

"That is a bunch of bullshit. We need to go right now!"

Lela was so shocked she could not respond.

"We can steal one of those fancy cars Sister Mary has and go to Mexico or Canada," Kelly continued. "I can get a job and we can change our names. We have to go! We have to go right now!"

Lela was amazed at how much thought and planning her daughter had put into this escape plan.

"We're not going to steal any cars," Lela lectured. "We aren't thieves."

"You can kill Daddy, but you can't steal a car?"

"You watch your mouth young lady," Lela scolded. "I don't care if I killed a hundred people, I'm still your mother."

"What are you going to do?" Kelly asked. "Kill me too?"

Kelly started to cry hysterically. Lela rushed to her. Kelly quickly backed away from her impending embrace.

"I wouldn't dare hurt you," Lela reassured her daughter. "You're my baby."

"I'll never forgive you," Kelly shouted. "I'll never forgive you for what you did to Daddy."

"I don't want you to forgive me," Lela stated. "I just need you to never stop loving me."

Kelly's tears stopped racing down her face. Her tough exterior and anger returned. She ran passed Lela and Cheryl, who was now standing in the doorway. Lela started to run after Kelly. Cheryl put up her hands in a stop motion.

"You have to give her a whole lot of time and plenty of space," Cheryl insisted.

"I didn't handle that very well at all," Lela said disappointed in herself. "I should have shot myself like I had planned. It would have been better than this slow death."

Cheryl stood for a moment wondering what was she going to say next to her only child. What are the proper words for consoling your daughter after she has committed murder?

Cheryl had been a single mother for many years. This was the first time she had ever longed for a husband. She needed a partner to consult. She needed someone to step in with the right voice and words to soothe both her daughter and her grandchildren.

Cheryl looked at Lela like she was seeing her for the very first time. People had always congratulated her on producing such a beautiful baby. The constant comments of admiration for being the mother of such a gorgeous child had just went in one ear and straight out of the other ear. Today was the first day she was overwhelmed by the actual physical beauty of her daughter. She finally realized why Curtis had worked so hard to marry Lela and keep her in his home. Lela was her prize child and Curtis' prize wife.

Guilt for not acknowledging the heartache that Lela struggled for years to make visible to everyone suddenly consumed Cheryl. Curtis had kept Cheryl sedated with gifts of jewelry and cars. He had sent her on trips around the world and handled all sorts of financial bills when she came up short.

Cheryl realized she had accepted payment in full for her child. She was ashamed of being more influenced by the continuous charm and money supplied by Curtis rather than the increasing pain of her daughter.

"Why didn't you just leave him?" Cheryl harshly questioned.

"Why didn't you tell me to leave him?" Lela harshly retaliated. "Curtis is a good man. You'll never find someone that can give you what he can. You must be crazy to think of leaving him. Sometimes I thought you were Curtis' mother instead of mine."

"So you killed him to punish me?" Cheryl shouted.

"I killed him because he made me sick," Lela yelled back. "I was sick of him. He had no respect for me or my children. He thought his money and his mother gave him the right to treat me any damn way he pleased. I loved and worshiped him with every ounce of my soul and he didn't even care."

"He treated you the way you let him," Cheryl informed. "You let a man walk all over your stupid ass for years. Then one evening you just expected him to walk through the door and be different? You wanted him to just suddenly show you some respect?"

"You're right," Lela agreed. "You're absolutely right. I was weak and stupid to marry him and too weak and too stupid to leave him."

"So killing him was your solution?" Cheryl asked.

"You think I meant to kill him?" Lela questioned her mother.

"No," Cheryl admitted. "I know you didn't mean to kill him. You think I haven't been there before? Do you see your father standing around here. I didn't kill him, but there were days when I thought I would. The fights I had with your father. It probably was just God or good luck that kept me from killing him or him from killing me. I know exactly what that pain feels like. You can love them so much and they can hurt you so bad, but damn Lela!"

Lela sank down on to the bed almost defeated. Cheryl sank down on to the bed next to her daughter.

"I knew that Curtis was a son-of-a-bitch from day one," Lela revealed. "No one believes me. I loved his smile. I loved when he played with the kids. Sometimes, he was really wonderful. Sometimes, he was a cruel, mean monster. I'm not even sure how to live without him. I let him do everything for me. He controlled my entire life. I may not have to worry about it. Ashley said the prosecutors still haven't taken the death penalty off the table."

Cheryl pulled Lela toward her and locked her into a mother's embrace.

"I know your heart is righteous and you didn't mean to kill Curtis. You made a terrible human mistake. We are all imperfect and make errors that we wish we could get back. There is no way they can kill you. God still lives in your soul and God can't be destroyed. You have family and friends that aren't willing to lose you. Your children cannot afford to lose you. Our faith will be the light to pull us all through this terrible fog. Just concentrate on the love for your children. I will concentrate on my love for you. It will give us the strength to fight this together."

"I can't even cry anymore," Lela said. "I'm all cried out."

"Me to baby," Cheryl said with a smile. "I'm dry as a bone."

The mother and daughter fell back on the bed and shared a rare moment of laughter. Cheryl did something she had not done in a very long time. She smothered her beautiful daughter with kisses.

***

twenty eight

Doris And Tracey

"What does she know?"

"She is just mean and crazy."

"No, she knows something that I don't. Mary is my sister. We aren't blood sisters, but living life together has made us real sisters. I know when she is keeping something from me. She doesn't care that much about Lela and she loved Curtis like he was her own son. Why is she doing this?"

"I'm the last person on earth to try and explain Mary Dandridge."

Tracey's lies echoed around the room and bounced off the walls. The lies landed like arrows straight through Doris' heart. She didn't know what was the truth. She could see it resting safely in Tracey's eyes.

Doris looked at her daughter and saw herself, yet someone different. Doris had prided herself on being a tough, no non-sense businesswoman. Her daughter had taken that attitude to a higher level. Doris suddenly realized she had made the mistake of raising her sons to be boys and raising her only daughter to be a man.

"I need to take the twins to the movies tomorrow after-noon," Tracey told her mother. "Do you want me to bring them by after the movie?"

"Yes, I need to see them," Doris replied. "Tracey, are those twins really my grandchildren? Is Curtis really their father?"

"I'm their father," Tracey said. "It doesn't even matter anymore who their real father is. They belong to me now and forever."

"Do you think Curtis had feelings for Roni?" Doris asked.

Tracey was annoyed by all her mother's questions.

"Listen Mama, Curtis probably fucked every woman in town except for you and me. Curtis didn't give a shit about Roni Paige or any other woman. No matter what he was doing out there in the streets, he actually loved that crazy-ass Lela."

"What about you?" Doris wanted to know. "Do you really love Tommy?"

Tracey just laughed. Her mother was always trying to make her commit. It was obvious that Doris believed Tracey would turn into a softer female if she had a husband and children.

Instead of answering the question, Tracey asked about her other brother.

"What about Charles?" Is he still losing his mind?"

Doris' thoughts quickly shifted to what she thought was a bigger problem than Tracey.

"I really am worried about Charles. I truly am scared he is slipping deeper into some type of depression. Do you think he could still truly be in love with Lela after everything that has happened?"

"It doesn't matter," Tracey reminded Doris. "Lela is going to jail. Once she is in prison, Charles will have no choice but to forget about her. I have never ever thought it was real love anyway. It's just some sick obsession. He has always had this one-sided rivalry with Curtis. He just wanted anything that Curtis had. He will have to stop with this childish obsession and concentrate on his own wife and child once Lela is finally gone."

"Euryale Washington called me today," Doris informed. "She is one of the state campaign coordinators for the Democratic Party. She adamantly believes she can groom Charles into being a candidate for city mayor. She wanted to set up a meeting. I'm sure that will come with a big price tag."

"Good for Charles," Tracey gave her approval. "He needs to get fixated on something else besides Lela. I say it will be worth every dime we can give to get Charles back on track."

"I'm just not convinced my baby boy is strong enough for doing something that will put him on such a public platform. Our entire family would be under total scrutiny. I'm not sure Charles can handle that type of mental stress."

"Why can't you let him try to do something else besides be your baby boy," Tracey snapped.

Doris heard the calm in Tracey's voice suddenly turn back to anger.

"Have I been too easy on the boys and too hard on you?

"Oh please."

"No, I'm serious," Doris reiterated. "I have let my boys turn into mush and I've turned you into stone."

"Well, it's nice to know how you feel."

"It's the truth. I've been a horrible mother."

"What's done is done, Mother. Curtis is dead. Lela will be out of our lives. Charles will come to his senses soon. Let us just do what you and Sister Mary always do. Let's just forget past sins and move on from here. We'll all be one big happy family again, Mother."

Doris knew she was Mama or Mommy when things were good with her daughter. However, she was Mother when that reoccurring bitterness rose up in Tracey's voice and attitude.

"Tracey, I admit that I have not been a good mother to you. I probably should have never been anyone's mother."

"I need to leave," Tracey interrupted.

"No, I need you to hear this," Doris pleaded. "I especially need to say this out loud to you."

"I'm leaving," Tracey said. "I need to go see about the twins."

Tracey began walking out of the room.

"I apologize for being so hard on you," Doris blurted out. "I apologize for not giving you as much attention as I gave to Curtis and Charles. I really do love you. I love you Tracey."

Tracey stopped walking and whirled around with a face filled with fury.

"Stop it," Tracey shouted. "Just stop it. You don't love me. You have never loved me. You just need me! Roni just needs me. Tommy just needs me. Charles just needs me. Curtis needed me more than any of you. You all just need me. None of you have ever loved me, especially you."

Doris was shocked by this outburst from her daughter.

She could see clearly, for the first time, the pain she had blindly inflicted on her daughter over the years. Hurt, jealousy, and rage was spewing out with all of Tracey's searing words.

Tracey would not allow her anger to bring forth tears. Just as she had done since birth, she refused to show her mother any form of weakness. Doris could see that this re-fortified wall of armor was protecting more than resentment toward a strict and neglectful mother.

"Tell me what Mary knows," Doris strongly demanded.

"She doesn't know a goddamn thing!" Tracey screamed back.

"I do need you. I do love you very much too. Now that Curtis is gone, we do have to be a stronger and better family. You have to trust that all of this has made me different now. I am getting old. I need to trust you to be my right hand. I need you to be my confidant and advisor. We need to love and trust each other."

Doris once again strongly demanded the truth.

"Tracey, tell me what Mary knows."

"Good-bye, Mother."

Doris felt a sinking, sick feeling in her stomach as she watched her defiant daughter whirl back around and march out of the house.

***

twenty nine

Mary And Nadine

"Did you love Daddy?"

"He was a nice man."

"Did you love him?"

"No, but he didn't love me. He only married me because he couldn't have Doris. Marrying me was the only way he could stay near her."

"How can you care about her so much when you know that Daddy wanted her so bad?"

Sister Mary took a long deep breath. She searched her mind to try to come up with some way to explain to Nadine her relationship with Doris Mercer.

"When I was in the seventh grade, I had a detention in my cooking class. I can't even remember what the hell I did to get a detention in cooking class. I was always burning up something. All we ever cooked was cookies. Anyway, it was just me and Big Mean Jean. We called her Big Mean Jean because she was about as big as a country barn and about as mean as a junkyard dog. We were suppose to sit there and write recipes. Can you believe that? That bitch wanted us to write some damn recipes on file cards. Who gets detention in cooking class? It was cooking class for God's sake. All we ever made was peanut butter cookies."

"Mama, stay focused," Nadine interjected.

"Oh yeah, Doris. You want to know about me and Doris," Sister Mary remembered. "Well, the cooking teacher left the room. Me and Big Mean Jean got up in the window and watched all the other kids going home for the day. Donny What's His Name was standing with his buddies looking cute and cool."

"You don't remember his last name?" Nadine said smiling.

"I have trouble remembering your first name and I gave birth to you." Sister Mary laughed even harder.

"Okay Mama. Enough with the jokes. Go on with the story before you forget the ending."

Sister Mary tried to regain her composure.

"All of a sudden, Doris came running back to Donny. She threw her arms around Donny and kissed him right on the lips. He was in total shock and his buddies were howling. Now keep in mind, Big Mean Jean loved her some Donny What's His Name. It was crazy. Donny looked more like a girl than Jean. She didn't care. She loved that little gender confused rascal. When she saw Doris kiss him, Big Mean Jean went straight up in total flames."

"Why are you telling me this silly story?" Nadine questioned.

"Just wait, I'm getting to the point," Sister Mary assured. "I knew of Doris at that time. We weren't friends. That night I could not stop thinking about what was going to happen the next day. Doris was always pretty and flamboyant. I knew Big Mean Jean was going to pound her into the next century. Right after school, Big Mean Jean stepped right to Doris. Doris was always good at talking lots of bullshit. She was too pretty to be a fighter. All the kids gathered around and waited for the slaughter. I don't know what came over me. When Big Mean

Jean threw that first punch, I grabbed her fist with my right hand and the fight was on."

"You beat Big Mean Jean!" Nadine said with admiration.

"Hell no! Big Mean Jean beat the living snot out of me while Doris stood there watching. Doris walked me home and cleaned me up. She even put a little lipstick on me so you couldn't notice my busted lip. She was always into makeup and hair."

Sister Mary and Nadine could not stop laughing until tears came rolling down their cheeks.

"Mama, you took a beating for Doris?"

"I've been taking a beating for Doris for years. It is just habit now."

Nadine needed to ask a serious question.

"Are we getting in the right fight this time?"

"I don't know Nadine," Sister Mary admitted. "I've put all my chips on this Portia Lee. I know she is determined to win. Her track record is a good one."

"Church members are getting concerned. They can't see how the church is going to benefit from any involvement."

"Nathan Senior wanted his son to take his place in the pulpit," Sister Mary told her daughter. "I told him that you were the oldest and should follow in his footsteps. He told me absolutely not. You were a woman and you had no ability to lead his church."

"Daddy gave me his blessing and was overjoyed when he turned over the leadership to me," Nadine reminded her mother. "Everyone in the church gave me a warm welcome when I took charge."

"I have had to threaten, fight, or pay for whatever I wanted in life," Sister Mary said. "I did all three to get you in that pulpit."

"Why?" Nadine asked in amazement.

"I do love my son," Sister Mary explained. "However, Nathan Junior is a nice man just like your father. When you're a leader of a flock as large as we have now, you have to know how to kill wolves. You know how to kill wolves like me. You have to be ready and willing to fight the Big Mean Jeans of the world."

Nadine had to think for a moment.

"I think that was a compliment, but I'm not quite sure."

"Believe me," Sister Mary said with pride. "You're just like me. That is truly a compliment."

***

thirty

Ada And Portia

"Your father is a lot like Curtis Mercer."

Portia sat at her desk going over notes and reports concerning the case. She was trying her best to ignore her aunt. However, Ada continued her quest to distract and loosen up her intense niece.

"Your father is not as handsome as Curtis. It doesn't matter. Robert can get a woman in about ten seconds flat. Robert has had a bunch of women. He only was in love with your mother. That's why he never divorced her."

Ada was finally successful. Portia slammed down her file folder on the desk.

"My mother is married to my step-father," Portia stated.

"But she never divorced your daddy," Ada informed.

"That is just a lie. My mother would never marry someone else if she was still married to Daddy. I mean Robert."

"Hell, Robert has been married to three other women since your mother. Your mother is the only wife the government recognizes. He never divorced your mother."

"Why would my mother not divorce Robert?" Portia asked.

"We were poor people," Ada said. "Robert never had no money to divorce nobody. I can't speak for your mother. I don't know why she never divorced Robert. She just left town with you and acted like we were a bad dream."

Portia shook her head in disbelief and returned to reviewing her case files.

"Ada, I don't believe anything you say"

"Ask your mother. What was her name?"

"I'm not asking my mother nothing."

"You're a lawyer. Look it up."

"I'm a little busy right now."

"Oh yeah, poor little Lela. I bet nobody else will disrespect that girl ever again."

"Ada, please."

Ada got up from her seat trying to stop her laughter.

She looked out of Portia's huge office window at Lake Erie.

"Why haven't you gotten married and had some kids?" Ada asked. "You were a skinny, black, ugly child. I can't believe you turned into such a damn pretty woman. Who you saving all that good stuff up for?"

"There are fools out there that actually hire you to be their lawyer?" Portia asked in amazement.

"Are you gay?"

"I was engaged for several years to a man."

"What!" Ada yelled. "When was this? Who was the man? What happen?"

Ada sat back down in her seat again and anxiously waited for the details.

"I intend to be a partner in this law firm one day very soon. My career and his requirements for a wife and mother just didn't mix well. We decided it was best to go our separate ways."

"Did you love him?"

Portia had to summon some courage to say what she really did not want to say out loud.

"No, I didn't love him. He was perfect. Tall, dark, and handsome. He had an job as an executive with a major corporation. He was more than financially stable. He is what every woman wants. Every woman except me."

"Now you know how Curtis Mercer felt. He made love to a lot of women. Beautiful and ugly women, rich and poor women, young and old women. It was all for show. He didn't love any of them. He was raised to have anything he wanted so he took everything that was offered. I don't think he realized how much he was hurting Lela until that knife went gliding across his throat. He thought his life was normal. He thought she was happy. He was just a good, lovable, spoiled brat. Curtis' idea of what constitutes manhood and Lela's requirements for a husband and a father just didn't mix well."

"Why did you stop coming to see me?" Portia questioned.

"Your mother hooked up with that high society cat," Ada explained. "You started calling him father. Your mother had two other kids. It got more and more uncomfortable. It seemed like a better idea to just let you move on to a much better family and life."

"Are you speaking for my father or for yourself?"

"I'm speaking for the both of us."

Portia stood up and walked to the window. She looked out at the rough, choppy waters of Lake Erie.

"I hate that lake," Portia told her aunt. "Every year it swallows somebody whole. It looks very beautiful and enticing. It's very dangerous and should not be underestimated.

"Yeah," Ada agreed. "Curtis shouldn't have underestimated Lela."

Portia turned to her aunt and smiled.

"No one should ever underestimate me."

thirty one

Damage Control

The news about Zanzibar spread like the flames that burned it to the ground. The various versions of why and how Butter, Hector, Sweet, and the bachelor party met their violent end had even penetrated prison walls.

Wallace Penny was overly confident that he was in a place totally safe from the claws of Tommy and Hunter. He had no real sympathy for his former friend, Hector. Wallace felt the horrible way Hector died was actually justified.

However, nothing is secret that happens on the streets and nothing is secret that happens in prison. There was a low murmur that was slowly turning into a roar that Wallace Penny was in possession of information that could greatly benefit the Lela Mercer defense team.

The state would not dare let anything bad happen to a lifetime resident in their correctional system. This was a foolish belief shared by both the defense as well as the prosecution.

Even prisoners who had committed the most heinous criminal acts were paralyzed into silence. They all sat motionless behind steel restraining bars listening to what could easily be their same fate. Darkness made the sounds of torture and murder echo endlessly throughout the prison for all to hear.

When the light returned, it was officially ruled that Wallace Penny had self-inflicted wounds that resulted in his untimely death. Everyone knew there were several prison guards as well as prison inmates that owed favors to Tommy Dancy.

Wallace Penny had not been worth saving from a false guilty verdict. He surely was not worth saving from an unpleasant and sudden trip to hell.

***

"What have you done!" Tracy screamed.

Tommy tried to pull together his bathrobe to conceal his naked body. He was also trying to rub the sleep from his bloodshot eyes. His continuous yawning indicated he had not completed his requirement for a good night's rest.

"I don't know what you're talking about. "Oh my God? Do you realize how many people died in that fire at Zanzibar? Everybody in this town knows that Butter didn't deal in drugs. That old school clown did gambling, women, and booze. He never in his life did any kind of drug deal. Everybody knows that was a blatant setup. You are going to bring the wrath of God down on our heads."

Hunter came out of the kitchen to hear this conversation better. Tracey did what she always did when Hunter was around. She totally ignored his presence.

Tommy plopped down on the sofa and continued fighting his need to go back to sleep. Tracey was being a morning nuisance that he hoped would soon go away. He tried to speed up her exit.

"You're being a silly woman. Go home."

Rage made Tracey lunge at Tommy with full force. He put up his arms to shield himself from her continuous blows.

Hunter grabbed Tracey and flung her to the floor. He had been waiting for years for an opportunity to express how he truly felt about her.

Tracey tried to break the hold that Hunter had on her air passageway. The force from Hunter pounding her head into the floor was causing her to feel faint. Tracey was fighting with all her might not to lose consciousness and regain her breath.

The sound of Tommy commanding Hunter to stop fell on deaf eyes. Hunter was determined to end his loathing of this woman. Her unnatural love for Curtis had led them all into this legal turmoil. Her hatred toward Lela had contributed to Lela's unhappiness and that fatal night. Her sick relationship with Roni had robbed him of his children. Her domineering attitude had turned Charles into an emotional cripple. Her resentment toward Doris had resulted in an unlimited number of lies and secrets that were still ruining lives.

As far as Hunter was concerned, Tracey was the source of everyone's misery. He felt it was his duty to end the spread of her venom. He pounded her head harder into the floor and tighten the grip he had around her throat.

The cold barrel of a gun brought Hunter back into reality. Tommy stood using one hand to keep his bathrobe together and using his other hand to point a gun in Hunter's eye.

"Hunter, let her go now!"

Hunter looked up at Tommy and knew his desire would not be fulfilled. He released Tracey and slowly got back up on his feet. Tracey choked and gasped for air to come back into her body. She rolled to her knees and got up on the sofa. Hunter walked back into the kitchen to get a cold beer.

"Sorry about that Tracey. Hunter is like my big protective brother. He doesn't like people beating up on me, especially girls."

Tommy laughed at his own sarcastic remarks and fell back into a chair. His bathrobe came loose revealing his massive chest. He sat the gun down on an end table next to his chair.

Tracey continued trying to regain her normal breathing pattern. She searched for Hunter so that she would not experience another surprise attack. Hunter cut his eyes at her smiling as he drank his cold beer standing in the kitchen.

"Dead men can't talk Tracey," Tommy said. "Don't worry sweetheart. Hunter and I will clean all the mess up. When Lela goes to prison, everything will go back to normal. We only have one more mouth that needs to be sealed."

"You and that rabid dog have done enough."

"I need to correct myself," Tommy revised. "Dead men and women can't talk."

"You better not touch Lela," Tracey warned. "If one hair on her head is out of place, it will come right back on me."

Both Tommy and Hunter started laughing. Tommy picked up the gun and playfully pointed it at Tracey.

"Lela is not the woman I'm talking about."

thirty two

Witness Protection

"They killed Wallace because he talked to you. They killed Butter for no reason. Poor Sweet never hurt anybody and look what happened to her. My beautiful Hector is gone. My baby's daddy is dead. Now you want me to talk to you. I'll be dead next. Get out and leave me alone."

"Listen, the FBI has already moved Roni Paige into protective custody. If my sources led me to you this fast, then who you really need to be very worried about is right behind me. You had better talk to me fast so that I can figure out how to protect you."

"Talk to you about what?"

"We don't have any time for games. If Hector is dead, why would they need to waste any more time on you? You must know something."

Rita Foxx got up from the motel bed and went to the bathroom. She ran warm water over a face towel in the sink. She wiped the tears from her eyes and then washed her face.

Delia and Keisha studied her as she walked back into the room. They were a little nervous about their current situation.

They were not sure how to get Rita out of this motel room alive and exactly what to do with her afterward.

Both women felt sinful for looking at Rita in such a sexual manner, but it was impossible. She earned her living by doing all types of sexual jobs. There was a good reason it had been a lucrative form of work for her. Rita's honey bronze skin was smooth and flawless. Her hair fell softly down to her shoulders. Her large breasts were bulging from her tight top. She had eyes that were light brown and almost mystical. However, when you looked deeply in those eyes, she was just barely above being classified a teenager.

Keisha could not believe it when Rita stretched out across the bed. Keisha loudly sounded an alarm.

"I know you don't think we have time for you to lay around this room. You need to get your shit together so we can go right now."

"I'm pregnant. I don't feel very well," Rita whined.

"Getting murdered is going to make you feel real bad," Keisha advised.

Delia sat down on the bed beside Rita.

"Honey, you don't understand. This situation is not getting ugly. It is already beyond ugly. If someone thought they needed to burn down Zanzibar, regardless of who was inside just to kill Hector, they meant serious business. We need to get you someplace a lot safer than this motel room."

"I just want you to leave me alone," Rita cried. "Without Hector, I'm already dead."

"Fine!" Keisha said with disgust. "Just tell us what we need to know so we don't have to stay here long enough to get killed with you."

"Tommy Dancy killed Hector, didn't he Rita?" Delia asked. "You know he did!"

Rita rose up crying and shouting.

"Everybody in this town knows Tommy is bad news. Nobody does anything about him because he dates Princess Tracey. He and that white guy, Hunter, just harass poor folks on the street all the time and nobody does a damn thing about them."

"Why Hector?" Delia asked again. "After all these years, why would Tommy need to kill Hector now?"

"Miss Lela killed Curtis," Rita said as she fell back on the bed. Rita tried to bury her head in the pillow.

Keisha was angry and too scared to waste anymore valuable time. She took out a pistol from her purse before throwing the purse to the floor. She rushed over to the bed and pulled up Rita's head by her hair. Keisha stuck the gun barrel right in Rita's face.

"I'm sick of playing with you. If I kill you right now, everyone will think Tommy Dancy did it. Start talking sister or you, Hector, and that baby will all be one happy family in heaven in seven seconds."

Delia was not concerned about Keisha rough tactics. She was just as anxious to get somewhere safer than this motel room.

"Come on Rita tell it," Delia urged. "Do you want your baby to live? Do you want to live long enough to be a mother? Let us help you."

"Get that gun out of my face first," Rita strongly requested.

Keisha released Rita and backed away from the bed.

Rita sat up on the bed and clutched the pillow to her stomach.

"Hector and Sweet were old friends. They both have been hustling for years. They once did a pornographic video together that is out there on the internet. They were both pretty high on booze and drugs when they did that video. Hector had the master copy on a disc. The master is the extended version. What is out there on the internet is just the cut down version."

"What's on the extended version?" Delia eagerly asked.

"Hector crying and confessing to Sweet on that video about everything that happened the night that police officer, Terrell Monroe, got killed."

Delia and Keisha looked at each other in astonishment.

"Does he name names?" Delia questioned. "Does he say anything about Tracey Mercer."

"No, he didn't even know Tracey Mercer. He did know Curtis Mercer well and talks a lot about him. On that disc, he tells it all about how he worked for Roni Paige and how they were selling drugs. He tells how Tommy and Hunter worked for Roni too and all what they did to protect her. Then on the video he goes into detail about what happened that night when the police officer got killed. He also explains why he lied in court to put the blame on Wallace Penny. He tells Sweet everything on that disc. When he got sober, he said he was going to erase it. Hector told me he realized that the master disc was a way to keep Tommy and Hunter from retaliating on him. They both know the disc exist."

"How did Lela killing Curtis change anything?" Keisha wondered out loud.

"Hector tells on the video how Roni was laundering the drug money through Curtis Mercer's auto shops. Tommy and Hunter were not worried until Lela killed Curtis. Hector had two master copies. He kept one and he gave the other one to Curtis Mercer. The disc by itself most people would think was just some amateur porno actors, high on drugs and alcohol, rambling about nothing. The disc plus what Curtis had in his secret books together would probably put Tommy and Hunter in jail for life for killing that cop."

"Secret books!" Keisha yelled. "What secret books?"

"Where is Hector's disc?" Delia cautiously asked.

Rita opened up the drawer in the table next to the bed. She pulled out the Holy Bible. Rita turned to the book of Revelation and pulled out a round compact disc.

She handed it to Delia.

Keisha pointed her gun at Rita again and gave instructions.

"Get your shit together now girl! We got to get our asses out of this motel room and I mean right now!"

***

"Why are we doing this," Fran complained. "This is police work and we aren't the police."

"Stop being a scary cat," Mavis told her friend.

"She called Lela," Ashley explained. "You know Lela can't leave the house. I wouldn't have let her go if she could leave the house."

"Didn't you hire that big fancy lawyer to handle this type of situation?" Fran asked.

"Portia Lee works for Sister Mary," Mavis corrected. "Ash let Sister Mary step all over her."

"What did you want me to do?" Ashley shouted. "I make good money at my job, but I don't make the kind of money needed to pay a lawyer like Portia Lee."

"If you had looked a little faster at Curtis and Lela's legal papers, you would have saw our dear buddy, Lela, is a millionaire," Mavis scolded. "When this is all over, Lela better take us shopping."

"I'm not buying nothing with drug money?" Fran declared. "Curtis dealing drugs with that rich mamma of his. That is just ridiculous."

"Portia Lee has not fully proven that Curtis was all bad like that yet," Ashley said.

"Then why are we sneaking around like we are undercover agents?" Mavis asked.

"I can't believe you would be defending Curtis," Fran added. "He hated you more than any of us."

"He didn't hate her that bad," Mavis snickered. "He left all his money in her hands. He liked her more than we knew."

"Both of you just shut up and help me find the address," Ashley yelled.

"I don't think we should be on this side of town," Fran warned. "This is hunkyville over here. These poor white crackers don't even realize the civil war is over in this part of town."

"Just shut up and look for the address," Ashley repeated.

"Ashley, if I see any of those skin-heads with them Nazi tattoos, you better floor that gas petal," Mavis advised.

"There it is," Fran shouted while pointing to the house.

Ashley parked the car in front of a large dirty white house that was badly in need of paint and repairs. All sorts of children's toys littered the front lawn. Several junk cars that had not been driven in years littered the backyard.

The three African American women cautiously got out of the automobile. Mavis and Fran jumped at the beep made when Ashley remotely turned on the car alarm. They let Ashley lead the way to the front door. After several hard pounds on the front door, an old white woman with snow white, stringy hair opened the door.

She greeted the three women with what seemed like an endless smoker's cough. When the cough finally did end, the old woman took a long drag on a cigarette before asking for a reason for this unexpected visit.

"Can I help you?"

"Is Amber Gail here?" Ashley asked.

"Who wants to know?" the old woman bitterly replied.

"Tell her Lela Mercer sent us."

The door quickly slammed in their faces. Mavis and Fran turned to see a gathering of small white children with dirty faces, uncombed hair, and shabby clothes looking at them with curiosity. They looked farther across the street to see several young white men with shaven heads and numerous tattoos and body piercings staring at them with the same amount of curiosity.

"We need to get out of here now," Fran advised.

"I'm feeling a little like Fran," Mavis agreed.

The door suddenly flew back open and the old white woman reappeared.

"Come on in," she said with a hoarse deep voice.

Ashley opened the door and motioned her head for Fran and Mavis to follow.

The inside of the house was just as cluttered with junk as the outside. The old woman sat down in a big easy chair and lit a fresh cigarette. After a long drag on this new tobacco stick, she hollered at the top of her blacken lungs.

"Amber!"

A pale young blonde slowly walked into the living room. She was clutching in her arms a baby that was clearly fathered by a man of African descent.

"Oh shit," Mavis mumbled.

Ashley lightly tapped her to prevent her from saying anything more out loud. Fran was speechless.

"Amber Gail, I'm Ashley Powell. Lela Mercer sent me to talk to you."

"I know who you are," Amber answered. "You just never spoke or paid any attention to me when you came into the auto shop office. I was an invisible woman to you."

Ashley looked more closely at Amber. She realized she had passed this young woman numerous times sitting at that desk outside of Curtis' office. She had never said one word to her until now. She felt a twinge of guilt for her past superior attitude and behavior.

"I apologize for my rudeness in the past."

"Is this your baby?" Mavis anxiously asked.

"Yes," Amber proudly announced. "He will turn one in three weeks."

Ashley's tone was hard and dry when she asked the next question.

"What's his name?"

"Curtis James, but we call him CJ."

Fran turned to Mavis and whispered in her ear.

"Another Curtis James?"

Mavis whispered her acknowledgment.

"Damn, damn, damn!

So much cigarette smoke was bellowing up they could barely see the old white woman's face when she spoke.

"Sit down ladies. Make yourselves at home."

"That's a scary thought," Mavis mumbled.

Fran poked Mavis in the side to stop her mumbling.

The three women sat closely together on the old worn couch. Amber sat down in a chair across from them. She let the baby get down on the floor to stumble and crawl around looking for play items.

"You told Lela you had something important that she needed to know."

"She needs to know about the other set of books."

"What other set of books?" Ashley asked.

"Curtis kept one set of books that he let the IRS see. Then there were the other books just for him and his sister, Tracey."

Ashley was not sure if she should be happy or sad with this new information. Would secret financial books hurt Lela's case or help? Ashley quickly realized that she needed to get those secret books to Portia Lee before the prosecutor, Marian McNair, got her hands on them.

"Where are these books?" Ashley asked.

"I need some guarantees first," Amber demanded.

"Everybody wants something," Mavis said.

"What do you want from us?" Fran asked.

Amber got up and lifted the baby from the floor. She sat back down and held him in her lap.

"My son needs to be treated just like all of Curtis' children," Amber insisted. "He needs to go to good schools and have an opportunity at a good college. Curtis had us living in a very nice apartment with a nice car to drive. When Miss Lela killed Curtis, CJ and I had to leave our apartment and everything we owned in seconds. We left with just what we had on our backs. We have been living underground. We need to start living above ground again in the same fashion Curtis wanted his son to live."

Ashley sprang from the couch like a cobra.

"You wanted my Lela to come over here so you could blackmail her?"

Mavis and Fran both leaped to their feet in reaction to Ashley.

Mavis quickly jumped in front of Ashley to prevent her from moving violently toward Amber. Fran realized she needed to take over the negotiation process.

"How much does little baby CJ need to live like Curtis was his father?"

"Curtis is his father. I know how much is in those accounts. Miss Lela will have millions when this is all over. I just need one of those millions. She has Portia Lee for a lawyer. She is going to come out of this smelling like a rose. I need my son to come out of this smelling the same way."

"Done," Fran quickly agreed. "Where are those secret books?"

Ashley was outraged and tried to get passed Mavis.

Mavis gripped Ashley by the arms and used all her might to keep her from moving forward.

"What the hell do you mean done?" Ashley shouted. "This little bitch was screwing Lela's husband and now she is trying to screw Lela too. We're not paying her nothing. Oh hell no!"

Amber stood up and gripped the baby tightly in her arms. There was fear beginning to surface when she realized that Ashley was determined to put physical hands on her body.

The old woman remained calm and comfortable in her easy chair. She even lit another fresh cigarette.

"Forget what Ashley is saying and doing. You just look directly at me," Fran advised. "We need those books, immediately. You will get your money. You have my word."

Mavis continued holding Ashley back, but added her commitment.

"You have our word and we speak for Lela. You will definitely get your money. Now give us those books."

Amber sat the baby on the old woman's lap and left the room. The baby began coughing along with the old woman. He closed his eyes and rubbed his nose in an effort to keep all the cigarette smoke from clogging his lungs too.

When Amber returned, she handed Fran a key and a small piece of paper.

"This is a key to a safe deposit box at the Tyche Federal Credit Union. That is the account number. Everything you need is in that safety box."

"Whose name is this account under?" Fran asked.

"Curtis had me open the account under the name of Ashley Powell."

***

Ashley still could only see red. Mavis had to drive. She drove like they needed to get out of this neighborhood as fast as possible.

"I can't believe everything that is happening," Ashley said in amazement. "He had that little white bitch impersonating me. What the hell else are we going to find out?"

"Amber is just trying to protect her family," Fran explained. "Let's face it. Little CJ is really our family too."

"We just paid for what?" Ashley asked. "We're going to pay that little heifer for fucking that dirty dog, Curtis. How did anything she said help us? How will anything in that safety box help Lela?"

"I'm betting that Amber is hiding out with the Cancer Lady because she is sure there is something in that safety box worth more to somebody than a million dollars," Fran assured her friends.

"I know one thing for sure," Mavis added. "I'm going to stop smoking tomorrow."

thirty three

Justified

"You have got a lot of goddamn nerve to justify your sorry ass by putting the blame on me. You have been looking the other way since you were appointed police chief. You've let Tommy Dancy and Hunter Lynch shit all over this town and now the shit is blowing up in all of our faces.

"I'm the first black police chief this town has ever had. Do you know how careful I have to be if I throw a police officer off the force. If I got rid of Tommy, the black leaders would have been beating down my door saying that I was catering to the whites. If I fired Hunter, the white leaders would have beat down my door saying I'm favoring the blacks."

"So you just let those two scum bags do as they pleased. Do you know how many innocent people went down in that fire at Zanzibar? Nobody in this town believes that was a drug deal gone bad." "You have to have evidence to arrest and charge people with crimes in this country. Isn't that law 101? Why don't you give me a reason to throw them off the force if you think they are scum bags? Give me some evidence to make an arrest."

Shay Newman stood up from her desk to emphasize her words.

Claudius Langford braced himself for her sharpened tongue.

Claudius looked more like a linebacker for a professional football team than the head of the city's police force. The suit he wore barely enclosed his huge body. He always carried a handkerchief in his hand to wipe away all the sweat that poured down his face. His large size, dark color, and facial expressions could be frightening to most. However, he was more frightened that Shay was not going to help him get out of this predicament.

"Don't think you're going to take me down with you. Somebody's head is going to roll over Zanzibar. I have no intention of it being mine," Shay informed Claudius.

"If I have anything to say, we will go down the drain together as one loving couple," Claudius told Shay.

Marian McNair got up from her chair to make an attempt at getting the discussion back on a productive track.

"Let's all sit down and cool down. Everybody in this room has a career on the line if we don't figure a way out of this mess. The black community is not going to rest long if we don't serve up somebody on a silver platter for what happened at Zanzibar. Butter was a scheming, two-time hustler for years, but he was a beloved scheming, two-time hustler."

Shay and Claudius exchanged intimidating glares. They both retreated to their seats. Marian continued laying out their current status.

"It's very obvious that Zanzibar was burned down just to kill Hector Alonzo. The low murmur on the street is that folks are sure it was Tommy and Hunter. Why was it that important to kill that many people just to get Hector? Most of all, why did Lela Mercer killing her no good husband trigger all this chaos?"

The door flew open and FBI special agents, Asia Wang and Lorenzo Flores, entered the office.

"So you don't have to have manners when you work for the FBI?" Shay asked.

"Look where being polite has gotten us," Asia said. "Wallace Penny was tortured and murdered in the middle of the night in his prison cell. We have had to put Roni Paige in federal protective custody, innocent family men were shot and burned to death at Zanzibar. And to top it all off, we still haven't located Meghan Reilly, Rita Foxx, or Amber Gail."

"And Lela Mercer sits by the pool at Sister Mary's mansion sipping sweet tea," Lorenzo added. "While her headless husband, Curtis Mercer, spins in his grave. It's very clear that the police department and the prosecutor's office in this city are both worthless. The time for being polite is over."

"Thank God Almighty, the sleeping giant, called the FBI, has arrived to save the day. You finally woke up and realized some federal laws may have been violated," Claudius laughed. "Well, wipe the sleep out of your eyes and get caught up on what has been happening in this city for the last several years."

Asia and Lorenzo sat down in chairs to join the conversation. Marian began laying out her plan of attack.

"Portia Lee is young, beautiful, and flamboyant. She has never once taken a single legal case to trial. Plea bargaining is her specialty. I will take the death penalty off the table. I intend to offer her life in prison with no possibility of parole. In exchange, Lela has to cough up some evidence against Tommy and Hunter for their role in Roni Paige's drug operation."

There was a moment of silence in the room. Claudius looked stunned and sat up in his chair.

"That's it?" Claudius asked in disbelief. "You think it will be that simple?"

"What choice do they have?" Marian wanted to know. "The woman has admitted to killing Curtis Mercer and their children are the main witnesses. I don't think this will be a hard decision for Portia Lee or Lela Mercer to make."

"What makes you think Lela knows anything worth a damn about Tommy Dancy and Hunter Lynch?" Asia asked.

"Yeah," Lorenzo added. "Curtis may have been the sole mastermind of that entire drug enterprise that Roni Paige was supervising. Lela Mercer may really be just a trophy wife that turned a blind eye to more than her husband's philandering."

"I don't give a rat's ass," Shay shouted. "Portia Lee had better come up with something on Tommy and Hunter if she wants to save her client's pretty head."

Marian was astounded by Shay's response.

"We don't want Portia Lee manufacturing something on Tommy and Hunter," Marian told her boss.

Claudius, surprisingly, came to Shay's defense.

"We have two major crimes in this small town that need to get closed out like right now. There is no doubt that all these murders are related. Portia Lee needs to get them all linked and neatly packaged up for us to close out. Now, I'll be honest, I'm a red-blooded man and my eyesight is working just fine. That Lela Mercer is a sweet badass piece of honey. It would hurt me dearly to see that black beauty get a lethal cocktail shot in her veins. Her high priced lawyer better earn her keep and manufacturer, rebuild, or buy some damn evidence against Tommy and Hunter if she wants to save her client's beautiful body and soul."

"We pulled Hector's cell phone records," Asia informed the group. "He made a phone call to a cell phone registered to a Robin Hawkins shortly before the fire at Zanzibar."

"Robin Hawkins is her real name. She is known in the strip clubs and on several pornographic internet websites as Rita Foxx," Lorenzo said. "There is a strong possibility that Miss Foxx can actually place Tommy and Hunter in Zanzibar before it burned down."

Claudius was overjoyed and almost sang his reaction.

"There you go! We squeeze Lela about the drug ring and get that little booty shaker to testify about Zanzibar. We kill too birds with one stone."

Shay was feeling better about their situation also.

"Well, it's up to you Marian. You have to get Portia Lee to play our type of ball game."

Marian smiled and shook her head in amazement that this was all going to fall on her shoulders.

"Life in prison with no chance of parole is the big carrot to offer that female dog named Portia Lee? With everything that is coming to light, you really think Portia Lee will think that is a plea bargain?"

Shay relaxed her stiffened body and reluctantly conceded to Marian's realization.

"Keep 15 years to life in your back pocket. Use it only if necessary."

"I'll do my best," Marian reluctantly agreed.

"We have Roni Paige in protective custody. She's not talking," Lorenzo announced. "She has a new lawyer whose name is Portia Lee."

"Imagine that," Shay said with disgust.

"You all know Roni Paige legally can't be forced to testify against Hunter Lynch?" Claudius asked.

"We know now," Shay yelled. "It would have been nice if we had been told this little technicality sooner."

"He married her long before he joined the police force and never seemed to get around to divorcing her. We didn't know ourselves until our two lovely FBI representatives brought it to our attention just recently that it was actually a valid legal marriage."

"It's good to know your police officers take the crooks off the streets and then marry them," Marian laughed.

"He married her in Las Vegas years ago and it never came up on any background check for us or the Internal Revenue Service," Claudius explained. "Hunter was on the police force long before I took over the job as police chief. There is no doubt that his background check was botched. You can thank my great white predecessor for that blunder."

"Just more incompetency that we will need to keep a jury from hearing," Shay informed. "Keep it coming Claudius. With your help, Portia Lee will be able to get this Lela Mercer murder case down to a misdemeanor."

Asia and Lorenzo stood up to leave.

"We don't have time to listen to you love birds squabble," Lorenzo announced.

"We're fairly sure Meghan Reilly is dead," Asia confessed. "There is not much hope that we'll find her body. The signs indicate that Rita Foxx and Amber Gail are both still very much alive and are still right here in this town somewhere."

"We'll step up the pace locating those two to get the deal done with Portia Lee," Lorenzo offered.

"What are you going to do Claudius?" Shay playfully asked.

"I'll keep a steady watch on Tommy and Hunter," Claudius promised.

"That's what got us in this mess to begin with," Shay mocked.

Claudius' joyous expression turned back to a hateful glare. He struggled to raise his big body up on to his feet. He took his handkerchief and wiped the massive amount of sweat from his face.

The floor seemed to rumble like an earthquake as Claudius stormed out of the prosecutor's office.

thirty four

Sister Friends

"You knew about that baby?"

"Sometimes women confront you when they are sleeping with your husband. They think it gives them power over you. They believe your husband loves them much more than he could ever love you. It never seems to enter their stupid minds that you legally and physically have the house, the cars, the kids, the money, and the man. Curtis wouldn't have left me even after hell had totally frozen up. How could all those women actually believe he cared about me less, but gave me more? He may have not truly loved me, but he did care. He didn't give a shit about any of them. Grown women can be so silly and stupid. Amber Gail is young and just as silly as all the rest. If Curtis had ever known she had approached me, he would have crushed her like an ant. He was adamant about keeping his dirty business done in the street from coming into our nice clean home. If he even thought one of those bitches had come near me or had said one word to me, he would fly into a rage and cut them completely off immediately. Isn't that ridiculous? In his heart, he believed only those women could break my heart. He didn't realize it was him that was breaking my heart every day. He thought he had every right to be unfaithful to me simply because he was a man."

Ashley had no response to what Lela was saying. She was dumbfounded that Lela knew about little CJ and had never said a word until now. Fran was also in shock. However, Mavis wanted to know more.

"Are those twins Curtis' kids too?"

"No," Lela quickly revealed. "It may be hard to believe, but Curtis really didn't lie to me very much. When he did lie, it was more than obvious. He was not a very good liar. He told me up front that everyone in town thought those were his twins. He said he would have never touched Roni. Curtis said his sister had put her tongue in places on Roni's body that would have made it incest if he had done the same."

"What the hell?" Fran was finally able to speak.

"Tracey Mercer was fucking Roni Paige and Tommy Dancy too?" Mavis screamed with joy. "Mean, crazy, and freaky too!"

"Back up," Ashley insisted. "You said you didn't know Roni Paige."

"I didn't know her as Roni Paige," Lela said. "When Portia Lee finally showed me a picture of her, I realized who she was. She was introduced to me by Tracey as Veronica Lynch."

"That white cop that is Tommy Dancy's good friend has the last name Lynch," Fran stated.

"That's right," Lela agreed. "I was told Veronica or Roni was his wife."

"Shut up," Mavis instructed. "I can't take no more!"

Ashley was just outraged.

"This is just crazy. How did all of that not come out when Roni went to trial."

"There was no trial for Roni," Mavis reminded everyone. "She got sent to federal court and quietly, and I do mean quietly, took a plea bargain. When she went off on her federally sponsored vacation, there barely was two lines in the newspaper about the entire situation. I had seen her with that white guy. He was a cop. I just thought he probably was riding her ass because she sold drugs?"

"He was riding her ass alright. How could a police officer be married to one of the biggest drug dealers in this town?" Fran asked. "Especially a white police officer?"

"Obviously, it helps to be fucking Doris Mercer's son or daughter," Mavis said giggling.

"The white guy is probably those twins' daddy," Fran realized. "Curtis really wasn't their father."

"You both already knew about Roni and those twins?" Ashley asked Fran and Mavis.

"Fran told me," Mavis blurted out.

"What!" Fran shouted. "Everybody in town knew about those twins, including Lela."

Lela was amused at Fran and Mavis attempting to explain their silence to her and Ashley.

"So, I'm the only one clueless in this room," Ashley admitted.

Lela tried to comfort her disappointed friend.

"Ash, Curtis and his family did so much dirt that sometimes I just didn't tell it all, because I didn't want to hear it come out of my own mouth."

"I told Portia Lee about Amber Gail," Ashley reported. "She promptly sent her private investigator to put Amber and the baby in a better hiding place."

"Ada came to the house and already told me," Lela confessed. "Ada was really excited. She said everything was coming together and looking better for me. I don't know what that means. I don't see how anything could be looking better for me"

"If you get out of this mess, what are you going to do?" Mavis asked.

"I don't really know," Lela said. "I have never thought about getting out of this mess. I don't really believe I can get out of this mess. I did kill Curtis."

"Portia Lee really is a pretty damn good lawyer," Fran confessed. "She has got people shaking in their boots since she took your case. Lots of folks have been whispering that Zanzibar burned to the ground because of you."

"What the hell are you talking about?" Lela inquired.

"You were right Lela," Mavis told her friend. "Curtis and his family did so much dirt in the streets that you didn't tell it all to us and they didn't tell it all to you."

"I'm with Fran," Ashley said. "It was looking pretty bleak for you, Lela. Now I'm starting to believe Portia Lee may actually get you a better deal than I thought. She may have been right about Curtis being your savior. He was out there in the streets doing more than what we knew."

Mavis made a cutting gesture across her neck.

"Live by the sword, die by the sword," Mavis stated.

Fran's scolding facial expression signaled her urgent need for Mavis to be quiet.

"You always know the right thing to say," Fran said sarcastically.

"How are you going to deal with Doris and her gang?" Ashley asked. "She is still the children's grandmother."

"I would never try to keep Doris from my kids," Lela declared. "Doris and Tracey never liked me much to begin with, but they love my children. I don't think much will change. Curtis was always the go-between when it came to the kids. Now you, Ashley, or my mother will have to be the go-between."

"What about that crazy Charles?" Fran wondered.

"Charles is not crazy," Lela said with pity in her voice.

"Come on Lela," Mavis interrupted. "You know that Charles' obsession with you is not normal. I could see having a crush on you for a while. There should have been some point when he realized this is my brother's wife. She doesn't even love me that way. He should have known that a Charles and Lela matchup was hopeless. Instead, it has gotten worse over the years. Now that Curtis is dead, Charles is spiraling right out of his mind."

"I wouldn't say he is spiraling out of his mind," Lela disagreed.

"You don't call trying to choke the life out of Ashley a little bit crazy?" Fran asked.

"Charles is a sweet and wonderful man," Lela stated. "I wish to God I had met him before Curtis. I wish right now that I had loved Charles like I still love Curtis. This is a traumatic situation for everybody. Charles' heart is broken. Time will bring him back to his family. Eden is a beautiful woman that has given him a beautiful son."

"You are as bad as his mother," Mavis informed. "You both won't face the fact that Charles is in some type of depression. Charles has actually been in a funk for years and we all have been just ignoring it. Everybody has been telling him time will heal, God will get you through it, and a child of your own with your wonderful wife will make you forget all about Lela. Well, none of that has happened. Charles needed some type of counseling long before you sliced up Curtis. Now that Curtis is dead, Charles has gone right off the edge. He is going totally insane right in front of us all."

"So you all feel I have killed Charles too?" Lela questioned.

"Charles isn't dead," Ashley announced. "Just grieving over both you and Curtis. He'll be okay."

"He's grieving more about Lela," Fran corrected. "Now that Curtis is dead, Charles feels his chance to have Lela is dead too."

"The boy is sick," Mavis insisted.

"We're all killing Charles," Fran revealed. "We all see his problem, but nobody will admit he has a problem. None of us are trying to get him the help he needs. With Curtis dead, Charles is going into a deeper darkness. I just hope he comes back to the light before it's too late. All of us in this room will get over Curtis's death and move on. Even Curtis' own children are dealing with his death and trying to move on. I'm not sure Charles knows how to move on."

"Nothing we can really do," Mavis conceded. "That is really for Doris and Tracey to handle. Charles is their problem."

"Lela is our only problem," Ashley declared.

"Yeah," Fran agreed. "Lela is our friend and time has made her our sister. We can only be concerned with saving her stupid behind."

"Thank you," Lela smiled.

"That's right," Mavis added playfully. "We can live without all those damn Mercers, but we can't live without you baby. We don't care how many people you kill."

"Mavis!" Fran scolded.

Mavis put her hands over her mouth too late to stop her last statement. There was an awkward moment of silence.

Lela's smile was broader and brighter than it had ever been since the unfortunate incident. She shouted to her sister-friends.

"I love you all to death. I mean until death."

Lela's outburst of laughter was contagious and rapidly infected each woman. The women laughed until tears began to flow.

The women all grabbed hands and formed a circle. Mavis led the prayer.

"Lord," Mavis shouted. "When I come calling, you know it's bad. I don't ask for much and you haven't given me much. But, I'm begging this time. These women are more than my friends. Our years together has made these women my sisters. Please Lord, help us. Please shine the light for that uppity, high-priced Portia Lee to show us the way out of this hell hole. If you grant us this one tender mercy, I'll try to stop smoking cigarettes and weed. I'll cut back on drinking hard liquor. I won't fool around with any men younger than twenty-five. Please Lord, help me and my sister-friends get through this as one. In the name of our Lord Jesus, Amen!"

"Mavis, what am I going to do with you," Fran asked laughing.

"What kind of prayer was that?" Ashley asked outraged

"The best kind," Lela said as she hugged and kissed Mavis.

"Group hug!" Fran yelled with joy.

"Oh please," Ashley said still outraged.

The women playfully pulled Ashley into their group hug.

"I couldn't get through all of this without my girls," Lela roared.

thirty five

The Other Wife

Pierce Drake looked like he should be in Los Angeles taking an actors' casting call or in New York doing a male model photo shoot. A small town in Ohio did not seem to be the appropriate home for such a fine looking male specimen. Pierce's body frame was tall and slender, yet muscular. His jet black hair was wavy and neatly trimmed. His piercing blue eyes made it hard for any woman not to notice. He was handsome, a successful attorney, and very wealthy. He was a pleasing sight to the eyes and his deep masculine voice was pleasing to the ears.

Harsh threats were all she heard when Portia Lee looked directly into those angry blue eyes.

"If you try to drag my wife's name into this circus, my law firm and I will not rest until you have to rent office space from Ada."

"If you are trying to insult me, it's not working," Ada proudly informed Pierce. "My niece and I are already a legal team."

"A team of fools that need to get off my property," Pierce warned.

"You need to save all those words of intimidation for your real clients," Portia advised. "Your wife can talk to me now or answer my questions under oath in court later. It is definitely your choice, Mr. Drake."

It did not take long for Pierce to realize he had no choice. He opened the front door wide enough for Portia and Ada to enter his lavish home. The two women followed Pierce through the house to a family room where his wife was nervously waiting.

Paula Drake stood up and extended her hand when they entered the room. She was almost as tall as Pierce in high heel shoes. She was a woman who looked sensual even in business-like attire. Her dark brown hair flowed down to her shoulders. Her light brown eyes made her smile seem almost sinful. She looked as rich as she was and smelled like heaven must. She was a perfect mate for a perfect husband like Pierce Drake.

"The one and only Portia Lee," Paula said. "Your reputation is becoming legend. And you brought with you, our own famous Ada Stinson. Ada, who would have thought you would be one of the lead attorneys on the biggest criminal case this town has ever seen?"

"Nice to see you too, Paula," Ada responded. "You don't normally speak to me when I see you at the courthouse."

"If I had known you were the aunt to legal royalty, I would have brought you candy and flowers," Paula admitted while laughing. "There is not a female attorney on the east coast that would not love to get an office at Endress, Neal, Tuthill, & Cruz. I hear your niece is their golden child."

"We didn't come here to be flattered," Portia said. "This is strictly business. Unfortunately, it is very ugly business. You might want your husband to leave the room while we have this discussion."

"I have no secrets from my husband," Paula insisted.

"I'm not sure if that is totally true," Ada reminded Paula. "You and me may be more alike than I ever thought."

"I doubt that," Paula replied in a nasty tone.

"What you say to my wife, you can say to me," Pierce demanded.

"Let's not start out on a sour note," Paula requested. "Ladies please have a seat. Would you like something to eat or drink?"

"What do you have?" Ada asked.

"Ada and I just need answers," Portia overruled.

"Let me save you some time," Paula quickly explained. "I did handle some legal matters for Curtis Mercer. Mica Goldman is the Mercer family attorney. However, there were certain matters that Curtis felt it was not really necessary for his mother to be aware of. I'm sure you know by now that Doris Mercer has her hands filled with running Mercer Health and Beauty Supplies. She didn't need to have to deal with her son's business affairs also."

"Does that include helping him conduct fraud?" Portia asked.

"I don't know what you're talking about," Paula calmly answered.

"Listen, we are all attorneys in this room," Ada said. "No need to act like anybody in this room is brain-dead. We already know what went down with you and Curtis."

Pierce leaped from his seat and pointed to the door.

"If you know everything, then you can get the hell up out of my house," Pierce commanded.

Ada stood up and tried to calm the irate husband.

"We really need to have a woman to woman talk with your wife, Pierce," Ada pleaded. "Just give us some time alone with Paula."

"If it's a woman to woman talk, then maybe you should leave the room with me, Ada," Pierce harshly advised.

Despite their relationship, Portia did not tolerate anyone else insulting her aunt. Her growing irritation with both Pierce and Paula Drake was evident in her bitter tone of voice.

"You had better tell this son-of-a-bitch to leave the room right now unless you want him to hear the gory details of how far down your throat Curtis Mercer stuck his big black..."

"Pierce!" Paula quickly interrupted. "Ada is correct.
This is a girls only conversation."

Pierce looked at his wife with anger and disgust.

"You get that black bastard, Curtis Mercer, out of my house for good right now," Pierce instructed his wife before storming out of the room.

"You didn't have to get racial on us," Ada shouted at Pierce.
Ada watched Pierce leave the room and then sat back down.
Portia now had a sense of ease in her voice when she spoke.
"Now that it's just us girls, let's talk dirty."

"I'm sure you came here for some salacious details of my sexual encounters with Curtis," Paula said. "Those are private matters that have nothing to do with your case. Lela Mercer almost cut her husband's head clean off. Nothing I have ever done caused her to commit that horrendous crime."

"You don't think her husband getting dressed up to go to a fancy hotel to repeatedly bang your big white ass might not have made her insane enough to involuntarily kill him?" Portia asked. "I'm actually wondering why she didn't kill you too?"

"I know you're not going to try to go with that type of defense?" Paula questioned. "That would make you certifiably insane."

"Ashley Powell is the executor over Curtis' estate. That gives her access to all his accounts," Portia stated. "Credit card statements that show numerous hotel charges. Wonder why a man would need to get so many hotel rooms in the same city where he has a large home. I first though he might me taking his little administrative assistant, Amber Gail. Then we saw in his paperwork that Curtis was paying for Amber Gail to live in an upscale apartment complex. There was no need to take her to any fancy hotel. We were confused again. Just who was he meeting in those hotel rooms? Just who was he going to meet the very night he was killed?"

"You will be amazed at how little cash you have to give to hotel maids for them to positively identify a rich white woman going into a hotel room with a good looking black man that looks a helluva lot like Doris Mercer's son," Ada added. "It even amazed me."

Paula smiled at Portia and Ada's description of their recent discovery.

"Sister Mary hired me to handle some business affairs for Curtis," Paula explained. "Curtis and I developed a strong friendship that crossed over into a sexual relationship. We both liked to explore different sexual avenues. There was never any form of love involved. Our relationship was just fun and games for him. I'm sure most people would never believe it, but Curtis truly loved his wife. He talked about her all the time. Lela was his prized possession."

"Did the business affairs you handled for him include sign-ing Lela Mercer's name on house deeds? Portia asked.

"I'm not the best lawyer in town," Ada admitted. "I wasn't aware lawyers can impersonate their clients too."

"Where are you getting these wild accusations?" Paula asked.

"From a scared assistant to personal banker, Meghan Reilly, whose name is Sherry Ferguson. She told her story to both the prosecutor and to my team. She felt I was more interested in keeping her alive much more than the prosecutor. I think I may have forgot to say she is the assistant to the same Meghan Reilly that has been missing for days and presumed by most to be dead."

"Sherry Ferguson can make a positive identification from the same photographs I showed those hotel maids," Ada confirmed.

Paula leaned forward confused on exactly where Portia Lee was going with this conversation.

"What exactly do you want from me?"

"I have been retained as the new lawyer for one of your former clients. I'm sure you remember Veronica Paige. You may know her as Roni Paige."

"No, no," Ada reminded. "You may know her as Veronica Lynch."

"I have a technicality problem," Portia revealed. "Mrs. Lynch cannot be made to testify against her husband, Hunter Lynch. Even if she did testify against him, it may not seem very credible. The jury may think she is just an angry black woman mad with a white husband that has not acknowledged her as his wife and who actually make the arrest that sent her to jail for the last three years. A jury may think she has an ax to grind. However, her lawyer knows everything and is a very respected member of the court system. Her attorney's testimony against Tommy Dancy, as well as Hunter Lynch, would be no problem to a wise and informed jury."

Paula sat back in her seat. She thought for a moment before speaking.

"What if I said that I can't help you?"

"Technology has allowed us all to do many things we would have never done in the past," Portia explained. "I am a very private person myself. It is extremely hard for me to understand how two grown people would agree to videotape their sexual escapades."

"Girl you is a freaky freak," Ada announced.

"I hope you have a copy of the sex tapes you made with Curtis Mercer," Portia said.

"If not, we can get you some good quality copies," Ada offered.

"Ashley Powell has provided me with copies that Curtis was keeping in memory of his fondness for you," Portia revealed.

"Girl you is a freaky freak," Ada reiterated.

"You want me to testify in a court of law against those two killers?" Paula asked. "Tommy Dancy and Hunter Lynch are vile and vicious. That could endanger my family."

"You can walk into the courtroom as a witness or as a defendant," Portia offered. "In this state, impersonating Lela Mercer and falsifying her signature for personal gain or to make sure you can fuck her husband over and over again would be called fraud. It also could get you disbarred and jail time."

"You are a golden child," Paula admitted. "You apparently have me in a delicate position."

"Not as many positions as Curtis had you in," Ada clarified. "But the position we have you in may be a bit more painful."

"You know my reputation," Portia assured. "I don't like to go to trial. If I have to make a deal with the prosecutor, I need to have the guarantee of your possible testimony as a bargaining chip."

A new voice invaded their conversation.

"You can count on my wife being at your full beck and call. We need to get Curtis Mercer finally dead and buried physically and mentally for everyone in this town."

The three women turned to see Pierce Drake standing in the doorway. They all waited for Paula to confirm Pierce's statement.

"I suppose I do owe her. She lent her husband to me on many occasions. I guess I can lend her my testimony. I'll be on call for you, if needed. I'm sure that's the least I can do for Lela Mercer. However, let me clarify something for you. Curtis and I had totally ended our physical relationship at least nine months before he was killed. Curtis' sexual attention span was not very long. He was actually spending more and more time with some other woman. No, I don't know who she was. It was obvious from his very uncharacteristic behavior that he actually cared about this new woman. I actually think the mystery woman had a real possibility of doing something none of his other women were able to do, including me."

"And what would that be?" Portia asked Paula.

"Dethroning the great Lela Mercer."

thirty six

Unbearable

You could smell Euryale Washington five minutes before she appeared. She doused herself in perfumed water, adorned herself with clanking jewelry, and decorated herself with massive amounts of makeup. You could only hope that she did not greet you with a kiss. The red stain from her lips would be almost impossible to remove.

Euryale had been a minority coordinator for the county's Democratic Party for several years. Her voice was suited for politics or preaching. However, she decided she needed to combine the two when trying to convince Charles to accept her proposition.

"You would be the first African American mayor of this city. We are only thirty minutes outside of that giant political machine sitting up there on Lake Erie. They have had several black mayors and we still have not had one. A black mayor will give our black community validation. It will show that we are a political and economic force in this city that has to be reckoned with. The two richest citizens in this town are African American. We need to stop being a force behind the scenes and starting being a force in the public eye. We need someone to lead the way. I know that leader could be you, Charles. You already know that we have some very influential people in this community that are ready to get behind your candidacy. Your brother Curtis also believed you were right for the job."

"You had already discussed this with Curtis?" Charles asked.

Doris cringed when Curtis' name came rolling out of Euryale's mouth. She knew it would not be accepted well by Charles. She hoped that Euryale would not say any more about conversations she had with Curtis. Her wish did not come true.

"Before his untimely death, Curtis and I had long talks about putting together a campaign to go after that mayor's office," Euryale revealed. "I actually thought Curtis might have wanted to take a shot at running for the office. He felt it was a job more suited for his baby brother."

"You really wanted Curtis and not me is what you are trying to say," Charles clarified. "Now that Lela has sliced him up, you are just stuck with me. That's the real truth."

"That is not what she is saying," Doris intervened. "You know Curtis could have never been mayor of nothing. He was my son and I loved him dearly. His lifestyle was not compatible with politics. He and I both realized you would make a perfect mayor."

"You and Curtis had already made the decision," Charles said. "Curtis is dead and he is still making all the decisions with you."

Doris looked in her son's eyes and saw something that made her afraid. Euryale saw the conversation was going in the wrong direction. She tried to steer it back to the right road.

"No, no Charles," Euryale insisted. "We all had been bouncing the idea off of each other before approaching you. You are the first and last choice that we want to get behind and build a campaign."

They were all startled when a second to Euryale's motion loudly filled the room.

"Euryale is absolutely correct," Sister Mary announced. "You would be the perfect candidate to run for the office of mayor."

Charles was shocked that his mother's facial expression disclosed that she was fully expecting the arrival of Sister Mary.

Euryale was surprised by Sister Mary's sudden entrance, but extremely elated.

"Sister Mary!" Euryale shouted. "I am so glad to see you."

"Doris told me about your proposal," Sister Mary said. "I believe this is something that both Doris and I need to get behind."

Charles exploded with anger. His words came hurling out with such force at Sister Mary that it took Euryale completely off guard.

"So all is back to normal. Curtis is dead and Lela is facing the death penalty and we just go back to our lives like nothing ever happened. You and Mama are back in love again. The two of you just go right back to ruling over everything and everyone."

"Charles, what is the matter with you?" Doris asked. "We both are trying to help you and your family."

"Help me and my family!" Charles yelled. "The other day you were ready to slay Mary like she was the evil dragon helping Lela. Now you and her are going to work together to help me and my family. I don't understand you two crazy women."

"Sister Mary can influence the church members to get behind your candidacy," Euryale said trying to sooth Charles mounting outrage. "The House of Mary Baptist Church is the largest church in this city. Sister Mary also could give a big financial boost to our efforts. It does take a large amount of funds to run a successful campaign."

"I don't need Mary's money," Charles shouted.

"Mary's money is my money too. You stupid fool!" Doris roared. "Why are you so damn mad anyway. Mary is helping your precious Lela. You have been licking Lela's ass for years.

Now you're suddenly upset because Mary is trying to keep Lela's neck off the chopping block."

"I thought you wanted Lela dead?" Charles blasted back.

"I don't want Lela dead," Doris told her son. "She is still the mother of my grandchildren. They can lock her up in prison and throw away the key. If they kill her, they will kill my grandchildren too. If you would stop whining and crying long enough to go home and be a father to your son, you would realize the sacrifices you have to make for your children."

"If I'm so stupid, why do you want me to be mayor of this city?" Charles asked. "I already know why. You and the great Sister Mary want to finish your goal. It's not good enough to have all the money in this town. You want to have all the power too. You and Mary want to be the real mayor of this city. You just want to use me to be your puppet. This is not about helping me and my family. It's about two evil bitches who made a pack years ago that was sealed by the devil."

Doris slapped Charles across his face before she could stop herself. Sister Mary jumped between Doris and Charles before the fight could escalate any further.

"You ungrateful bastard. I have worked my tail off to give you and your brother and sister everything the world has to offer. Look how all three of you have repaid me."

"Charles, you just need to calm down," Sister Mary urged. "Once you think about this proposal, I'm sure you will see what a career opportunity it will be for you. Being mayor could lead to governor, senator, and who knows what next. Doris and I may have made lots of mistakes along the way, but we can do something right for once by helping you and your family. Charles, you are a good and honest man. You could be good for this city."

Charles was still steaming from the heat filling his body caused by Doris striking his face and his pride.

"That is the last time you or Tracey ever hit me again," Charles vowed. "I am done with all of you women. I'm done with this family. You want me to be Curtis now that he is dead. Well, I will never be Curtis. You never let him be a real man. He let women run and ruin his life and then you killed him. I don't need you to figure out how to kill me too."

"Charles, your mother and I love you," Sister Mary said. "We are not trying to stop you from being a man. You take your time and decide what you want to do. Doris and I will back any decision you make for your family. Isn't that correct Doris?"

Doris was so upset she could barely collect herself to be civil. She forced herself to offer her support.

"You know I love you Charles," Doris admitted. "I just want you to be happy. That is all I have ever wanted for all of my children. I just want you to have more than I ever had and achieve more than I ever could. I just want my children and grandchildren to be happy."

"I can never be as attractive and charming as Curtis and as strong and smart as Tracey," Charles stated. "Most of all, I can never live up to being the great Doris Mercer's son."

Doris saw the disillusion in Charles' eyes. However, she could not find the right words that could wipe it away.

"Charles, you will be a great mayor of this city," Euryale insisted. "Let me organize your campaign. Go home and discuss it with Eden. We can win this election. The people of this city need you to bring us all together. You can do this Charles. You can make a difference in this town and a name for yourself."

Charles smiled at Euryale. He looked up to see a sight he had seen all of his life. A vision that he suddenly realized was permanent. Doris and Mary standing side by side.

"Thank you Euryale. Doris and Mary, don't ever think I didn't love you both with all my heart. I wish I could have made you proud."

Charles walked out of the house leaving behind a stunned Euryale. She recovered quickly and reassured Doris and Sister Mary that Charles just needed time.

"Don't worry ladies. It may have been too soon for us to approach him with all that has happened. He's still grieving over his brother. Let's just give him some time. He'll come around. He'll see our vision."

***

"I can't thank you enough, Nadine. I really appreciated the dinner and the conversation. I needed a little time away from both Charles and the baby. I really needed to talk. It felt so good to just let it all out."

"Now that we both have the full story, you know we are family in more ways than one. Anytime you need to talk, you can call me. Don't think of me as your minister, but as your sister. We can get through this if we stick together like a family."

"Charles has hurt me terribly and I'm not free from blame in our relationship," Eden admitted. "I still can't walk away yet. I had convinced myself that it was over. When I looked in my baby's eyes, I realized I need to try one more time. Charles is more devastated about Lela than he is about Curtis. His moods are swinging like a pendulum. Sometimes, I'm scared that he is losing his mind. It's ridiculous. I should be outraged. I love him so much. I love him like he loves Lela. I just need to see if we can start over. I want to try for me and the baby this time. I'm sure after all I told you tonight that you think I'm crazier than Charles."

"Remember what I said tonight. You and Charles will only be able to move on if you both reveal your true feelings," Nadine advised. "The truth really will set you free. Then you both will know when enough is enough. I have faith that you and Charles will eventually do what is best for yourselves and your child. Now, exactly where is Charles and that precious little man."

"Charles went to have dinner with Doris. When the dragon summons, you must go. My mother is keeping the baby for us tonight."

"Oh no," Nadine said disappointed. "I wanted to see that sweet little boy."

"Don't worry," Eden guaranteed. "You are included on the list of babysitters. We will surely be calling."

Nadine grabbed Eden and hugged her tight.

"After what I told you, you still care," Eden asked.

"I love you and the entire church loves you. God is your judge and not me or any member of the church. When you are in need, that is why there is a church family. Any of us will come running with help, love, and faith."

Eden kissed Nadine on the cheek and thanked her.

"I thank you so much!"

Eden locked the back kitchen door after Nadine had left. She turned off the lights and reset the home alarm. She was filled with a renewed spirit as she walked upstairs to the bedroom.

When Eden turned on the bedroom light, she was startled to see Charles sitting in the rocking chair by their bed. They had just bought the rocking chair to help rock their new baby to sleep. Charles was doing the intended purpose of the chair. He was rocking their newborn who was sound asleep.

The beautiful sight of her husband cradling their sleeping child made Eden smile. It was a wonderful sight that brought her joy until she saw the gun resting on the night table next to Charles.

The joyous feeling that had initially filled Eden's heart quickly transformed into terror that rippled down her spine.

Charles totally ignored the sudden illumination of the room and his wife's presence. The look in his eyes was wild and menacing. He was totally soaked in sweat. Charles was looking directly at his child. He seemed disconnected to reality.

"Charles, I thought you were having dinner with Doris tonight?"

"I stopped at your mother's house and picked up the baby. I told her that I had changed my mind. Little Charles Curtis Mercer needed to come home with his father tonight. I desperately needed to see him. I needed to study his face again. There is just something about his face that I needed to see again. He doesn't look anything like me. He doesn't look anything like you. It has just been racking my brain. Where have I seen this face before? Who does my precious child look like? I named him Charles Curtis Mercer in honor of my dead beloved brother. What should his name really be? Should his name really be Charles Curtis Mercer or Curtis Charles Mercer?"

"What are you talking about?"

"I have been sitting here looking at my son who looks just like my dead brother. Have you ever seen pictures of Curtis when he was a baby? My mother has mountains of photo albums filled with baby pictures of Curtis. My son looks just like my brother when he was a baby."

"Charles, you are under a lot of stress. You are not thinking straight."

"It has been bothering me every day since he was born. My son looks just like my brother. How is that possible?"

"You and Curtis are brothers. That is not unusual for children to look like their aunts or uncles."

"My son looks exactly like my brother."

"Charles, you are talking crazy."

"My son looks exactly like my dead brother."

"Stop saying that!"

"Tell me the truth."

"Charles, can't you be happy about our child."

"Tell me the truth."

"Why can't you be happy for once in your life?"

Charles whipped the gun off the night stand and pointed it at Eden.

"Tell me the truth now!"

"That's what you want. You want me dead so you can have Lela. That is what you have always wanted. You have wanted me out of the way so you can go running to your precious jewel, Lela. You don't give a damn about Curtis. You are grieving over your beloved Lela. If you want her that bad, go ahead and shoot me. Go ahead. Go right ahead. Shoot me!"

Charles quickly turned the gun on the baby. Eden screamed with fear.

"Charles!"

"Tell me the truth now!"

"Yes! Yes! You want the truth? Curtis is his father. Is that what you needed to hear? Curtis is his true father. Maybe if you had not been trying to get his wife, you would have been able to stop Curtis from coming over here taking yours. You should have been my husband. Curtis had no choice but to be Lela's

husband and my husband too. You spent all your time just slob-
bering over Lela when I needed you here. Who else could I
call to help me with anything and everything? And yes, some
nights I needed Curtis to help me make believe I was making
love to you."

Charles put the gun back on the night stand. He looked
more intensely at the baby and began slowly rocking in the
chair again.

"When my mother and Sister Mary realize this is Curtis'
son, they will eat him alive."

"He is our son, Charles. No one has to know, but us."

"You told Nadine."

"She is my minister and my friend."

"She is a minister and her God is Sister Mary. Doris and
Mary will know the truth before the sun comes up in the morning. By morning, I will have totally lost my brother, the only
woman I have ever loved, and the only woman that has ever
really loved me. Most of all, I will have lost my son. I will be left
with nothing."

"Charles, you have not lost me. He is still your blood. We
are still a family. Why can't you try to love me as much as I love
you? Why can't you let him be your son."

"I apologize from the bottom of my heart. I don't blame
you for sleeping with Curtis. He was a better man than me. I
regret that I let any woman come between our brotherhood. If
I had been a better brother, he probably would be alive today.
I failed my brother. I have disappointed my mother. My sister
hates me. I have put Lela under horrible pressure for years.
I should have just been Lela's friend and brother-in-law. I
should have stopped fighting so hard to be her lover. As my
friend, she would have been mine forever. Most of all and my
biggest crime, I have failed you as a husband and as a man. I

married the best woman a man could have for a wife. Then I offered her up to my brother on a silver platter. There is no one to blame for everything that has happened to this family except for me."

Tears streamed down Eden face. She was paralyzed with fear and regret.

"We can start over Charles. We can make this marriage work."

Charles looked down at the baby and kissed him gently.

"Doris and Sister Mary will love all of Curtis' children, but they will resurrect Curtis through him. Everyone will always think I'm his father. In his mind and heart, I will be a greater man and father in death than I ever would have been in life."

"Charles, I love you."

"He was going that evening to be with you."

"What are you talking about?"

"The night Lela killed Curtis. He was trying to get ready so that he could go and be with you."

Eden did not want to respond. She stood looking at her fragile family afraid to speak. Tears rushed from her eyes as she realized she had no choice. The truth was already known in his heart. A verbal confirmation was all Charles wanted.

"Yes, Curtis was coming that evening to see me. He said that he wanted to spend some time with me. He wanted to make sure me and the baby were fine. He never even knew the truth about the baby. He was all excited about his brother having a son. I never told him the baby was really his son. He said that he just needed to talk that night. All he ever talked about was Lela. Sex to him with other women was just sex. All those women he had didn't mean a thing to him. I didn't mean anything to him. He was a great father, a wonderful son, a beloved brother, and a good friend, but he was a terrible husband. I don't know why he was such a terrible husband. He loved Lela from the top of her head to the bottom of her feet."

Charles shook his head in agreement. He gently kissed the baby again. He looked up at Eden and apologized once more.

"I'm sorry for everything I have put you through. You will be free now. When I'm gone, Doris and Mary will take care of you forever and they will make this precious baby king of kings."

The sound of a single gunshot was like a cannon blast.

Charles released his hold on the infant. The blood sprayed out and covered the child in death and sorrow. The sound and feel of Charles' life slipping away caused the baby to awaken and cry out for his mother.

Eden fell to her knees to catch the baby before he hit the floor. After Charles rocked violently backward, he then came rapidly forward out of the rocking chair and crashed to the floor.

The color of red seemed to instantly coat the walls of the room as well as the floor. The cry from the child and the screams from the mother echoed throughout the house.

thirty seven

Safety Box

You could hear a pin drop when she walked into the west side branch of Tyche Federal Credit Union. Customers as well as employees knew exactly who she was despite the sunglasses. She stood with a handbag in one hand and a briefcase in the other hand just inside the doorway. She scanned the room for the branch manager. Clara Greene slowly rose from her seat to accept responsibility.

Ashley walked straight through the silence in the room right to the branch manager's desk.

"Are you the manager?"

"I am Clara Greene. I am the manager of this branch office. How can I help you today?"

"My name is Ashley Powell. I have a safe deposit box located at this branch. I need to get access to that box right now."

Ashley pulled off her sunglasses. She handed Clara the proper paperwork and her identification. Clara studied the documents and then examined Ashley's face.

"Yes ma'am. Your documents seem to be in order. Just follow me this way."

Ashley put her sunglasses back on and followed Clara. Clara was so nervous her hands were shaking uncontrollably. She could not get her key in the security door lock to get it opened. Ashley gently put her hand on Clara's shoulder.

"You need to calm down and take your time."

Clara could barely get her words out.

"Yes ma'am. I do apologize."

Clara finally got the key into the lock and opened the door. She led Ashley inside to her safe deposit box. Clara took the box out of the wall slot and placed it on the table in the center of the room.

"I will leave you alone now, ma'am."

"Don't you move, Miss Greene. I need you to stand right there."

Ashley took her key and opened the safe deposit box. She looked inside briefly. She closed the box and locked it again.

Clara was relieved this ordeal was finally coming to an end. She moved to put the box back in its' slot, but Ashley stopped her again.

"Don't put this box back yet. I need you to listen carefully and follow my instructions."

Clara resumed her fearful facial expression and nervous shaking.

"Please ma'am. I don't want to get involved."

"You got involved the day you let that white little piece of trash walk in here impersonating me. You know exactly what I'm talking about. Don't try to act dumb. You better listen and do exactly as I say or you and this credit union will have hell to pay. You understand me?"

"Yes ma'am."

Ashley smiled to try to put Clara more at ease.

"Very good. Now, listen carefully to my instructions."

***

Ashley was mentally exhausted when she arrived at her home. She was literally dragging her body as she shuffled from the garage into the kitchen. She placed her handbag and briefcase on the kitchen table. She examined her answering machine. She saw no indication of voice messages.

There was no need to turn the lights on in the living room as she was only passing through in her quest to reach her master bedroom. She turned the light on in the bathroom and began preparation for a hot, steamy bath. She felt the need to kick off her shoes and lie across the bed for a quick moment before shedding her clothes.

A shadow seemed to go across the bedroom doorway that made Ashley quickly sit up. She cautiously ventured out of the bedroom to investigate further. She walked back toward the living room. Lights switches were flipped on as she retraced her steps.

Ashley stood surveying her living room when a huge white hand covered her mouth and violently jerked her backward. She tried to rip her long fingernails across this masculine arm as she was put in a paralyzing choke hold. She felt her body being lifted up, carried, and thrown down on the couch. She looked in his eyes and saw familiarity.

"I should snap your neck. You're too pretty for me to kill right away. I think we need to have a little fun first."

Ashley swung her arms wildly as Hunter used his one hand to rip open her blouse. He used his other huge hand to clutch her throat and pin her head backward deep into the couch. He licked the side of her face and whispered in her ear.

"I'm going to have a hard time killing you after I'm done."

After franticly probing for any type of hard object, she finally felt the mini laptop computer that had been left on the living room coffee table. Ashley knew she had to get a stronghold on the laptop if she was going to be able to put any force behind her effort. Hunter was too pre-occupied with kissing and licking her body while using his one hand to get his pants undone.

Ashley slammed the laptop into the side of Hunter's head with enough impact to draw blood. The unexpected blow made Hunter briefly blind and dazed. He loosen his grip on her long enough for Ashley to push him to the floor and jump from the couch. As she tried to run, Hunter caught her left foot which threw her face down to the floor.

Hunter rose to his feet with blood streaming down the right side of his face. He was outraged that she was violently resisting. He stepped on Ashley's back to pin her to the floor. He vowed to make her death a slow torture.

"Why are you making this so hard on yourself? We have a very long night ahead of us together. You may even like some of the freaky things we are going to try tonight."

Hunter laughed as he took his foot away and tightly grabbed Ashley's hair to pull her up to her knees.

The glass shattered as the first bullet pierced the front window of the house. Hunter was struck by the bullet in the right shoulder. When the sudden excruciating pain made him release Ashley and stand straight up, the second bullet hit him in the left thigh. The combination of bullets made him fall backward to the floor like a cut down tree.

Ashley rapidly crawled away before Hunter hit the floor.

The front door was rammed open as law officers in full swat team gear stormed into the house. The swat team members surrounded Hunter on the floor as he moaned and groaned in agony.

Asia Wang and Lorenzo Flores calmly entered the house. Asia helped Ashley get to her feet and verified she was not seriously injured. Lorenzo sat down on the couch next to an ailing Hunter to make his request.

"Mr. Lynch, I need to know where you put Meghan Reilly's body."

"Who the hell is that?"

"Let's not try to be cute right now. I need to know the location of that personal banker's body. That young lady was a mother."

Hunter's words came flying out with bitter, bloody spit.

"I don't know what the fuck you're talking about."

Lorenzo stood up in an annoyed state and slammed his foot down on the gunshot wound on Hunter's left thigh. The pain made Hunter squeal like an injured pig. Lorenzo repeated his request.

"Mr. Lynch, I need to know where you put Meghan Reilly's body."

Hunter's bitter reply was mixed with pain and laughter.

"You will have to go fuck yourself first."

Lorenzo did not pursue his request for any further information.

"Take Mr. Lynch to get some medical attention. Maybe after he realizes the gravity of his situation, he will be more forthcoming in providing us with information."

"Is hell freezing up yet?" Hunter shouted.

The swat team did not wait for any medical personnel to enter the house. They lifted up Hunter and dragged him out of the house with enough roughness to cause him to yell obscenities every inch of the way.

Ashley sat at the kitchen table draped in a blanket and grateful for her rescue. Asia sat at the table with her ready to confiscate what she, along with her partner, actually had come to the house to retrieve.

"Miss Powell, we know you went to your safe deposit box at the Tyche Federal Credit Union earlier this afternoon. We need to have the contents of that safe deposit box. Please open your brief case."

Ashley inputted the combination to the briefcase lying on the kitchen table. She turned the briefcase around and pushed it across the table to Asia. Asia pressed the buttons and the briefcase opened.

Lorenzo walked into the kitchen just in time to see an empty briefcase. He scolded Ashley for her trickery.

"Miss Powell, why would you want to play games with us? Your best friend's life is on the line."

"That's why you need to speak to my lawyer if you want what was in that safe deposit box," Ashley advised. "What was in that safe deposit box is currently in the possession of my lawyer."

"We saved your ass," Asia reminded Ashley.

"No, you're trying to save your ass," Ashley corrected her.

"We are the federal government," Lorenzo warned. "You seriously want to insult the federal government?"

"As card-carrying members of the federal government, go back and read the U.S. Constitution," Ashley instructed. "When you're done, call my lawyer. Her name is Portia Lee."

thirty eight

Unbreakable

Their deaths were the same as their lives. Curtis' funeral was a public spectacle. Numerous family, friends, and strangers had come from far and near to pay their respects. There had been singing, testimonials, and loud wailing. It had almost turned into an entertainment event.

There were only gravesite services for Charles. Only the sounds of nature could be heard as Charles was lowered into the earth. Doris, Sister Mary, and immediate family members quietly witnessed Charles' final exit.

After the private funeral service for Charles, Doris sat in a dark room in her house for days that turned into weeks. Any ability to function normally had ceased. The thought of continuing through life without her sons seemed unbearable.

Sister Mary was willing to let Doris grieve for a certain period of time. However, Sister Mary felt Doris' hibernation would now have to come to an end. She entered the dark room and turned on the light.

"Did I tell him I loved him?"

"Yes, you told him. He said he loved you too."

"What did I do wrong?"

"You did more than the best you could ever do as a mother. There is only so much any of us can do as mothers. You could not live their lives for them. Their deaths were because of decisions they made for themselves. Their deaths had absolutely nothing to do with you. You gave them money, education, support, and as much love as a mother can give. At some point, they were responsible for their own actions and their own lives. Curtis and Charles both knew you loved them."

"The pain may break me."

"Nothing can break you. Nothing can break us."

Sister Mary walked into the room and sat down beside her long-time friend. She put her arm around Doris. Doris rested her head on Sister Mary. She continued blaming herself for the tragic fate of both of her sons.

"I excused every wild and crazy thing Curtis did. I knew he was out there chasing every skirt in town. I never said one word. Curtis was still such a sweet and kind person. I saw the sadness in Charles' eyes for years. I thought I could buy him happiness. The only thing he seemed to want in life was Lela. How could both my sons love the same woman so much? I should really hate her guts. She has taken away both my boys from me. It's very strange. It's hard for me to hate her, despite everything that has happened. She has given me my wonderful grandchildren. Lela is probably a curse that has been put on my head. I'm being punished for everything I did to Hoover, Mercer, and Nathan Senior. I've raised sons to be men that I would have never had for myself as a woman. I've raised a daughter to be harder than a man. I've made a mess."

"You're talking foolish. If you're being punished, I'm being punished too. Our lives have been one since the seventh grade."

"See, you're still mad at me too for Big Mean Jean."

"She wiped up the ground with my ass, Doris."

"Yeah, it was really bad. I thought she was going to kill you."

"We should go find her. I bet Big Mean Jean is as big as two houses by now. She probably has arthritis, high blood pressure, and a cholesterol level off the chart. I bet we could beat her down today."

"Who is we?"

Sister Mary and Doris laughed until they couldn't stop crying. The two women hugged each other like they were holding on for dear life.

"Mary, I've lost both my sons. What am I going to do?"

"You haven't lost me. We can't afford to break apart. We still have other children and too many grandchildren that need us even more now than ever. We've made it this far, Doris. We'll make it to the end, together."

"You knew what Tracey was doing," Doris acknowledged.

"If you want to know the latest project the Devil is working on, go to church. Just ask and you will be told."

"I go to that same church. Nobody told me anything."

"They're afraid of what you will do to them if they say something you don't want to hear. They're afraid of what I will do to them if they don't tell me everything."

"What were they telling you?"

"Tracy's girlfriend, Roni Paige, was actually doing all the dirty work. Tracey was like a silent partner. She handled laundering all the drug money Roni was making through Curtis' auto shops. The girl is actually a financial genius the way she worked those books. She made Curtis and Lela rich. That piece of shit, Tommy Dancy, and his police buddy, Hunter Lynch, were providing protection for their little profit-making operation."

"Is my baby girl just evil?"

"She was not doing it because she is a bad person. She was trying to be you. She didn't get being you quite right. She got carried away when Curtis came to her for help with his money problems and not you. She handled it the wrong way. She couldn't stop herself. The control she had over Curtis gave her power over you. I tried to clean it all up when I learned what was happening. I apologize for keeping you in the dark. I just didn't want you to be hurt."

"Always cleaning up my mess," Doris said.

"No, always taking care of my family," Sister Mary corrected her. "We weren't born family, but everything we have been through together over the years has made us family."

Mica Goldman came rushing into the room looking frustrated and breathless.

"I'm not sure how much more we all can take. You both need to get up and come see what is happening on the television."

Doris and Sister Mary broke their embrace and wiped tears from their eyes.

"Please, what now?" Doris asked.

Sister Mary was confused.

"What is on the television that we need to see?

Mica Goldman could barely get the word to roll off her tongue.

"Tracey"

***

Two helicopters flew overhead. Police cars blocked the street on both ends. The news media and curious citizens tried to physically get pass or see pass barricades. Police officers surrounded the house located at 202 Sugar Lane.

Claudius approached the police officer in charge of this hostage situation. He took out his white handkerchief to wipe away sweat before he issued one command.

"When your guys get a clear shot, drop him."

Inside the house, Tommy Dancy sat with a gun in his hand examining Tracey from head to toe. Tracey sat across from him clutching the seven year-old twin boys tightly to her body. One twin sat left of Tracey and the other twin sat on her right.

They both looked bewildered and afraid.

"Who did you have the best sex with, me or Roni?" Tommy asked. "I need to know. No way that bitch was better in bed than me."

Tracey urged Tommy to end this ordeal.

"If you're going to kill yourself, go right ahead."

"I'm not a weak little pussy like your brother Charles. I have no intention of killing myself."

"If you're going to kill me, then go right ahead."

"Lela cut Curtis's head almost clean off. Charles took a gun and blcw his brains clean out. I have not seen you shed one tear once. Is there a woman somewhere inside that body?"

"If women cried and fell apart every time some man did something horrible to them, the entire world would come to a complete stop."

"You are such a bitch. I was going to marry you. Do you realize that I was going to make you my wife?"

"That was your plan, not mine. Why don't you let these boys go? Then you can kill me."

"I didn't come here to kill you. Did you hear what I said? I wanted you to be Mrs. Thomas Dancy. Do you think I'm crazy like Lela? I would never hurt one hair on your head. I didn't even know you would be here. I came for these two little brats. They have Hunter sitting downtown in a jail cell wondering what he should say to get the best deal. I know my best buddy very well. Hunter won't say a word unless they dangle these little bastards in front of his face. Hunter is one of the most ruthless, bloodsucking son-of-a-bitches I ever met, except when it comes to these snot rags. He will do anything to make sure they're safe and happy. I actually was going to fulfill Hunter's dream. Everybody has been wondering who is their real daddy for years. I know my name is right after Curtis' name on the list. Well, I was going to step up to the plate and be their daddy. I was going to take these twins, get on the highway, and keep driving until we got to the ocean. Hunter wouldn't dare give me up if he thought his sons were with me. They were going to be my life insurance policy. Me and these boys could have lived nice and comfortable in southern California. I sure didn't count on you being here. Of all days for you to make an attempt at being nice. You sent their grandmother off shopping with her friends. What the hell, Tracey. It never occurred to you that the police might be following you around. You always did attract a crowd. I always loved that about you until now. Once again, you and your family have fucked up all my plans."

Tommy took a pack of gum out of his pocket. He motioned for the twins to take a piece. Both boys shook their head to answer no. Tommy laughed at their refusal.

"You say they aren't identical. I can't tell them apart. Which one is Curtis and which one is Charles?"

"Tommy, please," Tracey pleaded. "This is a hopeless situation. Let's just all walk out of here before someone gets hurt. You and I can take our punishment together for everything we have done."

Tommy laughed even harder.

"You really think you are going to get the same punishment as me? Hell, I will be doing good if I can get to the backseat of one of those police cruisers outside still alive. Doris Mercer will give you a strong scolding and Sister Mary will ask God to forgive you. That will be the end of it for you. We're not in this together anymore. It's just me alone now. I'm just like Lela. She was a fool to be with Curtis. I was a fool to be with you. You're going to get a better deal from me than Lela gave Curtis."

Tommy's cell phone rang. He answered the single question that was asked over the phone.

"Sure, come on in."

The front door slowly opened and Claudius cautiously entered.

"Hey Tommy."

"The great emperor, Claudius, has arrived."

"Tracey are you okay?"

"I'm fine," Tracey reassured the police chief.

Claudius came further into the room and flopped down in a chair. He took out his white handkerchief and wiped the sweat away.

"Now, Tommy how are we going to do this thing? You do realize it's all over for you. Don't wimp out on me. I really do like you Tommy. I need you to go down like a man."

"Claudius, if anything happens to Tracey, you will have to answer to Doris Mercer and Sister Mary. They will bring the wrath of God down on your head. That's why you're going to guarantee that no shots are fired. Then, you're going to walk me to one of those police cruisers. They will take me downtown and book me into custody. I'm not trying to have no shoot-out on Sugar Lane. I will call a lawyer and be out by morning. Maybe I can get that Portia Lee."

Claudius wiped sweat away again before replying to Tommy's request.

"Tommy, let me explain something to you. I love this city with all my heart. As the police chief, I get the inside view. What I see happening to this city is the same thing that is happening to you. This city is being destroyed by racism, greed, and stupidity. These are the exact same things that will be the reasons for your destruction. If you were a white man, you probably could get out of this mess clean. However, white folks don't like black men that think they're above them and the law. Black folks don't like black men that forget they're black. You've got both the whites and the blacks in this town calling for your head. Greed has clouded every judgment you have ever made. You should have said no to all that illegal crap Tracey got you wrapped up in. Look at her. Tracey is a damn gorgeous woman. You just needed to marry Tracey and all your troubles would have been over. The woman's mother is rich as sin. I don't care what she has said to you. Tracey would have married you so nobody knows about all the women she keeps in her not-so-secret closet. You could have married her and got paid to fuck as many women as she fucks. Nothing is ever enough for you, Tommy. You're just a greedy motherfucker. You didn't need one dime of that drug money you all were making. Stupidity is probably your worst sin. I can't even explain that one to you or myself. Tommy, you're just plain stupid."

"I appreciate your expert analysis. I'll try to consider the points you have made for the future. Now, can you arrest me and take me downtown? I surrender."

Claudius stood up and used his handkerchief to wipe the sweat away. Tommy stood up also and extended his gun for Claudius to take.

"Put the gun down on the floor," Claudius instructed.

Tommy carefully put the gun down on the floor as he was told. He stood up straight somewhat relieved this tense situation would soon be over.

"Just get me downtown so I can call a lawyer," Tommy requested again. "I'm sure with all the shit I know about everybody, including you Claudius, prison for me will be an option that I don't need to worry about. I'll just have to change my plans for survival. I don't really think I'm ready to be a father yet anyway. These twins can stay with you Tracey. You and your mother can fuck them up just like you fucked up your brothers. Claudius, I surrender."

Tommy laughed like he was actually delighted to be arrested.

"Nobody in this town, including me, can afford to be bothered with an idiot like you anymore," Claudius revealed. "It's over Tommy. I'm real sorry, but it's just over."

Tracey pulled the twins closer to her body and covered their eyes with her hands. Tommy looked directly into Tracey's eyes and saw his fate.

Tommy raised his hands up in a surrender motion. The attempt for a non-violent resolution was useless. The sharpshooter's bullet hit on the right side of his head. It quickly passed through his brain and exited out the left side of his head. The bullet made a small, harmless-looking hole when it lodged into the wall.

Tracey was his last thought and final sight as Tommy slumped back down into the chair with his eyes wide open.

The hostage situation had ended as quickly as it had begun.

Tommy Dancy was dead.

Tracey was still unable to shed any tears.

thirty nine

Devil In The Details

"Life without the possibility of parole."

Portia Lee looked around at Ada. The two women suddenly burst into laughter.

"Oh, you think this situation is funny?" Marian asked.

"We didn't come here to beg for anything," Portia explained. "We came to tell you what this office is going to give to our client."

Shay sat up in her chair with disbelief at Portia's arrogance.

"I know you think we're a bunch of country hicks down here. Despite your opinions, Marian and I plan to prosecute Lela Mercer to the fullest extent of the law. If you came in here to just insult our intelligence, you can get the hell out right now. I won't tolerate some pampered wife slicing up her husband because she suddenly felt a little disrespected. I won't tolerate some big city lawyer coming in my office acting like her rich client doesn't deserve the same justice as everyone else. We were nice enough to take the death penalty off the table for the sake of her poor children, who are probably mentally scarred for life. Life without the possibility of parole. You take it and you better be glad we offered it."

"Tough talk for a prosecutor who might have to explain why she prosecuted the wrong man for the death of Officer Terrell Monroe. The wrong man who got tortured to death in prison. The media and the public will certainly want to know how the real killers were allowed to continue working for the police department. Two men sworn to serve and protect who actually brutally harassed the poor citizens of this city and did more illegal acts than the criminals they arrested. Did I forget something Ada?"

"Well, there is that little matter of Zanzibar burning down with a whole lot of innocent, horny men and one poor stripper inside. Don't forget about that missing personal banker. The young, mother of two, who most believe has met with foul play."

"I'm sure you can bury a lot of what I call departmental fuck-ups with dearly departed Officer Tommy Dancy. However, another badly injured police officer called Ada's office yesterday from his hospital bed? Ada, what was his name?"

"Hunter Lynch."

"Mr. Lynch told Ada there is plenty he knows and plenty he might want to say depending on what type of deal he can receive. Mr. Lynch apparently knows a great deal about a drug operation that led to the death of Police Officer Terrell Monroe. I can't believe what Mr. Lynch is trying to insinuate. He is actually trying to imply that there was a major cover-up when Officer Monroe was killed."

"I think executed is a better term to use," Ada said.

"Thank you Ada. Mr. Lynch wants to get a deal in place to ensure that his twin boys are taken care of before he talks to this office or the FBI. Don't you hate when killers get sentimental. Apparently, the FBI have tried already to squeeze the truth out of Mr. Lynch. It's not going to work until he gets some guarantees regarding his children. All this time everyone thought Curtis Mercer was the father of those twins. Who knew Mr. Lynch was their real dad? Ada and I will have to find a place on our schedule so we can have a discussion with Mr. Lynch. I'm quite sure he has some bedtime stories we want to hear. We already have a meeting with two nice FBI special agents once we leave here. Ada, what were the names of those FBI special agents?"

"Asia Wang and Lorenzo Flores."

"They could care less about Lela or Tracey Mercer. They seem to be preoccupied with getting the real shooter in the Terrell Monroe murder and finding the body of that lovely young personal banker. They want to get their hands on the contents of a safety deposit box that Curtis Mercer was keeping. After personally going through that safety deposit box, I fully understand why. But, you know how I operate, you have to give me something to get something from me."

"You have your hands filled," Marian said with defeat in her voice.

"Busy, busy, busy," Portia said smiling. "I really just need a quick deal for Lela Mercer so I can move on to other matters. Lela is not going to kill anybody else. A lot of women and men in this town believe Curtis got what he deserved. However, I'm not here to pass judgment on how Curtis Mercer conducted his life. I just need to make sure his beautiful wife can live out the rest of her life in peace."

Shay slowly sat back in her chair. She was at a loss for words to respond to these thinly veiled threats. Marian quickly made another offer.

"Fifteen to life."

"We're not interested," Ada quickly answered. "We have recently acquired several new clients that have paid us in valuable information."

"Who might these new clients be?" Marian inquired.

"Sherry Ferguson, Amber Gail, Rita Foxx, and Roni Paige, who also goes by the name of Mrs. Hunter Lynch. All these lovely young ladies seem to be afraid for their lives. They have all requested our services. They have offered to pay us by revealing some little known facts that all seem to aid in Lela's defense. They all seem to have one piece of a very big puzzle that when put together, puts the police department and this prosecutor's office in a very bad light."

"Ada, you're turning into quite the lawyer in demand," Marian complimented. "I have a sudden new respect for her legal abilities."

"Yes, business has been extremely exciting lately," Ada said proudly. "I feel like a young practicing attorney again."

Shay slowly sat back up in her chair.

"Okay, Portia let's cut the bullshit," Shay reluctantly requested. "What do you want?"

"I want voluntary manslaughter. Three years in a minimum security prison and a one hundred thousand dollar fine. After she serves her prison time, two years supervised probation."

"You are fucking crazy," Shay shouted at Portia.

"You are fucking crazy if you don't think I won't dig up Officer Terrell Monroe's dead body and lay it right across the front of your office door for the FBI to find. They may never find that young personal banker's body, but they will find her name written in blood right across your forehead. I will set fire to this office like they lit up Zanzibar. You will be ringing up groceries and socks at the local discount superstore when I get through pulling all the skeletons out of your country hick ass."

"You really think Doris Mercer will ever go for such a light punishment for killing her beloved son?" Marian asked. "Three years in minimum security will just be bible vacation school for Lela Mercer."

Portia stood up and Ada followed her lead.

"I don't work for the prosecutor's office. You and Shay will have to make Doris Mercer believe it is in the best interest of everyone to take this deal, especially her daughter Tracey. If Lela has to go to hell's kitchen, I will make sure Tracey Mercer is cooking right along side of her. Like I said, no one has to worry about Lela Mercer ever again. She has killed the only person she ever wanted to kill. In three years, people in this town will have forgotten and forgave Lela. Fortunate for us, Curtis Mercer didn't live like a saint. Because of his devilish behavior while living, he is now a savior in death to Lela. People should really remember that how you live in life dictates how you are remembered in death. Write up the paperwork and we will seal the deal with Curtis' blood."

Portia and Ada walked out of the prosecutor's office.

Marian looked at Shay who was still in deep thought.

"What are we going to do?" Marian asked.

Shay looked up at Marian and gave the only answer possible.

"We make Doris Mercer take the deal."

forty

A Mother's Choice

"You've buried both your sons and Portia Lee will bury your daughter."

"Let her bury me," Tracey shouted. "I don't give a damn.

Lela has to pay for what she has done to this family. No damn way we will accept any type of plea bargain."

Shay looked at an unusually silent Doris Mercer. Doris looked weak and fragile. Shay lowered and softened her tone of voice.

"Doris, they have documentation from Curtis' own private files. They have witnesses that can back up everything Curtis put in writing. If we try to crucify Lela, Portia Lee will try to nail Tracey to a cross right beside her. Portia Lee is a good lawyer and she is only trying to protect her client. She's not out to get Tracey. Saving Lela is actually going to save Tracey too."

"Hunter Lynch is actually the key that can lock Tracey in a prison cell," Marian continued explaining. "His testimony would be the icing on the cake to put Tracey away for years. Your choice could mean the difference between state prison and federal prison for Lynch. There are a lot of enemies waiting in state prison. Hunter Lynch would prefer we hand him over to the FBI on federal charges. The words Tracey Mercer will never come out of Hunter Lynch's mouth in a federal court of law if you agree to take care of his twin sons for life. He knows everybody in this town thinks those twins belong to Curtis. Hunter Lynch wants your word that his children will continue being your grandchildren. The choice is yours Doris. Is destroying Lela more important than saving your daughter, Tracey?"

"Don't listen to any of this," Tracey screamed. "Three years for killing Curtis. Minimum security for driving Charles to kill himself. That bitch gets no bargain for ruining this family."

"The FBI will be more than willing to turn a blind eye toward Tracey if we hand them over the person that fired the fatal shot that killed Officer Terrell Monroe and who they are sure killed Meghan Reilly," Marian added. "Roni Paige is more than willing to help her husband, Hunter, take all the blame for the drugs and the death of that police officer. Roni will guarantee evidence that exonerates Tracey, gets her an early release, and sends Hunter Lynch away for the rest of his life. The twins are also her children too. Roni also wants an assurance that the twins will continue to be taken care of like they are your real grandchildren."

"Let them go after me," Tracey yelled. "I dare them to prove anything about me. Roni loves me. She would never turn on me. Curtis only knew what I let him know."

"Shut up!" Doris suddenly blurted out. "You shut up right now. You keep yelling about the damage Lela has done to this family. What about the damage you have done? I have to make a choice because of everything you have done."

"Voluntary manslaughter will be the official charge," Shay stated. "Lela will do three years in a minimum security prison with a one hundred thousand dollar fine."

"After she completes her prison term, she will be on supervised controlled release for two years," Marian added.

"That's all you think both my brothers' lives are worth?" Tracey asked.

"What about all the people whose lives and families were ruined by the drugs you and Roni sold just to keep your spoiled brother's pride from being hurt?" Shay asked. "What are their lives worth?"

Tracey had no answer for Shay's question.

Doris walked over to her daughter and examined her face closely. It was like she was seeing her Tracey for the very first time.

"I'm not going to even ask why you did what you did," Doris told her daughter. "It's not even important anymore."

"I will do what you want Doris," Shay promised. "If you want me to fight, my office will go to battle against Portia Lee with everything we have in our arsenal."

"If we do fight, it will be bloody," Marian informed. "Curtis' name will be dragged back and forth through the mud. There may be no way to keep his oldest daughter, Kelly, off the witness stand."

Her granddaughter's name made Doris swing around quickly to face Shay and Marian.

"My grandchildren cannot withstand anymore of this nightmare," Doris admitted.

Shay reminded Doris that it was her responsibility to decide.

"Doris, you make the choice."

It didn't take long for Doris to make her decision.

"I've lost both my sons. I won't lose my daughter too. She may not believe it, but I love Tracey more than she will ever realize. You tell Roni Paige and Hunter Lynch that their children are now my children forever. You give Portia Lee and Lela their plea bargain."

"Thank you," Marian said.

"I believe it will be the best choice for everyone involved," Shay agreed.

Doris turned back to Tracey. She grabbed Tracey by the face and pulled her even closer. She gently kissed Tracey on the lips and then hugged her tight.

Tracey closed her eyes, but was unable to keep tears from streaming down her face.

forty one

Judgement

"What should I say to her?"

"Tell her that her father will live through her soul. His soul was good and now her soul will be greater. Tell her that we are her family. Her father is gone, but we are still here. She will never be alone."

Sister Mary watched Lela's mother, Cheryl, walk out to the garden to confront Lela's oldest daughter. Kelly sat motionless staring at nothing. Cheryl sat down beside her.

"She will have to leave tomorrow."

"If she had listened to me, we could have been far away from here. We could have stayed together. He is dead and she will be gone. Our family has disappeared."

"The time will go faster than you can imagine. We will visit her every month. While she is gone, we will rebuild our lives day by day stacking love on top of love."

"I don't know if I still love her."

"That's not true. Loving her is your problem."

"I shouldn't love her after what she has done."

"She is still your mother. You don't have to forgive her for taking your father away. You only need to be strong enough to see the real truth. Your mother is a good person who made a horrible mistake. It doesn't matter if you do or don't believe she loved your father. One day as a grown woman, you will understand the thin line between love and hate that every married couple has walked down. I'm not excusing anything your mother has done. She was wrong and she has to be punished. What you do know as truth is that your mother would never physically harm you and your brothers and sister. She will never stop loving you no matter what you do or how you feel towards her."

Kelly stood up and looked Cheryl in the eyes.

"Will you take me to see her?"

"Once a month we will visit."

"She won't get hurt in there?"

"She will be able to survive anything if she knows you still care."

"Will I be able to touch her."

"Forever."

"I never got a chance to kiss him good-bye. I should kiss her good-bye."

"That would be nice."

Cheryl watched Kelly walk back toward the house. Kelly looked up and saw Sister Mary watching from the window. Sister Mary smiled and Kelly smiled back.

***

The courtroom was packed that morning with the news media and spectators. Portia Lee and Ada stood next to their client.

Shay and Marian stood on the opposite side of the room waiting to close their case. They all waited for Judge Susan Hoffman to give the stamp of approval.

Judge Hoffman quickly reviewed the paperwork and went through the legal formalities. After everyone acknowledged acceptance of the plea bargain, a final question was put to Lela Mercer regarding her actions that ended Curtis Mercer's life.

Lela turned and first looked at Portia and Ada. Then she turned and looked directly at Ashley. Ashley slowly moved her head up and down to signal her approval. Lela looked back at Judge Hoffman. Lela spoke loud enough to be heard by the judge, the news media, the public, the Devil in hell, and the God in heaven.

"Guilty."

forty two

Honorable Women

Candace Farrell stood at the home bar making alcoholic beverages for her bosses. The senior female lawyers sat comfortably in the living room contemplating Portia Lee's career with the firm.

"That turned out better than I had anticipated," Betty Endress admitted. "I thought poor Lela Mercer was domed."

"The firm collected a handsome fee for our services," Martha Neal said with delight. "Sister Mary has already paid the bill in full."

"Do you think we should make Portia a partner?" Donna Tuthill asked. "We don't want to lose her."

"It's too soon," Victoria Cruz stated. "Let's see how Portia handles a few more tough cases."

Candace passed out drinks to her bosses. They all raised their classes as Candace proposed a toast.

"To Portia Lee, an excellent lawyer and the future of this firm. May she one day soon stand shoulder to shoulder with the honorable women in this room. To the best law firm in this country, Endress, Neal, Tuthill, & Cruz."

All the women in the room gave an affirmative vote.

"Here, here!"

They made the vote official by drinking until their glasses were empty.

forty three

Revelation

"They all got what they deserved, except for Lela."

"How can you say that? You were her lawyer. You were responsible for getting her that nice and easy sentence."

"I didn't get her anything. If her husband hadn't been a no-good, skirt-chasing dog and her mean sister-in-law hadn't been a drug-dealing mastermind, they would have fried pretty Lela with bacon grease. I didn't do a thing. Lela has been living on luck and beauty all her life. Neither one has run out for her yet."

Ada sat back in her desk chair laughing at her niece's words. Portia looked around Ada's office in disgust.

"How can you work in this office?" Portia asked. "Don't you make any money?"

"Haven't we just learned that money and material possessions can't buy you happiness. Poor people need a lawyer too."

"Poor people don't pay."

"I don't need all those luxuries you have to have in your life. Simple things make me happy."

"I have to correct myself. I said everybody got what they deserved, except Lela. That was not true. Charles didn't deserve to even be in that family. I do feel sorry for Charles. He let other people dictate his entire life. He should have been more like my father and just walked away from them all."

Portia's reference to her father shocked Ada.

"Why did you decide to help me?" Ada wanted to know.

Portia slowly stood up and looked around Ada's office once again with disapproval. She took a deep breath before responding.

"You tell my father that I'm not just a lawyer. I am a damn good lawyer. I don't miss him and I didn't need him."

Ada's smile and laughter evaporated. She realized none of this had been about Lela Mercer. It was not about a woman who had been victimized by a cheating husband and domineering in-laws. It was not about Curtis Mercer who slept with women whose names he could not recall. It was not about children that gave Curtis the title of Daddy regardless if their DNA did or did not match. It had not been about the wealth of the Mercer family or the power of Sister Mary.

A commitment to getting Lela Mercer a slap on the wrist for almost cutting off her husband's head was a loud and visible statement Portia was trying to make to her own family. This had all been about a twelve-year-old child that Ada's brother had walked away from twenty years ago and never looked back.

"I know I can't speak for my entire family," Ada apologized. "I can only speak for myself. I am truly sorry for being absent in your life. I am sorry for any pain I have caused you. I hope that we can start off again beginning today. I want us to have a relationship. I'm not the best aunt, but I am your aunt. We are family."

Portia examined her aunt and the meager surroundings one last time.

"Ada, don't ever call me again."

Portia started walking out of Ada's office. Ada jumped up to follow her niece. Portia suddenly stopped at the front office door. She turned back to Ada for one last question.

"Do you think Curtis really loved Lela?"

Ada felt strongly qualified to answer the question.

"I know for sure that Curtis loved Lela with all his heart."

"How can you be so sure?"

"Because, I know exactly what it's like to love someone so much and treat them so wrong."

Portia was not impressed with Ada's explanation. She strongly reiterated her demand.

"Ada, don't ever call me again."

"I stopped making promises after my second husband."

Portia smiled and shook her head in total disbelief that Ada was her own flesh and blood.

Ada watched Portia leave the office and get in her expensive automobile. She walked out to the parking lot to continue watching Portia as she drove away. As Portia's car moved farther and farther into the distance, Ada whispered words that Portia never heard.

"I love you."

THE END

COMING SOON

ADA & PORTIA REUNITE TO UNTANGLE A NEW LEGAL DILEMMA

SACRIFICE FOR SINS

BY

Julie Williams

PREVIEW

It looked like a crucifixion. His arms were stretched out in both directions. Glass and metal were penetrating throughout his body. Blood dripped down the sides of the sports utility vehicle like red raindrops. His wide open eyes looked up toward the sky searching for a resurrection.

Blue and red lights lit up the streets. Traffic was backed up for miles. The crowd gathering was in amazement at the awful sight. The shaken owners, who had discovered their parked vehicle covered in death, were being comforted and informed by the police.

When the SWAT team arrived, the police officer in charge of the crime scene explained the situation. The investigators looked up to see sheer white curtains flowing out of the open glass balcony doors like the wings of an angel.

The SWAT team secured the building and advanced toward the suspected room of origin.

After bursting through the door, they found a hotel room void of any possible perpetrator. The room was in total disarray. The crumbled sheets on the bed suggested extensive use by more than one person. Lamps were overturned and broken.

Shattered drinking glasses looked like sparkling diamonds littering the carpet. Blood splattered the walls like an expensive, modern painting.

The law officers went out on the balcony and looked down seventeen floors to see the victim, who was naked and sprawled in a cross-like position atop of the large vehicle.

Moans and squeals from the bathroom put the SWAT team back on full alert. They carefully entered the oversized, luxurious bathroom of this extravagant hotel room.

The alarm was false again. Only a drunken Tias Lee was found lying in a bathtub full of water. His head was probably only minutes away from being totally submerged.

Tias' drunken stupor made him periodically moan and squeal like a pig being taken to slaughter. The sounds increased as the law officers dragged his naked body from the lukewarm water.

A blanket was found to cover the shame of Tias. He sat on the bed bewildered and wet as he was read his legal rights.

The victim was naked and dead and the suspect was naked and confused.

===

JXW Books

JXW COMMUNICATIONS

Providing reading entertainment for adults as
well as children. It is our goal to provide products
that are exciting and new for those who purchase,
read, and love quality fiction literature.

===